HERBS AND HOMECOMINGS

H.C. DE COSSY

1

Elizabeth Grace Sloane sighed as she passed the sign welcoming her to Fairweather Falls. She glanced over at her fifteen-year-old son, Joshua, who had fallen asleep in the passenger seat beside her. A quick glance in the rear-view mirror showed her eight-year-old daughter, Maddie, sound asleep in the back. Behind Maddie, suitcases and boxes filled the trunk. A moving van containing the rest of the things they could not leave behind would follow in the morning.

It had grown dark as Elizabeth drove up the coast from Connecticut. The drive to Fairweather Falls had taken almost six hours. Stuck in a car with two young people, one of whom had an insatiable curiosity about everything. Maddie had kept talking until she had abruptly fallen asleep mid-word just as they crossed over into Maine. Falling asleep mid-word was common for Maddie. She had been doing it since she could talk.

Driving through the town of Fairweather Falls was surreal. Elizabeth had never expected to return to the town where she had lived as a child. Fairweather Falls wasn't on any map. It was a haven for those beings that most regular people considered pure fairy tales. To Elizabeth, it had once been home.

Elizabeth sighed again as she drove through the center of town. Not much had changed in the almost thirty years since she had been home. The town center retained its old-world charm, stately Victorians surrounding the town square, interspersed with shops and the town hall. Off to the right, less than a mile away, was the sea. It was really the Gulf of Maine, as Fairweather Falls was not far from the border with Canada. Nova Scotia was just a short boat ride away. Elizabeth could remember taking the boat over on the weekends with her friends from school. Nova Scotia hosted its own magical communities, and there had been a lot of visiting back and forth. Elizabeth had even dated a guy from Dale's End, the closest magical community on the island. The ferry from Fairweather Falls put in at Dale's End. Elizabeth had met Jonah McClure while visiting the town with her friends the summer of her junior year of high school. The pair had dated for several months before the strain of living almost three-and-a-half hours away by ferry had become too much. There were beings who could teleport, but Elizabeth's parents considered it too much of a favor to ask. And the ones that would portal you somewhere for a fee charged too much.

Elizabeth drove through town and headed out the other side. The space between houses grew more expansive, the properties larger. About half a mile outside of town, Elizabeth turned right onto Seafarer Way, then right again into her Aunt's driveway. Hers, now. Aunt Gloria had left Elizabeth the house when she passed away several months ago. Inheriting the property had come at the perfect time for Elizabeth and her kids. She just wished that Aunt Glo was still there to share it with them.

Elizabeth was looking forward to ordering pizza and getting to bed as soon as possible. The exhaustion she had been holding at bay for the last year had finally set in. Elizabeth felt as if she couldn't take one step further. As she pulled up the driveway to the house, Elizabeth sighed again. The lights were on in the home, their warm, golden glow shining out between the curtains. Shadows moved in front of the windows, showing that more than one person was already in the house. Elizabeth had hoped to avoid her family until the following day. She hadn't told them she was coming home. Elizabeth hadn't spoken to her family much, except on holidays, during the entire time she had been away from Fairweather Falls. Her family had not approved of her leaving. They couldn't understand her need to see more of the human world that surrounded their community. Elizabeth had wanted to travel and see new things. She had felt that her family was trying to hold her back. They had wanted her to stay in the paranormal world. Elizabeth had left anyway and had never looked back.

Seeing the shadows of the people in the house, Elizabeth realized it had been too much to hope that she could hide their arrival from a family of talented Witches. Especially as her grandmother was a formidable Seer. Elizabeth looked over at Josh, still asleep in the seat beside her.

"Josh, Sweetheart. Wake up. We're here." Elizabeth patted her son's arm gently. He stirred, then stretched as much as possible within the confines of the car. Slowly, her words sank into his grudgingly waking consciousness. He looked around, noticing the lights in the windows.

"Is there someone in the house? I thought it was empty."

"Grandma must have told everyone we were coming. We might as well go inside. They won't let us sit out here for long."

Josh unbuckled his seat belt and opened the car door as the front door of the house opened. The tall figure of a woman was silhouetted in the doorway against the light. Elizabeth didn't recognize the figure. Had her family invited the entire town to witness their homecoming?

Elizabeth stepped out of the car. The person at the door of the house took a step forward. Suddenly, she started running, crashing into Elizabeth and flinging her arms around her.

"You really came! I didn't believe Grandma when she said you were coming back. I thought we were just humoring her, getting the house ready for you. I never thought you would actually show up."

Elizabeth stepped back from the embrace. She looked up into the face of the woman before her. The eyes shining down at her were familiar, though the last time she had seen them had been in the face of a much younger girl.

"Lucy?" Elizabeth gasped. "When did you get so tall?" Her sister, younger by three years, dwarfed her five-foot-six frame.

"About twenty years ago. You weren't there to see it. And you never came home, so....."

"You could have come visit any time. You know that."

"I meant to. Things kept coming up, and then suddenly it was now." Lucy shook her head. "Anyway, come in. Everyone is waiting for you. We all want to meet your kids."

Elizabeth turned to Josh, who stood waiting by the side of the car.

"Josh, this is my sister, your Aunt Lucy. You've spoken to her on the phone during the holidays a few times. Lucy, this is my son, Joshua. Maddie's asleep in the back."

The back door of the car opened.

"No, I'm not, Mom. I woke up," Maddie slid out of the car, rubbing her eyes. She looked up at her Aunt.

"You're tall."

"I get that a lot. You're still short."

"I'm eight. I'll grow. Maybe I'll be as tall as you."

"Maybe you will. I'm your Aunt Lucy, Madyson. Come inside and meet the rest of your family. You too, Josh. Your cousins want to meet you."

Lucy had children, too. Two boys and a girl. She had married a mage from another paranormal community and settled here in Fairweather Falls.

"I'm looking forward to meeting Thomas and your children in person," Elizabeth told her sister.

"They're looking forward to meeting you. Now quit stalling. Mom's about killing herself, holding back. Dad convinced her to let me be the one to greet you, to ease you into the family again. He won't be able to keep her back for long."

Sighing again, Elizabeth nodded. She walked around to the back of the car and grabbed her overnight bag. Josh grabbed his and Maddie's. The rest could wait until the morning.

Elizabeth approached the house with some trepidation. Her mother had never accepted Elizabeth's decision to stay away. Nora had tried to convince her to come home during every phone call. Which was why the calls were so few and far between. Elizabeth could only handle the guilt from knowing that her actions made her mother unhappy a few times a year. There was some resentment, too. Her mother never understood that Elizabeth had to make her own way. Nora had never accepted Elizabeth's choice to live in the human world. She hadn't come to visit, either. Not even when her grandchildren were born. Then again, Elizabeth hadn't asked her to, even though she had wanted her mother and grandmother there. Her partner, Jared, had tried to convince her to call them. Elizabeth had felt the guilt trip she would receive from Nora would be too much on top of the emotions of giving birth and having a new baby to take care of. So she hadn't called. And now, here she was. Returning home, just as her mother wanted. Elizabeth took a deep breath and stepped inside.

Lucy had gone into the kitchen and was pouring herself a drink. She quirked an eyebrow at Elizabeth, who nodded. It had been a long drive. Elizabeth turned back to the sitting room to the right of the door. Nora had Maddie by the arms. Nora was on her knees, looking up directly into Maddie's face. Elizabeth's father, Elliot, was shaking hands with Joshua. As Elizabeth watched, he pulled the boy into a hug.

Nora looked up as Elizabeth entered the room. Climbing slowly to her feet, Nora approached her daughter. She looked into Elizabeth's eyes, searching for something. Whatever she saw there seemed to make her sad. She pulled Elizabeth into her arms.

"My dear girl, I am so glad you came home." She kissed Elizabeth, then passed her over to Elliot, who hugged Elizabeth close.

Elliot kissed the top of her head, then tucked her under his arm against his side. Lucy came over and handed Elizabeth her drink.

"Thank you," Elizabeth said. Lucy nodded.

Elizabeth looked around for the person responsible for the welcoming committee. Deirdre Sloan rose slowly to her feet and made her way over to her granddaughter. She looked into Elizabeth's eyes, as Nora had done, then hugged her.

"I'm sorry we couldn't help more. You know we would have if you had asked. No one could have expected the fire, though. The way the house collapsed. I saw sorrow in your future, but I wasn't able to see more than that. I am so sorry, Elizabeth Grace."

Elizabeth's eyes filled with tears. She held on to her grandmother, sobbing into her neck. Her grandmother stroked her back as she cried.

Finally, Deirdre stepped back. Elliot led Elizabeth to the sofa and pulled her down beside him. Elizabeth rested her head on her father's shoulder.

"What made you finally decide to come home, Sweetheart?" Elliot asked his oldest child.

"I'm tired. I miss magic. After Jared died, I was just going through the motions, you know? Nothing interested me anymore. It was time to leave."

"What about your friends?" Nora asked.

"It's funny, but I never really made any close friends in Connecticut. I had friends that I would go on walks with or out to the occasional dinner with, but no one really close. I made some friends on my travels, but we mostly keep in touch through social media. We don't actually talk much. I had a few friends I thought would be with me for life, but even they've drifted away. I was already thinking about coming back when I got the letter from Mr. Lawrence."

Mr. Lawrence was Aunt Gloria's lawyer. Elizabeth had known him since she was a child.

Maddie curled up next to her mother on the sofa. Joshua sat on the other side of Maddie.

"Well, we wanted to welcome you home and to make sure that you knew we were here and we still loved you," Nora said. "We'll get going and let you get some rest. Come over to the big house in the morning for breakfast. We'll catch up."

"The movers are coming tomorrow."

"Then come over for lunch when they're gone. Let me know when you're on your way."

Everyone hugged Elizabeth and the kids, then the family left, leaving the weary travelers alone.

"Where's my room, Mama?" Maddie yawned.

Elizabeth stood and grabbed the bags. Joshua took his large black backpack from his mother. Elizabeth led the kids to the bedrooms.

There were three upstairs, along with a large bathroom. The bathroom had a large claw-foot tub, with a shower next to a window that looked out over the cliffs to the waves below. Elizabeth had always loved the room. Glancing into it as she passed it, she found that she still did. The tub was practically calling her name.

She led Maddie into the room next to the bathroom. There was an old metal-framed bed with curly ornaments and finials shaped like pine cones against one wall. The room faced the front of the house and had a large window with a window seat, complete with colorful pillows and a blanket. Elizabeth set Maddie's bag on the bed. Someone, most likely Nora, had made up the bed with clean sheets and blankets.

Elizabeth led Joshua to the next room. All the bedrooms were on the same side of the house, though the master actually extended across the house and had windows on both sides. Joshua's window looked out onto the front yard as Maddie's did. Here, too, there was a bed all made up and waiting. The linens in here were gray and blue. Nora had apparently already known which rooms the children would be in. Of course, she had. Deirdre would have told her.

Josh hugged Elizabeth before turning and setting his bag on the bed. Elizabeth continued into the master bedroom, Aunt Gloria's room. The queen-sized bed was to the left of the door. The window on the front side of the house had a window seat, as did both windows on the seaward side. A dresser sat between the windows. A wardrobe stood against the far wall. To one side was a bookshelf, filled with books. To the other, a comfy light blue rocking armchair complete with an ottoman. One of Aunt Gloria's yarn baskets sat next to the chair. Balls and skeins of yarn still filled the basket, bright colors just waiting to be knit into something warm and wonderful. A few even had sparkles in them.

Elizabeth set her bag on her bed. She stretched her arms behind her, then rolled her neck. Her back felt stiff after the long drive. Opening her overnight bag, she fished out her pajamas and bath kit before heading to the bathroom and a long, hot soak.

2

Elizabeth came awake slowly to the sound of waves crashing against the cliffs. Sea birds were calling in the early morning air, and she could hear the lobster boats heading out to check their traps.

She sighed in bliss. She had missed these early morning sounds. They were the soundtrack of her childhood. As a child, the early morning had been her favorite time of day. She loved the clear, clean light slowly lighting up the dawn. This felt like peace to her.

Elizabeth stretched, then threw off the covers as she sat up. She froze, staring at Aunt Gloria's chair against the back wall of the room. The chair was rocking, and sitting in it, knitting happily, was Aunt Gloria.

"Good morning, Sweetheart. I'm glad you made it in safely. I thought you might have forgotten the way."

Elizabeth's eyes were suspiciously damp. She brushed the moisture away as she stared at the ghost in the chair.

"I missed you, Aunt Glo. Why didn't you tell me you were sick? I would have come home."

"I wasn't sick, Lizzie Grace. I didn't pass on of natural causes. I thought you knew that."

Elizabeth shook her head.

"Hmph. I guess no one's told you yet. I was poisoned, Sweetheart. Caz found me when he came over to pick up the tonic I made for his mother."

"Who's Caz?"

"Oh, of course, you wouldn't know. His family moved here after you left. Caz is a shifter—his family is one of the rare ones that can take any animal form they choose. He's a few years younger than you and Lucy. Nice kid. He owns his own construction company now. Best work in town."

"And you make a tonic for his mother?"

"She's not been feeling well since her mate passed on. Bonded mates usually die within a year of each other; you know that. Caz isn't ready to lose her yet. He has two younger sisters, one of whom is still at home, and it terrifies him he'll have to take care of her when his mother goes. Also, he loves his mother very much. He moved back into the family home to help with her when his father died. Really, he already is taking care of his sister, but having Mathilda there enables the fantasy that she's still in charge."

"Huh. So what happened when Caz found you? Was there an investigation?"

"Of course there was, and it's ongoing. But for some reason, no one can scry the event, and the magical imprint was erased. There's no way to tell what happened other than good old-fashioned detective work, and that takes time. I think the police have basically come up against a wall. We may never know who killed me or why."

Elizabeth stared at her aunt for a moment.

"I know it wouldn't change anything, but I would like to know why someone thought they had the right to take you from us. It doesn't make sense. You've only ever helped everyone you met. Everyone loved you. No one in town would want to hurt you, much less kill you."

"Everyone has a dark side, Sweetheart. I was a bit of a wild child in my youth, much like you were. I think that's why we always got along so well. Maybe it was someone from the past. Though it pains me to think that I may have hurt someone so much that they still hated me enough to kill me so many years later."

"If it was someone from your past, why wait so long? Surely, if they hated you that much, they would have tried sooner?"

"Who knows, Sweetheart."

"Will you stay with me? I always thought we'd live here together someday. I don't want to let you go."

"I'll stay for now, Lizzy Grace. I'll help you with your magic. I don't suppose you've used it much, living out in the mortal world. You'll have lots to catch up on if you're going to be living here again."

"Thanks, Aunt Glo. I used my magic sometimes, but it felt like cheating when everyone around me had to do things the hard way. So you're right, I didn't use it very much. Besides, there's that whole 'Never show your magic to mortals' rule. I didn't want to get caught."

"Did your partner know?"

"That I was a Witch? Yeah, he did. His uncle married a Witch, so he recognized the signs. He used to visit them occasionally when he was a child. They lived out in the country, away from other people, and his aunt used her magic a bit more freely. When he was little, she put a geas on him so he couldn't tell anyone what he saw. When he grew up, she lifted it after making him promise not to tell. It really relieved him to have someone to talk to about it. I think that's part of the reason we got along so well. He could share that part of his life with me."

"Did you meet his aunt?"

"Yeah. Sheryl's lovely. She was happy to have another Witch in the family. We didn't get to visit very often, but I was able to let off a little steam when we did. I think that's why I was able to stay in the mortal world for so long; because I had Sheryl to talk to."

Aunt Gloria looked sternly at Elizabeth.

"Have your children shown signs of magical talents yet?"

Elizabeth blushed.

"Lizzie Grace, what did you do?"

"I bound their powers when they were born," she mumbled.

"Why on Earth would you do that?"

"Because we were living in the mortal world, and their father was a mortal!" Elizabeth exclaimed. "How do you think he would have felt, being the only mortal in a house full of Witches? I couldn't do that to him."

"And he never said anything?"

"I may have told him that magic doesn't always breed true in mixed marriages."

"Elizabeth Grace Sloan! That is a lie! You know the genes for magic are dominant!"

"I know, Aunt Glo. I had to do what I thought was right at the time. If it makes you feel any better, I was already planning on coming home before I got the letter from Uncle Teddy. Josh is starting to resist the bonds on his powers again, and I don't want to renew them anymore. He's almost sixteen. He deserves to learn about that part of himself."

"Well, I'm glad you're finally thinking straight, young lady. Why don't you get up and release both children from their bonds? We'll see what mayhem their new powers will create. It'll be fun."

BOTH CHILDREN WERE STILL OUT COLD WHEN ELIZABETH CHECKED on them. She knew from experience that Josh would sleep as late as she let him. Maddie was beginning to stir. Elizabeth stood in the hallway, where she could see into both their rooms. Planting her feet, she held out her hands to either side, one toward each child.

MOTHER, I ASK THAT YOU RELEASE THE BONDS ON MY CHILDREN, allowing their magic to flow free.

We are home now, and they are safe. We are among those who will help them grow in their Gifts and abilities. As I will, So mote it be. Thank you. Blessed Be.

THERE WAS AN ALMOST AUDIBLE SNAP AS THE BONDS ON EACH CHILD broke. A wind blew through the hallway, lifting Elizabeth's hair and blowing it into her face. She brushed it away. Josh rolled over and pulled his pillow over his head.

Maddie sat up, suddenly awake.

"Mom, what was that? And why are the lights twinkling? It looks like there are stars in my room!"

Elizabeth looked into Maddie's room. Several fairies were soaring around excitedly, their bell-like voices chiming in excitement. It looked like Maddie was an Elemental Witch. The Fae loved Elementals, whose magic was very like their own. Elementals were very close to nature. It sure explained why Maddie spent so much time outside.

"Maddie, look at the lights carefully. What do you see?"

Maddie rubbed her eyes and looked again.

"Fairies!" She gasped. "Mom, are they real? For reals real? Am I magic now? Is that why I can see them?" Maddie looked at Elizabeth, her eyes shining.

"Maddie, Sweetheart, our entire family is magical. And so are you. Oh." Elizabeth waved her hand and lifted the geas she had put on her children, preventing them from talking about the magical world. Sheryl had shown her how as soon as the children were old enough to talk.

"Fairweather Falls is an all-magical community, Maddie. We can all use our magic and talk about it whenever we want, here. These Pixies will be your friends if you let them. The Fae are attracted to Witches, especially Elemental Witches, who are very close to nature. You will probably make a lot more interesting friends the longer we stay in town."

"We're staying here for good, right?" Maddie asked as her gaze went back to the Pixies. The tiny beings had come to rest on her lap in the bed. They trilled up at the little girl.

"What are they saying, Mom? Can I learn their language?"

"Maybe, if they'll let you. Pixies can speak English, too, or any language they want, really. My guess is, when they are really sure that you want to be friends, you'll be able to understand them."

"Awesome sauce! That is so cool!"

"I'm going to take a shower and make breakfast, Maddie. I'll see you downstairs, ok?"

Maddie nodded, her attention on the petite Fae still sitting on her lap.

Elizabeth smiled and left her to it.

Looking through the pantry, Elizabeth discovered it had been fully stocked. She pulled out the ingredients for pancakes, then checked the fridge. Bacon *and* sausages. Excellent. Soon she had three skillets going on the oversized range in the kitchen. The kitchen was a fantastic mix of old and modern. There was a gleaming chrome refrigerator, large enough to hold food for an army, besides the old Aga range Elizabeth was cooking on. The range was powered by magic.

There was an island covered with a solid wood top in the center of the kitchen. Stools ranged around it. Over the island hung an oval arrangement that resembled a large, one-tiered chandelier from which one could hang the pots and pans. Dried herbs hung from it as well. There were windows in three walls, letting in plenty of natural light. Elizabeth had always loved Aunt Gloria's kitchen most of all. She had spent a lot of time there as a child, cooking and baking with her favorite aunt.

Elizabeth's stomach rumbled as she put a plate of bacon on the table. She added a plate of sausages, and with a wave of her hand, banked down the stove. She sighed. It felt so extraordinarily freeing to use her magic freely again.

Maddie came running down the stairs, the Pixies following her. Elizabeth had expected this and had set out a dish of chopped fruit for the little Fae beings.

"Maddie, get a couple of the tiny cups there on the shelf, and very carefully, pour a little bit of milk into them. Then add a tiny, tiny drop of honey to each cup. Your new friends will appreciate it."

Maddie hurried to do as she was told, setting the cups on the table near her place. Her new friends dove right in.

"These tiny ones are Pixies, Maddie. They can cause immense mischief, but if they call you friend, they will protect you above all else and make your life much more fun. You are very lucky that they like you."

Maddie was watching the Pixies drink their milk and honey. Her tummy growled. Maddie giggled and reached for her fork.

Joshua came slowly down the stairs.

"Morning, Sweetheart," Elizabeth greeted her oldest child.

"RRR. Morning, Mom." Joshua sat heavily at the table. He pulled the platter of pancakes over and started loading his plate.

"Did you sleep well?" Elizabeth asked.

"Weird dreams. Like Labyrinth weird. I could have sworn there was a gnome talking to me. He said I had to learn to talk to the rocks." Joshua picked up a slice of bacon and crammed it into his mouth.

A knock came from the kitchen door.

Elizabeth looked at her son.

"Josh, I think you had better get that," she said.

Grumbling, Joshua stood and opened the back door. He stood staring down in surprise.

Standing on the doorstep were two beings. One was a short woman, about chest high to Elizabeth. So about four feet tall. The other was a tiny Gnome, red pointy hat and all.

"Mom?" Josh looked around at Elizabeth.

Elizabeth stood and came to the door.

"We are honored by your visit. Please, come inside. We were just having breakfast. Would you care for some food?"

The short woman stepped into the kitchen. She had long brown hair that fell to her waist and wore jeans and a hand-knit cardigan over a long-sleeved tee-shirt.

"My name is Mary. I felt the children awaken. I am relieved to see that you have come home, Elizabeth Sloan. Your place is here. I will take care of your home. You will be too busy doing other things. Besides, it is an honor to serve in the home of both an Elemental and an Earth Mage. Your son is very strong in his magic. It will be a joy to see him grow. And my cousins are already in love with your daughter. Be welcome back to Fairweather Falls."

Elizabeth bowed to Mary.

"We welcome you to our home, Mary. All we have is yours."

The small woman grinned and began tidying the kitchen.

Elizabeth turned back to the Gnome on the doorstep.

"Be welcome in our home, Sir," she said.

"Thank you, daughter. I have come to train your son in his Gifts. My name is Magnus. He is coming late to his Gifts and will have much catching up to do. That's ok. We'll make it fun. I hope he is ready to work." The Gnome grinned.

Elizabeth grinned back. This should be fun to watch.

"Joshua, Magnus will teach you how to use your magic. It looks like you are an Earth Mage. That's a really, really powerful Witch. After breakfast, I suggest you spend some time getting to know each other. Let's all eat, first."

Joshua was staring at Mary, who had immediately made herself at home, and his tiny mentor. He looked back up at Elizabeth, a library's worth of questions in his eyes.

"Don't worry about it, Sweetheart. Remember, we're in the Havens now. We can use and talk about our magic freely. We are expected to, actually. In the fall, you two will go to school with other magical children. It would be best if you got caught up in your Gifts before then. Magnus will help you do that."

"And more. We will make a great Mage and craftsman out of you yet," the Gnome said. He had somehow managed to make his way to the table and was sitting on top of it, digging into a small plate of pancakes and fruit that Elizabeth had made for him.

Looking at her two newly magically awakened children, Elizabeth grinned. Life in Fairweather Falls was going to be fun.

⁂ 3 ⁂

The movers arrived as they were finishing breakfast. They were a magical moving company, used to moving supernatural beings to and from the magical world. They had everything moved in well before lunchtime. Just before noon, Elizabeth had everyone on their bikes and headed towards her parents' house on the next property over. Really, it was all one extensive property with several residences on it. They each had their own driveways and house numbers, though, so it was easy to pretend they were separate properties.

Mary stayed back at the house, tidying and cleaning, renewing the magics on the house that kept it alive. Once a Brownie took on a family, they went right to work. They were happiest when working and would get grumpy if denied their job. As Brownies had powerful magic and could go absolutely feral if angered, it was safer to let her get to it.

Magnus sat on Joshua's shoulder while Maddie's new Pixie friends flew after her as she rode. It only took a few minutes to reach the big house. The house had been in the Sloan family for several hundred years. Since the founding of the town, in fact. It was a beautifully constructed colonial house, with a large porch out front and immense gardens all around. Joshua was not the first Earth Mage in the family, and he wouldn't be the last.

Nora opened the door as they rode up to the house.

"Park your bikes along the side and come in! You're just in time. And I see that you have made a few friends already. Well done."

Nora turned to the Pixies and the Gnome.

"Be welcome in our home. Please, come in."

Elizabeth followed the children into the house. The front door led into a wide hallway. On the right was the living room, piano sitting by the window. To the left were the dining room and kitchen. After the living room was a set of stairs leading to the second floor. Behind the stairs was the downstairs bathroom. After that was a small library and stillroom. Nora did her potion work in there.

The dining room table was laid out with a wide variety of sliced meats and cheeses, loaves of bread, fruits, and condiments. How many people was Nora expecting for lunch? There was enough to feed a football team there.

"I hope you don't mind, darling. I invited a few people over to welcome you home," Nora said.

Elizabeth stared at her mother.

"Who could possibly care that I came home?" She asked, just as there was a knock at the door.

Nora hurried to answer it. Elizabeth turned around to see a woman about her own age step into the room. The woman had blond hair swept up in a ponytail. She wore jeans with a smudge of dirt on the right leg and a flannel shirt. She looked like she had been working outside. There was the faint smell of horse around her.

The woman looked nervous, as if she weren't sure what she was doing there or if they would welcome her.

"Elizabeth, you remember Sarah? You two were thick as thieves when you were small. Never saw one of you without the other. Sarah is the town veterinarian and Familiar caretaker now. She took over from her father several years ago. Sarah, sit down. We're just waiting for one more person; then we can eat."

Sarah smiled nervously at Elizabeth.

"Wow, Sarah. I didn't know you were still in town," Elizabeth said as Sarah sat on the opposite side of the table.

"Yeah, I did my training and apprenticeship in California, but my heart was always here. I came home about seven years ago when Dad started to talk about retiring. He still helps out, but I run the business and the Center now."

"That's great. Congratulations."

Elizabeth didn't know what else to say. She and Sarah had stayed in touch for a few years after they both left home, but being on opposite sides of the first the world, and then the country, had made it easy to drift apart.

There was another knock at the door. Nora stood again, looking somewhat nervous herself this time. Elizabeth groaned. What had Nora done now?

Nora turned from the door, allowing someone tall and broad-shouldered to enter the house.

"Elizabeth, you remember Jonah McClure, I'm sure. He moved here after college. He's a detective on our police force, now."

Elizabeth stared at the man standing just inside the door. Her heart felt like it was about to beat right out of her chest, and she felt the insane urge to hide under the table.

"Hello, Liz," Jonah said.

"Hey," Elizabeth mumbled back.

"Right, now we can eat. Elizabeth, your father is out back, tinkering on something. You can take him a plate after lunch, ok? Lucy couldn't leave the diner, but she said to come by after and she'd feed you all desserts. Jonah, Sarah, these are Elizabeth's children, Joshua and Maddie, and their friends. Kids, these are two of your mother's closest friends from childhood. Now, let's eat."

Maddie made a plate for her Pixie friends while Magnus sat on the table next to Josh's plate with his own in front of him. Nora began asking Magnus questions about his presence in Josh's life and was ecstatic with the answers.

"An Earth Mage, that's wonderful! Congratulations, Joshua. And it looks like Maddie is an Elemental Witch?"

"Elemental Mage, actually, Mom," Elizabeth said.

"How marvelous. What an exciting way to start your new lives here. Joshua, you are very lucky that Magnus has agreed to teach you. You'll learn a lot from him. Has a teacher appeared for Maddie yet?"

Elizabeth shook her head.

"No, but she's not as far behind. I'm sure one will turn up soon. The Pixies appeared as soon as I removed the bindings on her power this morning."

"Why were our powers bound, Mom?" Maddie asked.

"Because we were living in the mortal world, Sweetheart, and your dad was mortal. I didn't want him to feel bad, being the only one in the family without magic."

"But we would have loved him anyway," Maddie said.

"I know, Sweetheart. It just seemed better that way. But you don't have to worry about it. We're here now, and I won't bind your Gifts again."

"If Dad had lived, would you have unbound our powers, eventually?" Joshua asked.

Elizabeth stared at the table for a moment, then looked up at Joshua.

"I think I would have. You were already breaking through the bindings, Josh, and it wouldn't have been fair to keep putting you back under them. And I was getting tired of it. I was already planning to talk to your father about moving back here or somewhere closer to here so that you could get training. The fire happened before I could talk to him, and then we were all such a mess for a while. I was already starting to plan coming home, though, before I got the letter from Mr. Lawrence that Aunt Glo had left us her house."

Elizabeth looked up at Jonah.

"Aunt Glo says you haven't made any progress on her case yet? That there's no trace of a magical imprint or anything that could show what happened?"

"Gloria visited you?" Nora gasped.

"She's going to stay with us for a while," Elizabeth said. "She's going to help me get used to using magic again. And I think she wants to know why someone would kill her. If not who."

"Wait, Aunt Gloria was murdered?" Joshua exclaimed. Maddie looked up from the Pixies.

"She said she was poisoned."

Jonah nodded.

"She was. And she's right; we have hit a dead end. Even using mortal forensic methods, we've got nothing. Someone was very, very careful." He paused for a moment. "Gloria has no idea who could have wanted her dead?"

Elizabeth shook her head.

"Not a clue. Aunt Glo said maybe someone from her past, but that was a long time ago, and she didn't want to think that someone could hate her that much for so long."

"Hm. Please ask Gloria to let you know, or come see me directly if she has the energy if she thinks of anything else," Jonah said.

After lunch, Elizabeth decided to take the kids into town. They'd both been sleeping when they had passed through the previous night, and it had been dark, anyway. Before the lunch party broke up, Maddie had wrangled a promise out of Sarah to let them visit the animal rehabilitation and Familiar Center that she ran with her family on the outskirts of town. Maddie was excited to meet the Familiars. Elizabeth wanted to get a picture, or maybe a video, of the first time Maddie saw a real unicorn. Fortunately, Sarah said she had two at the moment, a mother and her foal. The women had parted on good terms, if still a bit cold. It felt strange to see her old friends again. So much time had passed, and they were different people now. Elizabeth hoped they would get the chance to know each other as they were now. They really had been close once.

Jonah had left when Sarah did, heading back to the police station. He had promised to let Elizabeth know if there were any developments in her aunt's case. He had smiled at her as he left. Elizabeths's heart had fluttered in her chest. She mulled the feeling over on the ride into town. Jonah had been the love of her teenage years. Yes, he was still handsome, and now he was here, rather than three hours away across the water. That didn't mean that they would get back together again. Or that they would even be friends. Honestly, Elizabeth knew nothing about the man Jonah had become. Maybe he was married or in a relationship. Maybe he had kids. Though she thought he probably would have mentioned it if he had, what with meeting hers. She shook her head, trying to dislodge the train of thought she was on. They were both living in Fairweather Falls, now. At the very least, they could be friends. Or casually friendly acquaintances. Whatever.

The family parked their bikes by the library in the center of town. Elizabeth focused for a moment, envisioning a ward around the bikes so they would stay put. Then she took Maddie's hand. Joshua walked at her side as they looked around the town. Fairweather Falls had always been a magical Haven. Occasionally, you would get the odd magical who married a human and brought them to visit or to live in the town. That didn't happen very often, though. It was much too hard on the humans, having to be placed under geases so they wouldn't give anything away to their mortal families. Not being able to invite their families to visit. It usually only worked out if the mortal partner in question had no family to speak of on the outside. Jared's family basically consisted of his uncle and Witch aunt. His parents had been killed in a car crash when he was eighteen. By then, Jared was already attending the fire science program at one of the nearby universities. That was why Elizabeth had thought it might work out if they had moved home. Or at least close by. After all, his uncle had married a Witch. They could come to visit whenever they wanted.

Elizabeth watched her children's faces as they walked around town. Maddie was staring at everything, her eyes wide in amazement. Josh blinked as a Naiad walked by, wearing very little. As this was a Haven, magical beings could walk around freely in their natural forms. A barrier around the town kept mortals out, so magicals didn't have to worry about being exposed. Witches flew by on broomsticks; Centaurs strode by in small groups; trolls guarded the doors to the bars. Various Fae went by, glancing down at Maddie and smiling as they passed. Even though the paranormal world had come out of the broom closet almost twenty years ago, it was hard to move forward from centuries of hiding. Many paranormal towns were now in the open, but the Havens remained hidden.

The center of town was pedestrian-only. Cars were rarely used, as most of the magicals in town had other ways of getting around. Only those that had a reason to leave town and go into the mortal world regularly kept vehicles. An enterprising hobgoblin had set up a car rental business on the edge of town for those that didn't own their own car but had a reason to go out into the mortal world and needed transportation.

There was a long, rectangular stretch of space in the town center that housed an open-air market. It was enchanted so that it was always the perfect temperature to encourage browsing and shopping. Vendors had stalls and tents set up on both sides of the central walkway. It was an excellent way for those whose business was seasonal or those who didn't want to have a permanent space in town to sell their wares. The family wandered past a tall Sidhe selling beautifully crafted musical instruments, a dryad selling handmade dresses, and a Brownie selling homemade sweets and baked goods from around the world. Elizabeth stopped at the Brownie's stall.

"Elizabeth Grace Sloan! I heard you were back. And straight to me, you come. I should have known," the woman came around the table at the front of her tent and put her arms around Elizabeth, hugging her tightly.

"And these must be Joshua and Maddie. I'm thrilled to meet you, children. Your mother ate her weight in my baked goods as a child. I fully expect the two of you to do the same. I often have new recipes to try out—I am always grateful for new people to try them on."

Maddie grinned at the little woman brightly. The group of Pixies that had followed her around since she woke up that morning were hovering over the sweets, arguing.

"Kids, this is Meg. She's the best baker you will ever meet. If she offers you the chance to taste something she's made, take it. No joke," Elizabeth told Josh and Maddie.

"Thank you, Elizabeth. That's very kind of you to say. Even though I'm sure that you're hoping your kind words will earn you a cake or two," Meg grinned at Elizabeth. Then she turned around and picked up what looked like a chocolate cupcake.

"Here. You deserve it for coming home. Chocolate cake, filled with coconut cream and strawberry jam, with a dash of contentment. I imagine you need a bit of a rest, after everything, after all."

"Thanks, Meg."

"And you kids choose something as well. Take your time; you can have whatever you like. I need to help my other customers. I'll be right back." Meg went to help the Pixies resolve their argument, which had grown quite shrill.

"One thing only, this time, you two," Elizabeth said, catching the look in Maddie's eyes. That girl did have quite the sweet tooth. No wonder the Fae liked Elemental Mages so much. They had too much in common.

Joshua chose a bear claw, and Maddie chose a strawberry parfait. Meg turned back to them as Maddie made her choice.

"Oh, very good. The bear claw has a shot of grounding, and the parfait a shot of joy. I can see that you two are going to be quite strong in your Gifts," Meg exclaimed.

"Of course, you know what Gifts they have already," Elizabeth said. "They only came into their powers this morning."

"Well, with Magnus there sitting on Joshua's shoulder, it's easy to guess that he's an Earth Mage, and the Pixies are a dead give-away that Maddie is a strong Elemental Mage. Magnus, you choose something, too. I have a few chestnut cookies here. I can dip them in chocolate for you if you like."

"That's very kind of you, Meg, thank you. I'll take two, please," the Gnome said, rubbing his hands together in delight.

Meg looked up at Elizabeth.

"Mary that's adopted you is my niece. She's a good girl. You can be sure she'll take good care of you."

"Thank you, Meg. That's good to know. Any family of yours is family to me," Elizabeth answered.

Meg patted her on the arm, then handed Elizabeth another cupcake. The Brownie was very pleased.

They said goodbye to Meg and carried on down the path. There were leatherworkers, toymakers, and down at the end a whole farmer's market, complete with prepared food stalls and seating. A group of musicians kept the diners entertained.

Joshua looked around.

"Doesn't the street market take away from the regular shops?" He asked.

"Not at all. It all works out very well together," Elizabeth said. "No one worries about it."

Lining both sides of the street around the market were the permanent shops and restaurants. The shops were slightly more upscale than those the kids were used to. There was a hardware store, a grocery store, an ice cream shop, several clothing stores, a magical supply store, the police station, the post office, a theatre, a real estate office, a health clinic, and the town hall. Every shop and restaurant was meticulously maintained. The outsides were all freshly painted, while many had potted plants and window boxes full of blooms decorating their fronts. The restaurants and the ice cream shop had outdoor seating areas in front, facing the market.

As they looked in the windows, Joshua and Maddie began to realize that the goods in the shops were not the same as those they were used to either. All of the clothing looked to be original designs, well made, and displayed with care. The hardware store had a weapons section in the back. ("The owner's brother is a blacksmith," Elizabeth told the astonished Joshua.)

Elizabeth came to a stop in front of a shop whose windows were still dark. The door was shut. The shop had the closed and empty feeling of a building that hadn't been used for a while.

"This used to be my favorite shop," Elizabeth said sadly. "I spent hours in here when I wasn't with Aunt Glo."

"Let me guess, it was a book store," Joshua said wryly.

Elizabeth smiled.

"It was. It had books from all over, not just the Earth realm. Some of the Fae books could sing or fly. It was amazing. I wonder what happened to it. I thought it would be here forever."

"Hmm, we all did, darling. About two years ago, old Jackson, the owner, decided to move home to England. Family business, he said. He told everyone the store would open again when the right person showed up to run it. So far, no one has."

Elizabeth looked up into a pair of deep blue eyes. The eyes were set in the pleasant, if somewhat pensive at the moment, face of a tall man with light brown hair that just reached his shoulders. He was dressed in clean blue jeans, tall heeled boots, and an almost blindingly pink top that looked like it came from the cover of a historical romance novel. He wore a lavender velvet choker around his neck, from which hung a cameo of another man.

"Are you new here, darlings? I don't think I've met you before," the man asked.

"I grew up here," Elizabeth answered. "We just moved back."

"Well, welcome. You must come into my store. We'll get your wardrobe taken care of. From the looks of you, you've been living in the mortal realm for too long." He looked at Joshua and Maddie. "The young man will probably prefer one of the other shops, though we may have one or two pieces that suit. The young lady, however, we will be happy to accommodate."

"Of course, you wouldn't be thinking of taking one of my customers, now, Calvin, would you?" A soft voice chimed in. A slender Aes Sídhe woman came to stand in front of Maddie. "This young lady is obviously an Elemental Mage, which makes her one of mine. We have everything she will need."

"Of course, Clara. I just thought we could have a little fun. I have several pieces that even you would approve of that would look darling on her," Calvin pouted.

Clara looked up at Elizabeth.

"I am Clara Morningstar. I own The Flower's Daughter, across the street. We provide all-natural clothing to the Fae and to any Elemental Witches and Mages in town. You know how much more sensitive we are to any dyes and chemicals. Please, once you're settled in, come see me. We'll have some fun getting the young lady fitted out."

Elizabeth smiled at the dueling shop owners.

"Thank you, both of you. I appreciate it. We'll visit both your shops. I will admit, it will be nice to have clothing that doesn't irritate Maddie's skin. You're right; she is extra sensitive."

Clara nodded, smiled at Maddie, and made her way back across the street.

"Mom, is that why I'm so sensitive? Because I'm a Mage?" Maddie asked.

"Yes, Sweetheart. Now that your magic is coming in, you both will become much more tuned to Nature and sensitive to chemicals and other things. You know I've always tried to buy eco-friendly clothing when possible? This is why."

"I like my clothes," Joshua said as he itched a spot on his hip where his waistband was rubbing.

"You'll like the clothes you can get here even better," Calvin assured him. "Trust me, darling. Come along to my shop. I'll show you. We can mimic any style you like. Though, there is a shop that caters to teens that you might like better, a few doors down. But come see us first."

Calvin grabbed Joshua's arm and started dragging him along. Calvin pulled Joshua into the next store over, Elizabeth and Maddie trailing behind.

"Paul, darling, we've got company!" Calvin sang out as they entered the store.

"Mama, he has tails!" Maddie whispered.

4

Calvin did indeed have five fox tails. Wow. A five-tailed Kitsune. Fairweather Falls was moving up in the world.

A second young man stepped out from behind a curtained-off doorway at the back of the shop.

"Calvin, you promised to stop dragging people in off the street, remember?" The new young man sounded exasperated with his partner.

"These people don't mind. They've been living in the mortal realm. They need our help. *Please*, darling."

The other man, Paul, sighed. Unlike Calvin's more flamboyant taste in clothes, Paul was dressed in black slacks, with a tight black sweater and shiny black low-heeled boots. He wore tortoiseshell glasses over his dark eyes. His skin was darker than Calvin's pale European tone. His black hair was short, save for one swath that fell over one eye. Paul brushed the hair out of his face as he observed the little group standing in the center of the shop.

"Welcome to Vix," Paul said. "I see you've met Calvin. I'm the other owner, Paul. Please, be welcome."

"Thank you," Elizabeth said. "Calvin's right; we have been living in the mortal realm. I would appreciate having clothes that more truly expressed who I am. Mortal clothing is largely uninspired."

"Music to my ears, darling," Calvin said. "Let's get started."

He walked around Elizabeth, eyeing her closely. "Earth Witch?" He asked.

"Yes, strong in potions," Elizabeth replied.

"Oh, good. Our last potion maker passed away recently. Such a tragedy. They still don't have a clue who was responsible."

"That would have been my Aunt Gloria," Elizabeth said. "We live in her house, now. I imagine I will take over her work, especially if there is no other potion maker in town."

"Oh my dear, I am so sorry. I had no idea. You poor things," Calvin was horrified. He swept Elizabeth and Maddie into a deep hug.

"We will certainly get you taken care of. And there is no other qualified potion maker in town. Of course, there are people who can do small things, but no one of Gloria's level. Even the Healers are having to order the complicated things from out of town. You'll do a good business. Will you work from home, like Gloria did? Or would you prefer a place in town? I must say that would be much more convenient for most folks." He paused for a moment. "The only store available right now is the bookstore. I wonder if it would open for you. It would be wonderful to have the bookstore open again as well. You could add a potions shop upstairs or in the back. Maybe have a little cafe upstairs? It would be perfect, darling!"

Calvin was becoming more excited the more he planned.

Paul rolled his eyes.

"Please forgive Calvin his little flight of fantasy. He loves to sort out everyone's lives for them. I always say he should have been a social director somewhere. Maybe on one of those cruise ships."

"Ugh. Boats," Calvin shuddered.

Paul shrugged. He rolled his eyes again as if to say, '*What can you do?*'

Elizabeth grinned.

They spent a little over an hour in Vix with Calvin and Paul. Calvin had tried to talk Elizabeth into some of his more outrageous styles before Paul stepped in and asked her what her preferences were.

"I actually prefer more Victorian-inspired clothing, with a twist," Elizabeth said.

"Ooh, I have just the thing," Calvin clapped his hands.

By the time he was done, Elizabeth had three walking skirts, one in deep brown, one in forest green, and one in navy blue. She had three shirtwaists to match, then three in plain white, and several fitted jackets. Calvin finished her off with two pairs of sturdy black boots with buttons up the sides and a low block heel. The boots felt as if they had been made for her feet, as if she were walking on air. Elizabeth sighed as she pulled them on.

"I have so missed magical clothing," she said. She stroked the outside of the blue velvet jacket she was wearing over her brown skirt and white shirtwaist.

Joshua and Maddie were staring at her as if they had never seen her before.

"I didn't know you liked clothes like this, Mom," Josh said.

"I love them. This is what I wore when I lived here before. I had a few pairs of high-waisted pants, too, for when I needed them, but I much prefer skirts. If I dressed like this in the mortal world, I got looked at funny, so I stopped. I feel as if this is so much more me. Thank you, Calvin and Paul."

Elizabeth grinned at Calvin, who held up two pairs of high-waisted pants in her size, one in brown, one in navy blue. Elizabeth nodded. Calvin squeed and hurried to pack them up.

Paul had given her a ridiculous discount as a welcome-home gift. He had also extracted a promise for reduced prices on potions for himself and Calvin. Elizabeth had been happy to give it. She liked the two men. *I think we could all be very good friends,* Elizabeth thought as she led the way out of the store. She turned left, and they stopped at Spice, the store catering to teens next. Magnus came up as they stood outside. He had stayed in the market to shop while they wandered.

"Oh, good. I was going to suggest replacing Joshua's wardrobe. His studies are likely to be tough on his mortal clothes. Let me help you choose, Joshua."

Elizabeth left Joshua in his mentor's capable hands and took Maddie across the street to The Flower's Daughter.

Clara was helping another customer when they entered the store. The Flower's Daughter was decorated to look like a forest bower. Clara had painted the walls a lovely, pale green. Several silver birch trees grew straight through the main room of the store. A soundtrack of bird calls and waterfalls almost convinced Elizabeth they had stepped through a portal into a sylvan glen.

Maddie looked around in complete delight as they entered the store. Her new Pixie friends fluttered off to look around while Maddie explored. Elizabeth smiled and sat in one of the comfortable armchairs by the window, looking out onto the street.

Clara finished with her earlier customer, a dryad, slender and with tiny green leaves throughout her long, chestnut hair. Waving the dryad goodbye, Clara made her way over and sat down across from Elizabeth.

"Your little girl is fortunate to have so many Pixie friends."

"They appeared as soon as she woke up and came into her Gifts this morning. After I removed the binding I placed on her. They've been with us all day. Maddie adores them."

"She is going to be a powerful Witch, you realize," Clara stated.

Elizabeth nodded.

"I know. Our family generally turns out very strong Witches. I think Maddie is the first Elemental in several generations, though. We are usually Earth Witches."

"Who is your family, if you don't mind me asking?"

"I am Elizabeth Sloan."

"Of course. The one that got away. It is a pleasure to have you back in town," Clara replied. She looked over at Maddie, who was being led through the clothing racks by her Pixie friends. One of the little Fae pulled out something florescent pink. Maddie shook her head, giggling. The Pixie's voice grew shrill as she argued her case for the brightly-hued garment. A silver squirrel bounced down through the branches of the birch trees and landed on Maddie's shoulder. She jumped, then stared at the squirrel, eyes wide. The little creature began arguing with the Pixie, gesturing emphatically with one paw while holding onto Maddie's hair with the other. Maddie was giggling again. In fact, as their voices grew louder, Maddie's giggles turned into full-blown laughter. Finally, she couldn't take it anymore. Maddie collapsed on the ground, laughing so hard she could barely breathe. The squirrel leaped for safety as she fell. He landed on a nearby table and promptly began chittering angrily at Maddie, who laughed even more loudly.

"Mom! I can't breathe!" Maddie gasped out.

Clara looked sharply at Elizabeth.

"She'll be fine. This happens every once in a while. Usually, when she needs to let off steam. It's been a while, so I guess she's due. I should really thank your Familiar. If Maddie goes too long without a laughing fit like this, she gets very, very cranky. That's no fun for anyone."

"You said that Maddie is the first Elemental Mage in your family for several generations. Do you have a mentor for her?"

"Not yet. As I said, she only came into her Gifts this morning. I'm sure one will turn up when the time is right."

Clara thought for a moment.

"I think I might know the perfect person. I will have to see if they are free. Your family can teach her the Witch side of her magic, I'm sure. I will arrange for the Fae."

Elizabeth looked at Clara in shock. This was an immense gift. Maddie must be stronger in her Gifts than Elizabeth had guessed.

"It will be my pleasure to arrange for her training," Clara continued. "In return, perhaps you could find it in your heart to help out from time to time, with such issues that a Witch is more suited to than a Fae," Clara said.

"Of course. I find your offer acceptable. I am at your service, provided it causes no harm to my children, family, or business."

"I believe our continued good faith will bring only benefits to all of us," Clara stated firmly.

"Done," Elizabeth stated, holding out her hand, palm up, to Clara. The Sidhe woman covered Elizabeth's hand with her own. A golden light wove around their joined hands, binding them together for a moment. A warm, tingling sensation filled Elizabeth's body as if her blood had become pleasantly carbonated with tiny bubbles of joy.

"Mom, come see what I found!" Maddie called. Elizabeth smiled at Clara and stood, making her way over to her daughter. Maddie held out a shining silver dress that looked incredibly uncomfortable but turned out to be made of a soft, supple fabric that flowed like water over her hand.

"That's beautiful, Maddie. That's a very special dress. You can have one ceremonial and party dress if you like. Why don't you give that one to Lady Clara, and we'll keep looking for regular clothes? I'm sure that you will find everything you need here."

Maddie skipped over to Clara with the dress, then dove back into the clothes amongst the trees.

Clara held the dress for a moment.

"This dress is made of water. I think Water may be Maddie's primary Element. It will be exciting to see what else she picks out." Clara laid the dress carefully on the counter. "I will go call the one I have in mind to be Maddie's teacher. I'll be right back." She disappeared into the back room.

Elizabeth wandered through the shop, looking at the beautiful things. She had always loved Fae clothing. It was literally made of the elements, concentrated into fabric form. It was the most comfortable and elegant clothing you could ever wear. Even children's clothes were made that way, among the Fae. Maddie would be one of the best-dressed Witches in town when they were done.

By the time Maddie had everything she needed, there was an enormous pile of clothes of every color on the counter next to the register. Clara found Maddie a couple of pairs of strong, sensible boots, too. The boots were perfect for tramping around outside all day, being immensely well made, yet were superbly comfortable as well. They fit Maddie like they were made for her. Fae clothing was good that way.

Clara, too, gave them a steep discount and bartered for an agreement for potions as well. Elizabeth left the shop feeling extremely happy with life. They both had a small fortune in new clothing, and yet her purse was still full. It was a wonderful feeling.

They met Joshua and Magnus at the end of the market by the stage. Joshua had a satchel slung across his body. That one bag was all he had. Elizabeth looked around, wondering where his new clothes were.

"I thought that Joshua should have a portal bag," Magnus said. "It will make it much easier on him during his training to be able to carry many things around without worrying about weight. Don't worry; this is my gift to my new apprentice. No strings attached," the Gnome said.

Elizabeth blinked. Portal bags, also known as 'bags of holding,' were prohibitively expensive for most people. This was another substantial gift.

"My appreciation for your thoughtfulness in taking care of my son," Elizabeth said slowly.

Magnus grinned.

"Of course, my dear. If you wouldn't mind sending a good potion or two my way now and again, I'd appreciate it, of course."

"Of course, Master Magnus. It would be my pleasure," Elizabeth replied. She was really going to have to get back up to speed in her potion-making post haste. It looked like the town truly had been without a Potions Master since Aunt Gloria died. And for a town like Fairweather Falls, that was way too long.

5

Mary was in the kitchen making dinner when they returned home. Aunt Gloria was hovering, chatting with the Brownie as she worked. Gloria turned and gave Elizabeth a good look as she entered the room.

"Well, you look much more like yourself, now, my girl. That's much better. Well done."

"Thanks, Aunt Glo. Mary, we saw your Aunt Meg at the market. She's one of my very favorite people. She speaks very highly of you."

"That's nice to hear," Mary said, blushing. She took a loaf of freshly-baked bread out of the oven and set it on the island in the middle of the kitchen. Elizabeth inhaled deeply.

"That is one of my very favorite smells. That's wonderful, Mary. It looks amazing."

"Baking in here with me was one of your favorite things to do when you were younger," Aunt Gloria remembered with a fond smile. Her eyes crinkled up at the corners.

"It really was," Elizabeth said. "So was potion-making. And about that—I already have several requests for potions. It looks like I'll need to get back up to speed sooner rather than later. Can we start on that right away, Aunt Glo?"

"Of course, darling. After dinner, why don't we go into the still-room and take a look around, see what's still good and what needs replacing? The gardens out back are all taken care of, as is the green-house. Nora's been checking on them for me. You know she can grow just about anything. Then tomorrow, we can start brewing. We'll start with the simple stuff and work our way up. Does that sound good?"

"That sounds wonderful, thank you," Elizabeth said.

"Dinner will be ready in about five minutes," Mary said.

"Wonderful. I'll tell the kids. I have to take my bags to my room anyway," Elizabeth said.

"I want to see what they got, too. I'll come with you. How did the day go?" Aunt Gloria asked, floating after Elizabeth as she climbed the stairs to the second floor, bags in hand.

"Magnus bought Joshua a portal bag, and Clara Morningstar is finding a Fae teacher for Maddie."

Aunt Gloria blinked.

"Elizabeth, Clara Morningstar is Aes Sídhe. Her uncle is the King in this area. If she is offering Maddie a teacher, Maddie will be incredibly powerful someday."

"I got that impression. It will be interesting to see who Clara sends."

THERE WAS A KNOCK ON THE DOOR EARLY THE FOLLOWING DAY AS the household was eating breakfast. Mary had made spiced oatmeal with raisins and chunks of apple mixed in. Even Joshua, who usually wouldn't touch oatmeal, had dug right in.

Mary went to answer the door, waving to Elizabeth to stay put and finish her bowl.

"Hi, My Aunt Clara sent me to teach a new Elemental Mage here in this house? My name's Maggie. You can call me Mags."

"Of course, come in. I will announce you." Mary led Mags into the house.

Elizabeth stood while Josh and Maddie looked up curiously.

"Elizabeth, children, Gloria, may I present the Lady Margarethe

Clíodhna Laughlin of the Silver Waters Fae Court. She is here to be Miss Maddie's teacher."

Maddie's eyes grew wide. Joshua had gone very, very still. He stared at the young Fae standing in front of them.

Mags was not your typical Aes Sidhe Fae. She was tall and slender, with gently-pointed ears and slightly up-tilted eyes. But her long, curly hair was dyed to look like flames, a deep purple on top, then red, then golden. There were flashes of teal here and there as well. The unconventional Fae wore a dark purple skirt that came down to her knees, with a deep ruffle on the bottom. She had on a jacket somewhat like the Victorian-inspired ones that Elizabeth preferred, with a cameo affixed to the left breast and the chain of a pocket watch hanging out of the right pocket. The jacket was edged with teal lace along the bottom. Her legs were encased in stockings, striped in red and purple. She wore black leather boots with low block heels. There were roses embroidered on the sides of the boots.

Joshua blinked and went back to eating. He quickly finished and excused himself, hurrying from the room.

Mags appeared to be the same age as Joshua. Elizabeth wasn't sure, as Fae aged very slowly. The young woman could be several hundred years old.

"I am Elizabeth Sloan. This is my daughter, Madyson, and my recently deceased Aunt, Gloria. The young man that just left is my son, Joshua. Be welcome in our home, Lady Margarethe Clíodhna Laughlin of the Silver Waters Fae Court."

"Call me Mags. So, Maddie. Aunt Clara tells me that you only got your magic yesterday? Has this lot been with you since then?" She pointed at the Pixies, who were still following Maddie around. They were currently enjoying their own tiny bowls of oatmeal.

Maddie nodded.

"If you don't mind me asking, Mags, are you quite sure that you are up to teaching a new Elemental Mage? Clara seems to think that Maddie will be quite strong, and you seem very young," Aunt Gloria asked.

"I'm one hundred and seventy-five. I finished my training myself, recently. This is my journeyman project. My Master, Anloriel, will be overseeing. I was trained to be a magical teacher, so this is perfect for me. And my magic is powerful, like Maddie's. You get my enthusiasm and energy along with my Master's experience. Win-win."

Aunt Gloria nodded.

"Well, sounds good to me. We are happy to have you," Elizabeth said. "Please, have a seat. Mary made the most wonderful oatmeal for breakfast. I'll be working in the gardens and the stillroom today if you need me. Joshua will be out with his teacher, Magnus, I imagine. Let me know if you go anywhere, and no taking her into the Fae Court without me, ok?"

"Sure thing," Mags smiled up at Mary as the Brownie placed a bowl in front of her.

"Will you be staying with us, or will you return home in the evenings?"

"I'll stay with Aunt Clara, I think. Maybe find myself somewhere of my own nearby after a while."

Elizabeth looked at Aunt Gloria.

"Is the guesthouse still open?"

"It is. Check with Nora if she has any plans for it. I'm sure that would be fine."

"If it's ok with my family, we have a small cottage on the property that we only use when guests are visiting. I'm sure you could stay there while you are with us," Elizabeth offered. "Magnus prefers to return home each night, and Mary had the house add on an extra room for her behind the pantry. Unless you would prefer we add another room for you here? Could we do that, Mary?"

The Brownie nodded.

"That's very kind of you," Mags said. "If I can convince one of our family Brownies to come with me, I would appreciate the use of the cottage. It would be nice to have a bit of space all to myself. And I would be close enough for when I need to be here early or leave late. I think that would do very well."

"If it would help you, Lady Margarethe, my cousin Mariah is available. She would be happy to serve. Unless you have your own Brownie already," Mary offered.

"I still live at home, so I have been taken care of by the family

Brownie. And my old nurse, but she is more a valued member of the family, and retired, now. She was my grandmother's nurse as well. I would love to meet Mariah."

"I will send her to you, then, as soon as Miss Elizabeth arranges your house."

Mags grinned.

"I'll go call my mother," Elizabeth said. "Please, take your time eating. I'll let you know what she says."

❧

"Clara sent her niece to be Maddie's teacher?" Nora exclaimed. "But they're Aes Sídhe! They're Royal Fae!"

"Yep. Maddie's going to be seriously powerful. I think Josh will, too. Magnus is no slouch as a teacher, either."

"For both children to be assigned mentors like this, I agree they will both be very powerful," Nora replied.

"So, can Mags have the cottage?" Elizabeth asked again.

"Of course. Are you sure Magnus doesn't need somewhere to stay, too?"

"His home is nearby, I think. He prefers to go home at night. Mags wanted to be closer to Maddie and liked the idea of having her own place. I guess she's never been on her own before. And Mary has pretty much promised her cousin Mariah will take care of Mags."

"It's a great honor for their family; of course she will. Well, this is certainly working out well for everyone. Ok. Well, keep me posted."

Elizabeth agreed and hung up. She returned to the dining room.

"Mags, mom says the cottage is yours if you want it. Are you sure you wouldn't be more comfortable staying here with us? Or at your Aunt's house?"

"The cottage will be perfect. I appreciate the offer."

"Ok, then. Maddie, I'll be out back if you need me, ok?"

Maddie nodded happily.

"Are we going to learn about magic today?" Maddie started in on Mags as Elizabeth left the room.

Elizabeth grinned, then went to call Clara. She was sure that Mags was who she said she was—Mary would have known if the Aes Sídhe harbored any ill intent towards the family. Still, she thought it wise to check in. It was always good to stay on the right side of the Fae.

6

Elizabeth stuck her bottom lip out, letting out a puff of air that lifted the fringe of hair hanging towards her eyes, softening her (to her) relatively high forehead. She had been in the stillroom all day, working with Aunt Gloria on the potions she already had requests for. While Elizabeth would have loved to be able to say that she dove back in like she'd never left, in reality, it had taken her several hours to feel confident in her potion-making abilities again.

Aunt Gloria had been very supportive. The ghost had hovered nearby, thankfully allowing Elizabeth to figure things out for herself, giving advice or help only when asked. They had taken a brief break around one for lunch, then jumped right back in.

Elizabeth looked with pride at the row of stoppered glass bottles on the table in front of her.

Aunt Gloria had shown her where her lists of regular potions were and the list of who got regular refills and when. Elizabeth had made the tonic for Caz's mom, Mathilda, as well as various arthritis potions and a few asthma potions for other town members. She had replenished the stock of first aid and healing potions too.

"Do you have any idea what potions Calvin, Paul, Clara, and Magnus would want?" Elizabeth asked Aunt Glo.

"Calvin used hair tonics to keep his hair looking perfect. I made an herbal shaving cream for Paul. I also made them a special spritz for the store to attract prosperity and goodwill. Occasionally, they'll ask for something else." She paused. "Neither Clara nor Magnus has ever asked me for anything. I think you will just have to wait and see what they want when they want it."

"Can we get started on the things that Calvin and Paul might want?"

"You might want to check the infusions I have going. They've been neglected since I crossed over. Some of them need several months to infuse properly, as you remember."

Elizabeth checked all of the jars containing herbs and oils that Aunt Gloria had infusing in the stillroom. She threw out one in which the oil had gone rancid. The others seemed to be ok.

Elizabeth checked her phone. It was after four in the afternoon. She stretched, arching her arms overhead and backward, leaning into the stretch. She rolled her neck, then shook all over.

"I think I've reached my limit for the day, Aunt Glo. I'll get started on Calvin's things tomorrow if that's ok."

"I think that's fine, dear. I'm sure he'll appreciate having them whenever you can get them to him."

Elizabeth locked the door to the little one-room-plus-bathroom cottage in the garden and returned to the house. Her clothes were dusty and had several spills and smudges on them, despite having been covered with Aunt Gloria's oversized white apron. Potion making was often messy. But the stillroom was now clean, the herbs and flowers she'd harvested from the gardens hanging to dry overhead. The shelves were gradually getting restocked. Elizabeth felt warmly satisfied with her first day back at work.

"You handled everything very well today, Lizzie Grace," Aunt Gloria said, following her into the kitchen. The room was empty, a plate of cookies on the table, the air smelling of cinnamon and sugar. Elizabeth helped herself to a cookie before putting the kettle on for tea.

"Thanks, Aunt Glo. It felt great to be working with you again. Thank you for being patient with me."

"No problem, dear girl."

The house was quiet. Josh and Maddie must still be out with their teachers. Elizabeth took her tea into the living room and sat on the couch, putting her stockinged feet up on the coffee table. She stared out the window at the front gardens. It was so peaceful here. Elizabeth felt the ever-present tension in her neck begin to release. She set her tea down on the table and leaned her head back against the cushion.

"MOM! LOOK WHAT I CAN DO!" MADDIE'S EAGER VOICE STARTLED Elizabeth from her nap. She had fallen asleep on the couch. A cookie still lay on her lap. The peppermint tea in her cup was cold. Outside the window, the light was fading.

Maddie ran into the living room.

"Look, Mom!" Maddie held out her hands, creating a rainbow between them.

"That's beautiful, Sweetheart! Did Mags teach you that?"

Mags followed Maddie into the room. She grinned.

"I did. The kid's a natural. We are going to have so much fun!"

Elizabeth hugged Maddie and stood.

"This is wonderful, Mags. I really appreciate you helping Maddie become comfortable with her magic."

"No problem. I'm glad Aunt Clara called me."

"Would you like to stay for dinner? I'm sure Mary will make more than enough food," Elizabeth offered.

"I think I'd better go home and meet Mariah on the first night in our new home," Mags said. "Another night, though?"

"Of course. Have a good night. Please let us know if you need anything."

Mags smiled, said goodnight to Maddie, and left to spend her first night in her new home.

"Let's see what Mary made for dinner, shall we?" Elizabeth held out her hand to Maddie, who took it with a grin. Mother and daughter skipped into the dining room together.

❧

Over dinner, Joshua showed everyone the small bear he had formed out of stone with Magnus's help.

"Magnus wants me to get used to working with the earth in many ways. He says that making something beautiful from the earth shows respect and honors it. There is a lot about earth that I didn't know, Mom. Like, a lot. It's going to take me forever to learn it all."

"Are you enjoying it, though?" Elizabeth asked.

"Yeah, I am. It's really cool. Magnus is an outstanding teacher. He says I might even be able to Heal a bit. He doesn't think that potions will be my thing, though. He says he thinks I'll be better with stone than plants."

"I can see that. Stone is solid, dependable. It can be stubborn, but it's also strong, good for protection. Earth Mages can make some of the strongest wards and barriers for protection. I'm excited to see what you will be able to do, Honey."

"Me too. Thanks, Mom. I'm glad we came here."

"Me too, Mom!" Maddie agreed.

Elizabeth looked up at Mary, and they both smiled.

7

The phone rang in the middle of the night, rousing Elizabeth from a lovely dream involving a field, her kids, their teachers, and someone whose arms wrapped around her from behind, leaving her feeling safe and warm. Elizabeth fumbled and almost dropped the phone when she picked it up. It was the house phone, an extension of which sat on the nightstand in case of emergencies.

"Hello?" Elizabeth's voice was raspy with sleep.

"Is this Gloria's niece? I'm sorry to wake you, but I need your help."

"Who is this?"

"This is Caz; Gloria made a tonic for my mother. I was trying to stretch the last bottle until you'd been home for more than a couple of days, but I ran out, and Mom's not doing well. I went to check on her before I went to bed, and she's lethargic and not speaking clearly."

"Maybe she's tired. It's the middle of the night," Elizabeth pointed out.

"No, you don't understand. Mom always stays up until around eleven reading. Look, Gloria always said you were as good as she was with potions, maybe better. I know it's late, but could you make one for me? I'll pay extra for the inconvenience."

Elizabeth sighed.

"I made a new batch of your mom's tonic this morning. It was the first thing I made. I can bring it by tomorrow."

"I can come get it now. Please, she needs it right away."

Elizabeth looked at the clock. It was eleven-thirty at night. She'd only been asleep for a couple of hours herself.

"My children are sleeping. If you can be very quiet, I will come down and get you a bottle now. But this is not going to be a repeat occurrence. From now on, you make sure that you have enough potion on hand. Otherwise, you wait until the next day."

Elizabeth hung up and groaned. She swung her feet off the bed and stood. She took out one of Aunt Gloria's cloaks from the wardrobe and pulled it on, then headed out to the stillroom. As she was locking the door to the workshop again, a voice spoke behind her. Elizabeth spun around, cloak swirling about her.

"I really appreciate this, Ms. Sloan," the voice started.

Elizabeth glared at the young man in front of her. He looked to be around thirty years old, with short, dark hair. The moon wasn't bright enough to see much more than that.

Elizabeth handed over the tonic. Caz passed her back a handful of cash.

"Listen, Caz? I realize that you aren't ready to let your mother go. But don't you think it's cruel to keep her here when she really wants to be with your dad again? They were bonded mates, right?"

"Yeah, they were. But my sisters are still young. They need her."

"Is your mother really in a state to be helpful with them?"

Caz didn't answer for a moment.

"Marley couldn't handle it if we lost mom, too," he said, finally.

"Marley is one of your sisters? How do you think she feels, knowing that you have to drug your mother to keep her with you and that she's suffering? How old is Marley?"

"She's fifteen. She was kind of a surprise. Tara is twenty-six. She just got married. She wants mom to be around to see her first kids."

"Look, Caz. I'm not a Shifter. But I know about the mating bonds. I've seen what happens when one partner dies. It's as if the other partner fades away until there's nothing left, afterward. It's like a large part of their soul is ripped away. You're old enough to take care of your younger sister. The older one is old enough to take care of herself. Does your mom really want to keep going like this? Have you ever asked her?"

"She knows we still need her. She takes the tonic willingly." There was a stubborn set to the young man's shoulders.

"Just think about it, ok? I know that your situation is different in that your dad is already gone, and your mom's the only parent you have left. But you are all old enough to handle it. My fifteen-year-old handled his father's passing, then being uprooted from everything he knew and being brought here into a new way of life, unlike anything he had ever known. You and your sisters have an entire community here to support you. Think about it, ok?

Caz stared at her for a moment, nodded once, then turned away. His form shimmered as he went, shifting into the shape of a large mountain lion that quickly vanished around the corner of the house.

Guess he felt threatened by my words, Elizabeth thought to herself as she stared after him.

"You always have been one to call it like you see it, Lizzie Grace," Aunt Gloria said, materializing beside her.

"Maybe it was none of my business, but do you remember Rosie and Todd? When Rosie died, Todd had a really hard time. His family wanted him to stay, too, and it was hell for him. He finally told them that they were old enough to handle it, and it was time. He passed almost a year to the day after Rosie did. And everyone survived. I don't enjoy seeing someone in so much pain being manipulated by family like that."

"I know. That's one potion I don't like making. I made Mathilda swear to me that it was what she wanted before I agreed to make it. I never expected it to go on for so long. It's been almost two years. They need to let her go."

"Well, I've said my piece. Maybe I'll pay a visit and talk with Mathilda myself. I'm going back to bed, Aunt Glo. I'll talk to you in the morning."

The following morning brought no respite. Elizabeth woke with a headache and groaned at the light streaming in through the lace curtains. She had forgotten to pull the drapes.

After breakfast, the children out and about with their teachers, Elizabeth got directions from Aunt Gloria and made her way into town. Caz's family, the Monroes, lived on the other side of the town from the water. Their house backed up against the forest, providing plenty of space for the family to run in their shifted forms.

Elizabeth took a breath, then lifted her hand and knocked firmly on the door. It was opened after a minute by a young girl of about fifteen with long, straight brown hair and brown eyes that matched her older brother's.

"My name is Elizabeth Sloan. I am here to see your mother. May I come in?"

Marley nodded and stepped aside.

"Mom's in the living room. She gets tired easily, so try not to stay too long, ok?"

Elizabeth took in the clean home as she entered the room. It looked as if either Marley was an unusually clean teen, or Caz was paying for someone to come in and keep the home. There was nothing out of place. Elizabeth could smell the remains of the family's breakfast of eggs and bacon in the kitchen.

Mathilda turned her head as Elizabeth stood in the doorway to the living room.

"Mom, this is Elizabeth Sloan. She wants to talk to you. I'm going to work, ok? I'll be back around five. I might go out for a bit with Clarissa after work," Marley leaned over and kissed her mother on the cheek, then left the room. A moment later, the front door closed behind the girl as she left.

"You're Gloria's niece. The one who moved away," Mathilda said. Her eyes were cloudy, her voice raspy. She was beautiful, but worn. Mathilda Monroe looked tired. There were deep circles under her brown eyes. Her wavy brown hair was tied back into a loose braid as if she hadn't the energy to do anything else with it. She sat on the couch with a blanket wrapped around her. A closed book lay beside her, and a mug of tea sat on the coffee table nearby.

"I am. Thank you for seeing me, Mrs. Monroe." Elizabeth took a good look at Mathilda. "Caz came by last night to pick up another bottle of your tonic. I understand that since my Aunt's passing, there has been no one else in town who could make it for you."

Mathilda shook her head.

"There are several Witches who make potions, but none as strong as Gloria. Everyone always knew to go to her first," Mathilda smiled.

"Aunt Gloria has stayed on in Spirit form. I will be taking over her potions business. Before I left, I was training with her. My abilities are stronger than even hers, or so she tells me," Elizabeth was still regarding Mathilda closely. Abruptly, she sat back.

"Look, Mrs. Monroe. I know that you love your children. I also know that staying for so long after your bonded mate passed on must be incredibly difficult for you. I have seen this before when I was younger. The man left behind, Todd Mitchell, finally told his family to let him go. He passed a year to the day that his wife died. He was so happy to finally go, to see his Rosie again. The year he stayed for his family was hell on him, even with the tonic. Aunt Gloria says that it's been nearly two for you. If I am going to keep making this tonic for you, I need to know that it's truly what you want. Honestly, you don't look so good. I think staying is taking a terrible toll on you."

Mathilda sighed and stared out the window. She turned back to Elizabeth, looking her in the eye.

"I love my children. I thought I was taking care of them, making it easier on them, by staying for as long as I could. But I am only making more work for them. I'm tired all the time. They are constantly taking care of me. I know that even Marley would recover if I were to leave now. She's fifteen. She's always been an independent girl. She has a good head on her shoulders. She does well in school and has good friends. Marley would be ok. She would miss me, but she would be ok. It's Caz I'm most worried about. He blames himself for his father's death, and I think he refuses to let me go because of it. I think the idea that he is responsible for both of our deaths is too much for him, even though it's not true."

"Why does Caz blame himself for his father's death?" Elizabeth asked.

"John was working on a job with Caz and a few other men when he died. John was an electrician, and he helped Caz get his contracting business off the ground. He worked jobs for Caz, putting in the electrical, or fixing it in remodels. That sort of thing. On that job, he was working on the wiring, and suddenly there was a massive power surge. Caz still doesn't know how it happened. They had turned the electricity off while John redid the wires. John received an immense shock, and it stopped his heart. He was unconscious and unable to shift. The house was some way outside of town, and by the time the paramedics got there, it was too late. There had been several other accidents there that day, and Caz had tried to send everyone home until he got it sorted out, but John was close to finishing his part of the job and insisted on staying. Caz blames himself for not insisting more, for not making John leave."

"I see," Elizabeth said. "So he is refusing to let you go out of guilt, mixed with love. That is a powerful mix."

Mathilda sighed.

"I know it's time to move on. Tara's married, expecting her first child in a few months. I will stay long enough to see her child born, and then I'll go. I'll make sure the children know that it's time." Mathilda turned to Elizabeth again. "You'll keep making the tonic for me until then?"

"I will. I suggest that you try to get Caz to seek help for his feelings of guilt. If he still blames himself when you cross over, it will be even harder for him. Did the police look into the accident? They are sure it was an accident?"

"Of course. What else could it have been?"

"I don't know. It's just strange. You said the power was turned off while your husband laid in the new wiring. That seems off to me."

"There was never any reason to suspect it was anything other than a freak accident. John was a good man and a wonderful husband and father. Everyone loved him. There would have been no reason for anyone to wish him harm."

Elizabeth stood.

"Thank you for seeing me, Mrs. Monroe. I'll keep making your tonic until Tara's child is born. I'll make sure you get a new bottle regularly."

"Thank you. And please tell Gloria hello for me. We were friends, she and John and I, years ago. Knowing that Gloria was living here is one of the main reasons we moved here ten years ago. She had always spoken so highly of Fairweather Falls."

A tingle zipped up Elizabeth's spine, fizzing coldly in her brain.

"I'll tell her. Be well, Mrs. Monroe."

"Be well, Ms. Sloan. I'm sure I'll see you again soon."

8

Elizabeth stepped outside the Monroes house and closed the door after herself. She stood for a moment on the top step, then made her way back to her bike, which she had left leaning against the side of the house. Elizabeth had intended to stop in town on the way back home. Instead, her mind buzzing, she rode straight back to the house.

"Aunt Glo!" Elizabeth called as she strode in through the front door.

Aunt Gloria appeared before her in the living room.

"What is it, Elizabeth? What's wrong?"

"Aunt Glo, Mathilda says that you knew her and her husband, John, when you were younger. Is that true?"

"Yes, we spent some time together before I came back here to live. We were part of a small group of friends that did everything together for a few years. Then Nora had you girls, and I decided it was time to come home."

"Did you stay in touch with the other people in that group?"

"With most of them. We were really close. We used to meet up at least once a year, but once everyone started having kids, that kind of stopped. I still sent holiday cards, and there were a couple I still spoke to every now and again."

"Did you know that John died under unusual circumstances?"

"I thought he died from an accident on the job? Wasn't he doing the wiring for one of Caz's projects?"

"He was. And the power was turned off. Mathilda says that he was killed by a sudden power surge through the lines. But Aunt Glo, if the power was off, that shouldn't have happened."

Aunt Gloria was silent for a moment.

"That is strange. I didn't know that."

"Aunt Glo, I think it might be a good idea for you to check in with the other members of that group you were all a part of. I would like to know if anyone else has experienced any strange accidents in the last two years. And, you might want to talk to Mathilda. Once Tara's baby is born, she's going to stop taking the tonic. You might want to spend some time with her before she goes."

Elizabeth thought for a moment.

"Can you leave the house, Aunt Glo? Or are you bound to it?"

"I can go wherever I like. Sometimes I visit your mother. She hasn't been ready to see me yet, though. She's actively keeping me out."

"Well, think about going to see Mathilda."

"I will. Thank you, Lizzie Grace." Aunt Glo disappeared.

Elizabeth wandered into the kitchen. Mary handed her a small plate with several cookies on it and a mug of hibiscus tea.

"That's just what I needed," Elizabeth sighed.

Mary smiled.

"Elizabeth, I was wondering. This house already has a lot of magic in it since Gloria lived here for so long, and your Great-Aunt Sarah before her. Would you mind if I made the house alive? It would be somewhat sentient, able to anticipate needs, rearrange and create rooms and furniture, that sort of thing."

Elizabeth blinked.

"I hadn't thought about it. I mean, it already does some things by itself, so I guess this would just be the next step. Would we be inviting in a House Spirit? I've never met an enlivened house before. I thought that was only something in the old stories we were told as children."

She blinked again. "You know, Mary, I think that would be fun. Maddie will love it. Josh might take a little longer to get used to it. Would the house be able to talk to us?"

"Not so much in words. It wouldn't have a House Spirit. But it would be able to let you know if it was happy or not. You would definitely know how it was feeling. And it could protect your family, should it need to."

"Let's go for it. That's a wonderful idea, Mary. I can't wait to tell the kids!"

Mary grinned. "We'll have to make sure they introduce themselves properly to the house when they come home this afternoon."

"I am very much looking forward to seeing that!" Elizabeth grinned back.

❧

ELIZABETH HAD GONE BACK INTO TOWN TO LOOK AROUND AND DO A bit of shopping. She had stopped outside of the old bookstore, contemplating it, imagining what it would be like inside if she were to take it on as a potions store. Elizabeth had even gone so far as to reach for the doorknob but had stopped before actually touching it.

Elizabeth had returned home and was unloading her bike baskets, which were filled with flowers and treats when Maddie and Josh came home with their teachers. Josh grabbed an armful of things from his mom while Maddie bounced around, talking excitedly about her day.

"Before anyone goes into the house, I need to tell you something," Elizabeth spoke over Maddie's excited voice.

Everyone stopped and looked at Elizabeth.

"Mary has Enlivened the house. The house now has its own consciousness. It can understand when you talk to it; it can make extra rooms and furniture and let you know how it feels. It can also protect us if needed. Each of you, including Mags and Magnus, will need to introduce yourselves to the House when you go in. The House needs to know who you are and that you are welcome here."

Maddie's eyes were wide.

"The house is alive?"

"Yes, to a certain degree."

"This is so cool! Do we get to name her now? She has to have a name, Mom."

Elizabeth smiled.

"I hadn't thought about it. I guess we can see if the House would like a name. It has to be one that the House likes, though."

"Woop!" Maddie yelled, running for the door.

Maddie put her hand on the door frame.

"Hi, House! I'm Maddie. I live here. Elizabeth's my mom. I'm an Elemental Mage. Do you want a name? Can I name you? Please?"

The door to the house opened. Maddie squealed and ran inside. Those still outside could hear her suggesting names to the house.

Josh moved towards the door. It closed in front of him. Josh put his hand on the door's frame as Maddie had done.

"Hi, House. My name's Josh. I'm Elizabeth's son. I live here too. I'm an Earth Mage. I specialize in stone."

The door opened, and Josh went inside.

Elizabeth motioned to her children's teachers. Mags grinned and approached the door.

"Hiya, House. I am the Lady Margarethe Clíodhna Laughlin of the Silver Waters Fae Court. I am Maddie's teacher and I will be here almost every day."

The house opened the door. Mags smiled happily and skipped inside.

Magnus went last.

"Good day, House. I am Magnus. I am Joshua's teacher."

The door opened again.

Elizabeth smiled and made her way inside. She patted the door frame as she passed through.

"Thank you, House. That was fun."

IN THE SITTING ROOM, MADDIE WAS STILL SKIPPING IN CIRCLES, trying out names. So far, the house had liked nothing the happy girl had suggested. Mary had come in from the kitchen and was watching with a smile.

"Alison? Carol? Susannah? Maia? Melissa?" Maddie stopped for a moment. "Come on, House. I'm running out of ideas."

"Maybe something in a different language?" Mags suggested.

"I don't know any other languages yet," Maddie said.

"Caoimhe, Sinéad, Siobhán, Fionnuala, Fíona, Elodie, Eloise, Eleanor," Mags chanted.

At 'Eleanor,' the house shook a tiny bit, and everyone felt a warmth flow up from their feet to their heads.

"Eleanor it is, then," Elizabeth said. "Good one, Mags."

Maddie frowned. She had wanted to name the house herself.

"Come on, Maddie, let's get to know Eleanor better," Mags said. "Maybe she can turn your walls pink."

Maddie shrieked and flew up the stairs to the second floor. Mags followed after her.

Elizabeth grinned at Mary, then turned to Josh.

"What do you think, Sweetheart?"

"I think my life keeps getting weirder and weirder, but in a good way," Josh smiled briefly, then went to set his bag in his room.

Magnus looked up at Elizabeth.

"I would like to introduce Joshua to the other Earth Witches and Mages in the area," the Gnome said.

"That would be great. It would be great for him to make some friends here. He kind of became a loner after his dad died."

"Why don't we have a house warming party to welcome you all home?" Mary suggested. "You could invite the whole town. That way, maybe all of you will make some new friends. I know my Aunt Meg will come, and she'll bring treats, too."

"I like that idea, Mary. Let's see, it's Monday now. Do you think this Saturday is too soon?"

"That should be fine. Everyone will want to come. They are all curious about your family."

"Then bring it on. I'll tell my mom. That's the quickest way to get the news out in this town. She'll do all the inviting for us. She'll probably invite people I never wanted to see again, as well as those I do."

⁂ 9 ⁂

Nora was, as predicted, thrilled to invite the town. She started making calls at once. Within hours, everyone knew there was a party happening on Saturday at Aunt Gloria's house. The local stores and market were swamped as everyone flocked to gather ingredients for whatever specialty they chose to bring. In Fairweather Falls, when you went to a housewarming, you brought food. And sometimes gifts.

Saturday morning Maddie bounced out of bed, full of energy and excitement. She ran down the stairs to the kitchen where Mary was making breakfast. Elizabeth was sitting at the center counter, sipping a cup of tea. Maddie climbed up beside her mother and started spinning around on her stool. She stopped when Mary placed a bowl of oatmeal with strawberries, yogurt, and cinnamon sugar in front of her.

"When are people getting here, Mom? Do you know who's coming? How many people are coming? Do you think a lot of kids will come?" Maddie held her spoon in her hand, bowl untouched in front of her.

"Eat your food, Mads," Elizabeth said. "I think Grandma Nora told people to start arriving around eleven. It's only eight now. You have three hours."

"What am I going to do for three hours? That's forever! Are we decorating? Can I help?"

"I wasn't planning on decorating. Maybe you could pick some flowers and find a few vases to put them in? Finish your breakfast first!" Maddie scooped three bites of oatmeal into her mouth, then jumped down from her seat and flew out the door. She came back in, grabbed the kitchen scissors from the caddy by the stove, then, holding them point-down in her fist, hurried out the door again.

"My poor herbs," Elizabeth sighed.

"They'll grow back," Mary smiled.

"I know. It's worth it to keep Maddie busy for a while. I'm feeling somewhat antsy myself."

"Why don't you go for a bike ride? It's a beautiful day. Use up some of that energy."

"Maybe I will. I don't think I could focus on potions this morning. A bike ride is a good idea."

❧

ELIZABETH TOOK HER BIKE OUT ALONG THE COAST, RIDING UP towards the border with Canada. She made it about a half-hour up before turning back.

I need to make regular rides a priority, she thought to herself. Her thighs and lungs were burning. *I thought I was in better shape than this.*

As she turned into her own driveway, Elizabeth was surprised to notice that there were already cars lining the driveway, spilling over to the road outside. Hopping off her bike, she checked the time on her phone. It was still only ten forty-five. People were arriving early.

Elizabeth put her bike away in the bike shed and let herself into the kitchen. Mary was at the stove, stirring a pot of something savory. Three other women, including Meg, bustled about, arranging food on trays and in bowls to be taken out to the picnic tables that had been set up out back.

"Elizabeth! There you are," Meg greeted her, putting down her tray and rushing to put her arms around Elizabeth in a massive hug.

"Do you remember Mrs. Lindsay and Mrs. Doyle? I think they were your teachers in school?"

Elizabeth smiled at the other two women. Mrs. Lindsay had been her first-grade teacher, Mrs. Doyle, her freshman algebra teacher.

"Thank you for coming," Elizabeth said with a smile.

"We're delighted to see you home again, Elizabeth," Mrs. Lindsay said. Mrs. Doyle smiled and nodded.

"It's a pity that Gloria isn't here to see you finally home," the algebra teacher said. Mrs. Doyle was an Earth Witch of considerably lesser talents than anyone in Elizabeth's family.

"Of course I'm here. Why would I not be? Someone has to bring Elizabeth back up to speed so she can take over my business," Aunt Gloria popped into view. Mrs. Doyle jumped.

"Gloria! I had no idea that you had returned," Mrs. Doyle gasped.

Mrs. Lindsay looked very much as if she were trying not to laugh. Her hand covered her mouth tightly as she turned away, fussing with something on the stove.

The corner of Elizabeth's mouth twitched.

"I'll be staying for the foreseeable future, Dilys, so don't go getting any ideas. Your Sandra could never hold a candle to my Elizabeth, and you know it. We are already taking orders."

"Sandra Doyle is a potion maker, or she is trying to be," Meg told Elizabeth quietly. The Brownie's eyes were twinkling. "Her potions have nowhere near the power of yours or Gloria's, and everyone knows it. I almost feel sorry for the poor girl. I think she actually has more power and potential than she knows, but her mother forces her to conform to ideals that are not her own."

"But Sandra's my age. We were in school together. Surely she's not still under her mother's thumb?" Elizabeth replied.

"Oh yes, she is. Sandra is so used to being picked on by her mother that any spine she might have started to develop was firmly squashed years ago. Like I said, I feel almost sorry for the poor girl. She's terrified of her mother, and rightly so."

"Sandra must surely have her own family by now?"

"Mrs. Doyle never approved of any of the very few boys that came calling," Meg whispered. "They were promptly sent packing or were so scared of Mrs. Doyle that they fled after one date. Poor Sandra never had a chance while she was living in this town, and Mrs. Doyle never let her leave."

"But surely she could have gotten a scholarship and gone away to college?"

"She did get a scholarship. She tried to keep it a secret from her mother. But Mrs. Doyle found out anyway, and as Sandra was still underage, she forbade her to go. She called the University herself and told them that her daughter would not be attending, that her health was such that she needed to stay home where she could be properly taken care of. The University offered to hold the place for a year, but Mrs. Doyle declined."

"What a hateful woman. I remember everyone being scared of her, but I don't remember her ever being that bad. Sandra would sneak out sometimes and come to parties in high school. I knew she didn't get along with her mother, but I didn't know it was that bad."

"It's only gotten worse as the years went on. Mrs. Doyle uses guilt and manipulation as well as actively putting poor Sandra down whenever she can to control her daughter. We've all tried to help the poor girl as much as we can, but it's a challenge since it makes it worse for her if her mother finds out."

Elizabeth shook her head.

"Does Sandra really have a gift for potions, or is it something she does because her mother wants her to?"

"I'm not sure, actually. I know Sandra is an Earth Witch, and I do find her walking in the woods sometimes. Her Gifts are focused on plants. But I'm not sure if potions are the best use of them. I don't think she's ever been given the chance to find out where her own interests lie."

Elizabeth made a vow to herself to look for Sandra at the party and talk to the woman herself. Sandra had been a quiet, nervous girl in school. She had been a fantastic artist, Elizabeth remembered. Sandra would sit at lunch and draw until the bell rang to go back to class. Maddie liked to draw. Maybe Sandra could give Maddie art lessons.

Plan made, Elizabeth turned to Meg.

"Is Sandra here yet?"

"She's helping set everything up outside. I was surprised that her mother let her out of her sight, actually. But Robin George took her in hand and got her outside before Mrs. Doyle could say anything."

"Thanks, Meg."

Elizabeth smiled and snagged a cookie off of a plate on the island before heading outside again. Looking around the property, Elizabeth saw Maddie running around in the field with several other children. She smiled and continued to search the people getting the area ready for the party.

Several men from the town had brought grills and were firing them up in preparation for barbecue. Another two pairs were carrying coolers and extra tables around the house from the cars. Several women were putting reusable tablecloths on the tables and setting out dishes full of food. Three teens had been given the job of setting up the wash station—all parties in Fairweather Falls were zero waste. People brought their own plates, cups, and cutlery and washed them up as they went. The town teens would take it in turn to man the wash stations, making sure that they switched out the water in the tubs and added soap whenever needed. Elizabeth remembered helping to man the washtubs at many a party during her high school years.

Elizabeth studied the women setting the tables. She didn't see anyone she would recognize as Sandra Doyle. Elizabeth did see Robin George, though. The Dryad looked just as she had over twenty years ago when Elizabeth had left Fairweather Falls. Her long, curly chestnut hair was pulled back into a low ponytail, flowing down her back. The Dryad was about five foot six and slender, with smiling green eyes and a cheerful personality. That cheerfulness often fooled people into believing that Robin was laid back and Pollyanna-ish, as she tried to find the best in everyone. Those that made that assumption were quickly disabused of it if they spent any time around the Dryad at all. Robin had a quick wit that could be cutting if she were angry and a well-developed sense of justice. It surprised Elizabeth not at all that Robin had been the one to rescue Sandra and hustle her away from her mother.

"Robin!" Elizabeth called.

The Dryad's head popped up, and she turned quickly, catching sight of Elizabeth standing by the back door.

"Liz!" The Dryad ran toward Elizabeth and threw her arms around her, hugging her tightly. "I'm so glad you're back. Life can get fun again now!"

Elizabeth laughed. "I'm sure you've been having plenty of fun while I've been gone, Rob," she told her high school friend.

"Well, of course, but it will be even better now that you're back. Hey, you have kids now, right? A teenager and a younger one? I think I saw your daughter fly by, chased by my two, not that long ago."

"You have kids too? How old are they?"

"The twins are eight. I married Ben Sly, do you remember him?"

"The Bear Shifter? Wasn't he always picking on us?"

"Turns out it was because it was the only way he knew to get close to me," Robin laughed. "Apparently, he had a crush on me all through school. Anyway, after high school, he joined the military for a while, while I was away at University, and when he came home after his four years, he proposed. I was home for the holidays visiting, and the rest is history." Robin grinned.

"What did you study in school?"

"Graphic design. It was a bit challenging, going to a mortal University, but I managed. I wanted to see how the rest of the world lived. Which I'm sure you can understand." Robin smiled up at Elizabeth.

"I heard your mother invited Sarah and Jonah over for lunch the other day. How did that go?"

"Oh my gods and fairies, Rob. It was so awkward. Thankfully, the kids had just come into their magic and met their teachers, so we were able to keep the conversation on that and other surface stuff. But it's weird. Sarah and I were so close, but we drifted apart, and I didn't really know what to say to her. She promised Maddie she could come out to the center and see the animals, though, so I guess I'll get a chance to see if we can fix things now. I want to get to know her as an adult, you know?"

"Sarah spends most of her time out at the center. She rarely hangs out with us anymore. She's become really reclusive. I don't know why. I think she'll be here today, though. Her dad loves a good party and usually makes her take him."

"What about her mother? No one has mentioned Sherry since I've been back."

Robin looked sad.

"Sherry left a few years ago. I don't know what happened. She was there one day and gone the next. She left a note for Dennis and Sarah, apologizing, saying that she loved them, but she had to go. And that was it."

Sherry was a Selkie. She had always sworn that Dennis had not tricked her and stolen her sealskin, that she was with him because she loved him. Her leaving this way didn't feel right. Elizabeth made a note to ask Aunt Gloria if Sherry had been a part of her little group like John and Mathilda had. However, the timing didn't seem to work. Sherry was already in Fairweather Falls when Gloria came back. Sarah was only two months younger than Elizabeth. Then again, Sherry was from Fairweather Falls. Dennis, an Earth Mage, wasn't. He was from the Midwest somewhere.

"I had no idea," Elizabeth said. "That's horrible. Honestly, I can't see Sherry doing that to Dennis and Sarah. She loved them both so much."

"Maybe the call of the sea got to be too much," Robin said.

"Maybe. Well, I hope Sarah and Dennis do come today. I'll have to make a greater effort to be friends again."

"I think you coming home is going to be good for all of us. I'm looking forward to getting the old gang back together again," Robin said.

"About that," Elizabeth said. "Meg was telling me about Sandra's life. I want to help her. No one should live like that. And no mother should have that kind of control over her child."

Robin grinned maniacally. She rubbed her hands together.

"Oh, Liz. I am so glad you're home. This is going to be so much fun. I've been trying to help Sandra grow a spine for so long. You were always the one she really looked up to. With you helping, we'll break that old harridan's hold on Sandra yet...and have fun doing it, too."

10

Robin led Elizabeth over to Sandra, who was helping another woman set out drinks on a table near the house.

"Sandra! Look who I found!" Robin called as they drew closer.

Sandra looked up sharply. She smiled nervously when she saw Elizabeth.

"Liz! It's lovely to see you. I'm glad you came home," Sandra said. Her voice was thready, almost a whisper, as if she were afraid of being overheard.

"Hey, Sandra. It's good to see you. I'm glad you came today," Elizabeth smiled at the young woman.

"We wouldn't miss it. Mother insisted on coming early to help out."

"Well, it gives us more time to get reacquainted," Robin said. She turned to the other woman at the table.

"Laura, I'm stealing Sandra for a bit, ok?"

Laura smiled and waved them away.

Robin hooked an arm through Elizabeth and Sandra's arms and led them away towards the cliffs. They didn't go far, just enough that they couldn't be heard from the house. Robin dragged them down so that all three were sitting on the ground.

"Tell us what your life's been like, Liz. We want to know it all," Robin said.

They talked for a while, telling stories about their lives until Elizabeth felt a tug on her energy and looked up. In the distance, she saw Sarah and Dennis coming around the corner of the house. Sarah was carrying something in her arms. Dennis had a dog on a leash at his side.

Elizabeth stood up and waved. She sent a pulse through the earth towards Sarah and her father, knowing that they both would feel it. They turned, searching. Dennis waved back and headed towards the three women, Sarah in tow.

Dennis headed straight for Elizabeth, drawing her into a hug when he reached her. He pulled away and held her at arm's length, looking at her with a twinkle in his brown eyes.

"Look at you, Lizzie Grace! All grown up. And Sarah tells me that you have two wonderful children now. An Earth Mage and an Elemental Mage?"

"I do," Elizabeth said. She smiled at the older man. "Josh is fifteen—he's the Earth Mage. Maddie is eight—she's the Elemental Mage."

"Well, I'm thrilled that you've all come home at last. My girl needs you around to pull her out of her head and help her have some fun. She spends all her time with me and the creatures. While that's not a bad thing, she needs to get out more with other people, too. I know you've tried, young woman," Dennis nodded at Robin, who grinned back, "but there's strength in numbers, and my Sarah always was a stubborn one."

Sarah looked embarrassed.

"Dad, I get out enough. I told you. Liz will be too busy settling into her new life here to pay attention to me."

"Sarah! Of course, I won't," Elizabeth protested. "I was just telling Robin how much I wanted to reconnect with you. I've missed my friends here. I know I'm not the best at staying in touch, and that's on me. But I hope we can be friends again, now. I'm not planning on leaving again. I would really like to get to know you again."

"See? I told you so," Dennis said.

"Lizzie Grace, I thought your children might like these two fine creatures for their Familiars if that's ok with you. They've been hanging around the Center waiting for their Witches, and lately, they've been restless, suggesting that their Witches were nearby. Would it be alright to introduce them and see if they're a match?" Dennis looked at Elizabeth, who looked down at the dog and then up at the kitten in Sarah's arms. The kitten had bright blue wings.

"Are you sure, Dennis? That's a huge, huge gift."

"I'm sure, Elizabeth Grace. And maybe now that you're home for good, you'll finally let me match you up as well. You know I've felt a Familiar waiting for you since you were small."

"But you said they weren't here yet. I've given up on ever finding them," Elizabeth said.

"I think, now that you are here, your Familiar soon will be, too," Dennis said with a smile. "They always show up at the right time. You know that."

"Thank you, Dennis. I see the cat's a Faery Cat, though I have never seen one with such fine wings before. So I imagine the dog's not a normal dog?"

Dennis chuckled.

"Not in the least. He's a Cù Sídhe, a Fae Dog. He can glamor and shift forms as needed. Right now, border collie seems to be his form of choice."

"Are you sure a Fae Dog is right for Josh? Maddie is the one with the ties to the Fae," Elizabeth asked.

"I'm fairly sure, yes," Dennis replied. "We'll find out when we introduce them."

The kitten was beginning to squirm in Sarah's arms.

Robin and Sandra stood, and the little group headed back towards the house.

"Maddie!" Elizabeth called as they approached the children, who were still playing tag in the field.

Maddie broke away from the game and ran towards them.

"Hey, Mom! Hi Sarah. Ooh, what's that? That kitten has wings! What a pretty kitty! Can I hold her?"

"It's a him, and yes, you can. Here," Sarah handed the kitten to

Maddie. The little black kitten had a white tuxedo patch and one white paw. He was genuinely adorable. The kitten snuggled right up to Maddie, arranging himself so that his face was buried in her neck under her hair.

Maddie's eyes grew wide as she seemed to listen to something that only she could hear.

"His name is Oreo! He says he's mine! Can I keep him? Mom, please, can I?"

"Yes, Maddie. You can keep him. Why don't you go show Mary and Granny Nora? Make sure you introduce him to Eleanore and Aunt Glo, too. And send Josh out here, please."

Maddie took off for the house, holding the little kitten tightly to her.

"I think you just made her year, Dennis," Elizabeth said. "Thank you both for bringing him."

After a few moments, Joshua stepped outside. He looked around, then headed over when he saw his mother. He looked down at the dog, who was sitting patiently at Dennis's feet.

"Josh, this is Dennis, Sarah's father," Elizabeth introduced.

"Nice to meet you, Sir," Joshua said. "Is it ok if I pet your dog?"

"Go ahead. He's friendly," Dennis said with a twinkle in his eye.

Josh squatted down and held his hand out to the dog. The Cù Sídhe sniffed his hand, then shoved his head into it so hard that he knocked Joshua right over. The Fae dog proceeded to wash Josh's face for him. Josh was on his back, laughing and wrestling with the dog in seconds. Elizabeth grinned.

"Well, I guess that answers that. Thanks, Dennis. Thank you, Sarah."

"Thank you, Lizzie Grace. These two needed a good home. I'm glad they've found one with you and your children," Dennis said. "I have their things for you in the car. We'll bring them in for you before the end of the party.

"We'll help you," Robin said. "Why don't we do that now, then we won't forget later."

Leaving Josh to play with his new Familiar, Elizabeth, Robin, Sandra, Sarah and Dennis went to get the Familiar supplies and bring them into the house. They carried the things in through the front door and up to the children's rooms. On the way back out to the party, they passed through the kitchen. Mrs. Doyle looked up sharply when she saw Sandra.

"Sandra! I thought you were helping with the party!" The former teacher said sharply.

Sandra looked tired.

"I wanted to see Sandra and catch up," Elizabeth said. "It's been so long. Laura didn't mind my stealing Sandra for a while. We'll be outside. Thank you for your help, Mrs. Doyle."

Putting her arm through Sandra's, Elizabeth led the other woman from the house and away from her overbearing mother. Outside, Dennis left to join the men by the grill while the young women stayed together. Elizabeth pulled Sandra over to a chair and sat, dragging the other woman down into the chair beside her. Robin and Sarah pulled up chairs across from them.

"Sandra, why do you let your mother mistreat you so much?" Elizabeth asked. "You are an adult. You deserve to have your own life; you know that, right?"

Sandra sighed.

"Mother has made sure that I am dependent on her for everything. I tried to go away to college, and she called the school and turned down my scholarship. I'm still not sure how she found out about it—I never told her I was applying. I didn't tell anyone. When I was twenty-one, I tried again. I applied for a job in another paranormal Haven and was all packed and ready to go when suddenly, they didn't need me anymore. I didn't tell her about that one, either. I tried one more time when I was twenty-five. She somehow found out about that, too, and stopped it before it could happen. She has never let me have a job or earn any money of my own. No one in town will hire me because they are all afraid of Mother. I have no resources and no longer have any hope of escape. If Mother so much as thinks that I might defy her in some way, something bad happens. It's easier not to fight it anymore."

Elizabeth looked at Robin and Sarah. All three were confused.

"But, Sandra. Your mother is a very low-grade Earth Witch. She doesn't have the power to hex you like this. And I don't like that she somehow knows everything that goes on in your life, even if you haven't told anyone. It sounds as if she has some way of spying on you. Are you sure she doesn't have a second talent in Air magic? Could she be scrying you?" Elizabeth asked.

Sandra shook her head.

"I suppose that wouldn't be it, anyway, since she would have to be reading your thoughts if you hadn't told anyone you were leaving. Scrying can't do that. Could she be a telepath? That's really unusual, but it could happen."

Sandra shook her head again.

"I don't know how she does it. It didn't use to be this bad. When I was little, we were really close. We had what I thought was a happy relationship. Then my father left, and Mother wasn't really happy anymore. She started not allowing me to go on sleepovers, and then she started restricting playdates. She allowed friends to come to our house for a while, but she hovered and tried to be a part of anything we were doing. It got worse as I got older. Soon no one wanted to come over anymore because she was so weird. I kept trying to have friends, but since I had to sneak out if I wanted to see them, it was hard. Then, things started to happen to the friends I snuck out to see. Do you remember the one time I snuck out at night in high school to go to that party on the beach?"

Everyone nodded.

"Remember that the bonfire surged and almost got out of control, and Mary Ellen Clarke got burned before they could control it again, even with two Fire Witches there? That was Mother. When I got home, she told me it was my fault, and bad things would continue to happen whenever I disobeyed her."

There was a beat of silence.

"Sandra, why didn't you say something? This is abuse. We would have helped you. The school would have helped you."

"Mother taught at the school. No one would have believed me."

"Yes, they would. We all knew there was something wrong. We all knew that Mrs. Doyle was way too controlling with you. We all felt sorry for you, but we didn't know what to do," Sarah said.

"My mother would have taken you in," Elizabeth said. "Nora is infinitely stronger than your mother. And she would never stand for someone abusing you like this, especially your own mother."

Sandra froze. She was facing the house, and Mrs. Doyle had come out the back door. The former teacher looked around, searching for someone. Her gaze caught Sandra's, and she started towards them.

"Sandra, do you want to stop this?" Elizabeth asked.

Sandra was frozen, watching her mother approach.

"Sandra?"

Sandra, looking terrified, nodded her head.

Elizabeth, Sarah, and Robin all stood in front of Sandra, facing Mrs. Doyle. Other people standing near them were beginning to notice that something was wrong. They saw the three women standing in front of Sandra protectively and noticed Mrs. Doyle bearing down on them. Other people joined Elizabeth and her friends, shielding Sandra from her mother. Sandra remained in her chair, hunched over on herself. Her arms were wrapped tightly around her chest as if she were trying to hold herself together.

Mrs. Doyle came to a stop before the friends.

"Sandra, I need your help in the kitchen. You've sat around long enough. Let someone else have a turn to enjoy the party."

"This is my party, and I want Sandra to stay out here with me. There are plenty of people here who are willing to help out. I'm sure that no one will mind my keeping Sandra. We used to be friends. I would like to be friends again," Elizabeth stated.

Mrs. Doyle's jaw tightened. It was Elizabeth's party. Elizabeth's request was not unreasonable. But giving in would allow Sandra to have some fun and make friends, something Mrs. Doyle had fought against for years. However, if Mrs. Doyle insisted on Sandra coming inside, then everyone would know there was something wrong. Mrs. Doyle desperately needed her neighbors to have a good opinion of her.

"Well, I suppose that's all right. It is your party, Elizabeth. Sandra can help with clean-up afterward." She turned and started to walk away.

"Mrs. Doyle." Elizabeth wasn't about to let this go that easily.

Mrs. Doyle turned back.

"Yes, Elizabeth?"

"How did you know that Sandra had gotten a scholarship to school? And when she got a job in another town? How did you find out? Sandra swears she never told anyone. You're just a low-level Earth Witch with a desperate need to control others. You can't scry, and you're not a Seer. So, how did you know?"

Those who had gathered nearby were listening curiously.

A throat cleared in the crowd.

"I'm afraid I'm the one who told Dilys about the scholarship, Sandra. I didn't know that you hadn't told her you'd applied. I felt horrible when I found out that she had turned it down on your behalf. You deserved that scholarship. You were a very talented artist and a hard worker. I do apologize. I should have apologized before now." The speaker was an older man in slacks and a sweater vest over a white button-down shirt. Mr. Phillips had been the school guidance counselor for years before retiring to take care of his wife and his beehives. He was a Bear Shifter.

"And I may have let slip that I had heard you had gotten a job in Silver Falls," an Air Witch said from the back of the crowd. "I knew that Dilys had been very controlling and thought it was wonderful that she was finally loosening up enough to let you live your own life. I congratulated her on it. My sister lives in Silver Falls. She was friends with the woman who owned the bakery you were going to work at. When you didn't leave, I felt terrible. I am so sorry, Sandra. I should have kept my mouth shut. I should have apologized before this now, too. I've always felt bad, but I was afraid to make things worse by getting involved again."

"What do you mean, controlling? I don't try to control my daughter. I take care of her the way a good mother should. Sandra knows that, and she takes care of me, the way a dutiful daughter should take care of her mother. Sandra loves me," Mrs. Doyle protested.

Sandra stood up. She moved to stand between Elizabeth and Robin. Sarah moved to stand behind her, placing her hands on Sandra's shoulders.

"You have controlled everything in my life since Dad left. If you were as controlling with him as you were with me, it's no wonder he left. I just wish he had taken me with him. Then maybe I would have had a chance at a life of my own. As it is, I've never had anything that was mine. You drove my friends away. You punished them if I tried to see them and told me it was my fault. You somehow hexed anyone that was nice to me. You never let me date. You never let me have a job or any money of my own. I've thought a lot about it. Maybe you were afraid I would leave, like Dad. You certainly stopped me every time I tried. But you've killed any love I might have had for you. I can feel sorry for you because you must be miserable to feel the need to control everything like you do. But Elizabeth is right. I deserve better than this. I deserve to have my own life. I don't know what's changed, but I can't live this way anymore. I won't let you control my life anymore, Mother."

The crowd had tightened protectively around Sandra as she spoke.

"What are you saying, Sandra? That you want to leave like your father did? After everything I've done for you? Where would you go? You have nowhere to stay, no money, and no skills. No one will give a forty-five-year-old with no skills a job."

"I will," Sarah said. "Sandra can work at the Familiar Center. We have an apartment over the barn that's just being used for storage space. We can clean it out, and she can live there. Sandra can stay as long as she likes while she figures out what she would like to do with her life."

"Sarah, she'll curse the Center. I can't do that to you," Sandra turned her head to say over her shoulder to Sarah.

"No, she won't," Dennis said. "I am a much stronger Earth Witch than Dilys Doyle is, and the Center is highly warded. The Familiars have their own protection magic as well, and they will never allow harm to come to the Center."

"Sandra, you say that this has been going on since you were a child?" Derek Simonson, the Chief of Police in Fairweather Falls, asked. He was fifty-five and had moved to town ten years ago.

Sandra nodded.

Derek turned to the crowd.

"And it seems as if at least some of you were aware of what was happening?"

"I don't think that anyone realized how bad it was," Mrs. Potter, who owned the grocery store, said. "Mrs. Doyle taught at the school. She put up a good front. She always said what a good girl Sandra was, helping to take care of her. That Sandra was shy and more likely to draw than make friends. But I think we all knew there was something wrong. I think we didn't want to believe it. That's on us, as a community. There was never a mark on Sandra, but she was not a happy child. We should have done better."

There were murmurs of agreement throughout the crowd.

Sandra was crying, fat tears rolling down her face. Elizabeth and Robin put their arms around their friend from the sides, while Sarah continued to hold on to her shoulders.

"I think that this young woman has had enough," Derek said. He turned to Mrs. Doyle. "As police chief, I declare your magic forfeit for having used it to cause harm and to manipulate and control for so long. Your magic will be bound. If, someday in the future, it is determined that you are truly sorry for your actions, and you show genuine remorse, I may consider having the bindings lifted." Chief Simonson turned to the crowd.

"Who will perform the binding?"

Nora stepped forward. So did several other Witches. Chief Simonson chose the strongest Witch of each magical element to cast the spell. They circled around Mrs. Doyle, holding hands.

"You can't do this!" Mrs. Doyle cried. "You can't take away my magic! You can't keep me from my daughter! She'll come to her senses, you'll see. She'll be back with me inside of a week. Sandra can't survive without me. You'll see! I need my magic to take care of her! She needs to be protected from herself! She can't be allowed to make her own choices; she'll never come back! She'll die."

Mrs. Doyle collapsed into tears as the binding snapped into place. She sank to the ground. Sandra watched her mother for a moment, then turned, burying her head on Sarah's shoulder. The four women stood in a huddle, holding Sandra while she cried.

"Sandra," Derek Simonson said as he approached the group slowly.

Sandra raised her head and turned, brushing tears away. Someone handed her a napkin so she could blow her nose.

"Sandra, I am so sorry that we as a community have failed you for so long. If you have any trouble with your mother, if she acts out towards you in any way, I want you to tell me, ok?"

He looked back at Mrs. Doyle.

"In fact, I think I'll place a restraining order spell on her. She won't be able to come within three hundred feet of you. Ok?"

Sandra nodded.

"Thank you," she whispered.

Chief Simonson helped Mrs. Doyle up off the ground and, with her upper arm firmly in his grasp, led her away around the side of the house.

Sarah led Sandra back to her chair. Sandra sat. Someone brought her a cup of chamomile tea and a plate of cookies. Maddie brought Oreo over and set the kitten in Sandra's lap.

"Oreo said pet him, and you'll feel better," the little girl told the crying woman.

Sandra smiled at Maddie.

"Thank you. That's very nice of you."

Throughout the day, many people approached Sandra, apologizing and offering to help her set up her new home. Sandra had nothing she wanted to bring from her mother's house.

"I suppose I need to get my clothes," she told Elizabeth and the girls. "But I can't face going over there right now. And I don't really like the clothes I have. Mother chose most of them." Elizabeth looked at the bland beige pants and blue blouse that Sandra was wearing.

"I'll go get your clothes," Robin said. "And as soon as you get your first paycheck, we'll go shopping."

"You will come to The Flower's Daughter tomorrow," Clara said, coming up beside them.

"I was not here when you were a child and missed how you were treated. We Fae do not take well to hearing of the mistreatment of children. You will come to me, and you will pick out whatever you like. On the house. I heard someone say that you liked to draw. Maybe someday, when you are feeling up to it, you can do a picture for me."

Sandra stared at Clara in shock.

"I'll make sure she's at the shop tomorrow," Sarah said.

"She must come to us as well," Calvin said as he and Paul

approached from the other side. "Clara's things are beautiful, and you will feel like a Goddess. But sometimes, it can be fun to have different clothes—to pretend that you are someone else altogether. I can help you there. Come to us after Clara's—we'll have fun. I insist. And maybe you can draw something for us, too."

Sandra stared. Others offered her furniture and linens, plants and flowers, and food for her kitchen.

Dennis picked a few people out of the crowd and left to empty the apartment so Sandra could move in right away. Those offering furniture promised to bring it over that evening.

"See, this is how the community should have treated you," Elizabeth said. "We all need to support each other and stand together. When you're settled at Sarah's, come see me. It sounds like, from what I've heard, that you were not allowed to really use your magic much or find out where your interests lie. I know your mother had you making potions. But is that something you enjoy doing? Is that what your Gift is telling you its focus is? Because if it is, you can work with me, too. Aunt Glo and I will train you."

"Thank you, Elizabeth. I don't know. I know I have an Earth Gift, but I wasn't encouraged to use it outside of school unless I was doing what Mother wanted. I think my talents lie more with animals. I think that's what my initial tests showed. But I don't know."

"We can have you retested if you like," Mrs. O'Shea, the secretary of the high school, offered. "When you're ready."

"Thank you, everyone," Sandra looked around at the crowd. "I don't know where I will go or what I will do from here, but thank you. I really appreciate it. Thank you."

"Well, I think that was a good day's work, don't you?" Elizabeth said to Robin.

Robin grinned.

"It was. Now let's have some fun. And Sandra, after shopping tomorrow, we're going to decorate your apartment."

"Oh, I have some good ideas for that," Sarah said.

"I'll bring some herbs and potions," Elizabeth said. "We'll get pizza and make it a girl's night. Someone else can watch the kids."

Sandra smiled.

“I think this is the start of a beautiful friendship, don’t you?” Robin asked.

Sandra’s smile grew.

“I think we’ll do great things together,” Elizabeth said. “We’re going to torch this town. Who knows what trouble we can get into.”

II

The answer to that question, over the next few days, was 'not much.' Robin, Sarah, and Elizabeth helped Sandra get settled into her new life. They arranged the furniture and decorated the apartment until Sandra had everything the way she wanted. By the time they finished, the one-bedroom apartment was cozy and felt like a home.

"I can't tell you how much this all means to me, you guys," Sandra said as they stood in the living room staring around at their handiwork. There was a comfy couch with brightly colored squishy pillows and a hand-knit blanket on the back. Plants were hanging from the ceiling and in pots on every available surface. Crystals were on the shelves and tables. Pretty white curtains fluttered in the breeze from the windows. Heavier purple drapes could be closed over them in the evenings.

The kitchen was fully stocked with food, pots and pans, dishes, and cutlery. The bathroom had plenty of towels, supplies, and toilet paper —the soft kind. The bedroom had a metal frame bed with scrollwork head and footboards. A firm mattress was on the bed, covered in clean white sheets and a pretty, multi-colored comforter. A velvety-soft light green blanket was folded across the foot of the bed for extra warmth.

"We're happy to have been able to help," Robin replied.

Elizabeth was grateful for her friends. It felt good to help Sandra set out on her own at last.

"I meant what I said, Sandra. If you want to do some potion work, you can always come to me," Elizabeth told the other woman.

"Thank you, Liz. I appreciate it."

❧

HELPING SANDRA AND RECONNECTING WITH HER FRIENDS HAD given Elizabeth a sense of belonging and rightness that she hadn't realized she had been missing. With every passing day, Elizabeth became even more sure that coming home had been the right thing to do.

Elizabeth smiled as she poured a potion into its shiny blue glass bottle. The stillroom was filled with warm, golden light. The day's work had gone well. She capped the bottle and set it aside. It was a little after four in the afternoon, and Elizabeth felt ready for a break. She left the stillroom, locking the door behind her.

Josh was sitting on the patio, looking at something in his hands. Magnus sat on the arm of Josh's chair, guiding whatever it was he had the boy doing. Maddie and Mags were down by the cliffs. Elizabeth could hear Maddie's excited voice on the wind as they went about whatever they were doing. She turned to watch them for a moment, feeling her heart catch as she saw her eight-year-old daughter rise up into the air. Mags was teaching her how to fly.

Elizabeth took a deep breath, then let it out. Mags would keep Maddie safe. Elizabeth turned back toward her son.

Josh sat back, holding the object he had been working on in his hand.

"Well done, lad," Magnus told his apprentice. Josh smiled. He looked up and saw his mother watching.

"Look, Mom," Josh held the object out to Elizabeth. It was a piece of jade, about three inches long and maybe half that wide. The jade was shaped like a bear. The bear held a fish in his mouth, tail flipped to one side.

"That's beautiful, Josh! It's so well done. Did you make this?"

Josh nodded.

"Magnus is teaching me how to control my Earth magic to shape things. He says I might as well make something beautiful while I'm learning control."

"I agree. I think you have a real talent for this, Sweetheart. If you wanted to, I think you could make more of these and sell them. I'm sure one of the stores in town would carry them. Or maybe you could have a tent at the market."

"That would be cool. It would be awesome to have my own money," Josh agreed.

"It will be a good way for the town to learn your skills and advertise your strengths," Magnus said. "You will be a powerful Mage once I'm done with you. It will be a good way to show everyone that you have such fine control over your magic. There are many that will appreciate it."

Magnus looked up at Elizabeth. "Have you thought about having a potion shop in town? I think you should try to open the bookstore. It's the best location."

"But didn't Calvin say that the shop could only be opened by the right person? I don't think that could be me." Elizabeth thought for a moment. "Do you know who owns the shop? Does Mr. Jackson still own it? Is there a property manager?"

"I believe that Mr. Jackson does still own the shop. I would ask at the realty office—they would know if Mr. Jackson had left someone in charge."

"Thank you, Magnus." Elizabeth paused.

"Let's go into town for dinner, shall we? We can get pizza or something at the market. Magnus, you're welcome to join us."

"Thank you, Elizabeth. I think I will go home. My wife is making something special for dinner. She won't tell me what, but she promised I would like it." Magnus grinned.

Magnus said goodbye and left. Elizabeth turned to call Maddie just as the girl and her teacher flew up the field and landed in front of her, Oreo held tight in Maddie's arms. Maddie's grin lit up the earth.

"Did you see me, Mom? I flew! Mags taught me how to fly! It's so cool!"

"I did, Sweetheart! That's amazing! Was it fun?"

"It's so fun, Mom! It's awesome!"

Mags was grinning, too.

"I am really enjoying working with Maddie, Elizabeth. She's extremely bright and learns very quickly."

"You honor us by saying so, Mags. Josh and I were just talking about going into town for dinner. You're welcome to join us."

"Thank you. I'd like that. Let me tell Mariah before we go."

❦

MARIAH AND MARY DECIDED TO GO INTO TOWN, TOO, AND HAVE dinner with their Aunt Meg. The whole group rode bikes into town together. They got pizza, then sat in the food court at the open-air market in the town center. There was a lively Celtic band playing as they ate. Mags jumped up and taught Maddie a jig to one of the songs. It was a wonderful evening.

After dinner, Elizabeth headed over to the realty office. It was still early, and the office didn't close until seven. She paused, her hand on the door. Biting her lip, she turned the handle and went in.

A chime over the door rang out as she entered the office. A young woman looked up from behind her desk at the back of the room. She smiled when she saw Elizabeth.

"Hello! What can I do for you? You're Elizabeth Sloan, right? My name's Amariah." Amariah stood and walked around her desk, hand outstretched.

"Hi, Amariah. Nice to meet you. Yes, I'm Elizabeth Sloan. I'm thinking about opening a store in town, and I was wondering if you knew who was managing the old bookstore, now that Mr. Jackson's gone."

Amariah smiled.

"Our office is handling the upkeep of the shop, of course. As much as we can, without being able to get into it. Mr. Jackson warded the property so that only the right person could open it up again. So far, no one has been able to."

"Have very many people tried?"

"Only three so far. Mostly people from out of town."

"I used to spend a lot of my time there when I was younger," Elizabeth said. "Mr. Jackson would let me help out sometimes or let me hide away with a good book when I needed to. If you don't mind, I would like to try getting into the store."

"Of course. Let me lock up here. If you aren't able to get in, don't worry. I'm sure we'll be able to find you another space."

Amariah locked up the office, then led Elizabeth several doors down to the bookshop.

"Normally, I would use a key, but as it is...."

"What do I need to do?" Elizabeth asked.

"Just put your hand on the doorknob and turn it. The wards were created to recognize the right person."

Elizabeth took a breath and grabbed the door handle. She turned the knob. Warmth traveled up her arm toward her heart.

The door opened.

"Oh, very good!" Amariah said. "Go on, go in!"

Elizabeth pushed open the door and stepped inside.

The store had been dark and empty. Now it was anything but. As Elizabeth walked into the shop, the lights came on. Music played from hidden speakers, quiet, instrumental music that somehow made the listener happy to hear. There was a sparkle to the air inside the shop. Books filled the shelves. There was a seating area in the center of the shop, with three cozy armchairs and a loveseat. A coffee table sat in the center of the seating arrangement. There was another seating area with two armchairs to the left against the wall. The walls were painted a beautiful royal blue color, with silver stars in the corners. It was a beautiful, cozy store, just as Elizabeth remembered it. There was even a bowl of mints on the counter, next to the beautiful old metal cash register.

There was a swirl of energy by the counter. Suddenly, Mr. Jackson stood before them, a large smile on his face.

"Elizabeth! You finally came home. I'm happy to see you, my dear."

"Mr. Jackson! I thought you went home to England!"

"I did, my girl. I felt the store open and came right away. I had to see you to explain all of this."

Elizabeth blinked.

"My dear girl, no one loved this store as you did. When I knew it was time to go home, I knew that you were the only one I wanted to take over the store here. If you hadn't come home, the store would have gradually faded until no one remembered it had ever been here. The store is magical itself, you see. It needs the energy and enthusiasm of its owner to exist."

"Mr. Jackson, I really appreciate you saving the store for me. How does this work? Do you want me to buy the store from you? Or would I be working for you while I run it?"

"Oh, no, my dear. The store can only be gifted from one caretaker to the next. It's yours, now. Don't worry. It already knows you and loves you. You can do anything with it that you like."

"I was thinking about a potions shop," Elizabeth said.

"You could have the bookstore downstairs and a potions shop either upstairs or in the back. The shop will expand and create whatever you want. Maybe a little cafe? I had often thought it would be a nice touch. You could serve Meg's excellent pastries," the older gentleman suggested.

"That would be wonderful," Amariah agreed.

Elizabeth thought about it.

"That would be cool."

"Do you accept the store, Elizabeth?" Mr. Jackson asked.

Elizabeth took a deep breath.

"Yes, I do. Thank you, Mr. Jackson."

"Excellent, my dear." Mr. Jackson took two steps forward and held out his hands. Elizabeth placed her own in his. A tingling energy passed from Mr. Jackson's hands through hers. Mr. Jackson smiled, then kissed her forehead.

"I leave it in your competent hands, then, Elizabeth. If you want anything, just ask the store. A House Spirit inhabits it. The spirit has no limits in time or space. So just be careful what you ask for." Mr. Jackson winked, and then he was gone.

Elizabeth turned to Amariah in shock.

"Well, I guess you have your store!" the realtor said with a grin. "I'm excited to see what you do with it."

12

Elizabeth wandered back outside in a daze. She closed the door, promising to be right back. Amariah said goodbye and returned to the realty office. Elizabeth made her way back to the market still in shock. Mags and Maddie were enjoying ice cream treats and talking with Meg. The Brownie looked up as Elizabeth approached the table.

"Elizabeth! Are you ok? You look like you're in shock."

"Mr. Jackson just gave me his store. It's magical. It's sentient, like the house, but more so. It has a House Spirit. He says the store will do whatever I like. He doesn't want rent, he says it can only be gifted, and it's mine."

Meg's eyes grew wide.

"That is an enormous, extraordinary gift, Elizabeth. I am very happy for you. What will you do with it? Will you keep it a bookstore? Or turn it into a potions store?"

"Both, I think. Mr. Jackson suggested I add a little cafe and sell your pastries, Meg. Would that work for you?"

"That would be wonderful, Lizzie Grace. It looks like you have a lot of work to do."

"I'm really glad that the kids are busy with their teachers," Elizabeth looked around. "Where is Josh, by the way?"

"He went to talk to some of the merchants in the market. He wanted to find out how they run their businesses. I think he wants to sell his carvings here."

"He can sell them in the shop, now, if he likes," Elizabeth said. "This will change everything for us."

"You'll do fine, Sweetheart," Meg said, patting Elizabeth's arm.

"Can we see the shop, Mom?" Maddie asked.

"Of course. Let's find Josh, and I'll show you both."

Josh and Maddie loved the shop. As they left, Elizabeth patted the wall of the shop and promised to come back the next day.

"We'll talk about what I'd like to have here then, ok?" A warm tingle ran up her arm. Elizabeth smiled. Life was definitely looking up. Maybe Calvin would have some cool decorating ideas for the potions area of the shop.

CALVIN DID, IN FACT, HAVE MANY IDEAS. HE SHARED THEM WITH Elizabeth the next day at the shop.

"It should be green, of course, to reflect your Earth magic and the plants you use in your potions." They were talking about how to decorate the apothecary portion of the store. "Maybe with gold accents, to balance the silver ones in the bookshop part of the store. Where will you put the potions room? Is there a way upstairs? And how will those without the ability to climb stairs get up there?"

"I hadn't even thought about that," Elizabeth said. "Maybe I can keep the upstairs as an office and open the back room as the potions area?"

"That might be better, darling," Calvin agreed. He sipped his latte.

"Where will you put the café area? It would be a shame to lose any of the bookstore space."

"Mr. Jackson said that the store has no limits in time or space. Maybe it can add a room onto the back and a little garden? Customers can sit out there when the weather is nice."

"Let's go look at the space," Calvin said.

They walked into the backroom to find that the store had taken her suggestion as a command. The back room was slightly larger than it had been before. If you were to look out the back, there was a small garden now, with three little wrought-iron tables and their chairs, painted white. Flagstones paved the ground, with planters around the sides filled with flowering herbs. Lavender and rosemary plants lined the sides of the garden. Somehow, the space looked as if it had always been there and didn't interfere with the little road behind the shop at all.

In the enlarged back room of the shop, there was now plenty of space for the potions area and a small café. The potions area would be in the front of the room, closest to the bookstore. The back half would be the café. The walls were painted hunter green, with shiny golden scrollwork and stars in the corners. Shelves lined the walls, and several tables with chairs were in the café part of the room.

"This is going to be lovely, Elizabeth. You'll have to hire help, of course," Calvin said, looking around. "I would suggest asking Meg to recommend a few people. Maybe high schoolers? You'll need a manager, too, for when you need to be home working on your potions. You won't be able to be in the shop all the time."

"I don't have the budget to hire staff," Elizabeth said.

"I'm sure something will work out. Remember, you don't have overhead. The shop is yours and self-sustaining. Maybe you could take on a few potions apprentices and have working in the store be a part of their duties? They'll learn a lot from you. It would be totally worth their while. Then you could pay them according to apprentice rules, a stipend rather than a wage. They could make extra money by selling their own potions in the shop when you think they are good enough. They could have their own lines, with their own labels. You could take a thirty percent cut, and they could keep the rest."

Elizabeth looked at Calvin.

"You're really good at this, Calvin. It's like you've thought about how to do this before."

Calvin smiled.

"My dear, I am much older than I look. I've had a lot of time to learn a lot of things. I am a veritable font of information. Information I am happy to share with my good friends, of course."

"And in return for free potions whenever necessary, I'm sure."

"There is that," Calvin agreed.

"Why not?" Elizabeth said. "I guess I have apprentices to find. And a manager. Someone who already has the skills to run a business. It has to be someone who appreciates the store's abilities and sentience. The store has to like them, too."

"I'm sure you'll find someone. I would suggest talking to the people in town first, though. Get the word out. Then if you need to advertise in other towns, you can do so."

"Thanks, Calvin."

"No problem, darling. Let's find you a staff."

ELIZABETH STOPPED BY MEG'S STALL ON THE WAY HOME. SHE LET the Brownie know she was looking for apprentices and why. Meg was thrilled.

"That's fabulous, darling! Such a wonderful idea. I'm sure young Earth Witches will be thrilled to learn from you. The town appreciates having a fully trained Potion Master around, even more so since the few months between Gloria's death and you coming home."

Meg promised to get the word out. Elizabeth went home with her mind buzzing, full of ideas for the shop. She called Robin as soon as she got home.

"Hey, girl, I need your artistic talents. I'm taking over the old bookstore and adding a potions room and cafe. I need a logo and menus and stuff."

"Congratulations! I thought old Jackson had warded the shop so no one could get in?"

"He warded it so only the right person could get in. It turns out he was waiting for me to come home. He portalled in and officially turned the store over to me as soon as I opened the door."

Robin was thrilled. She promised to have ideas drawn up as soon as possible and demanded a look inside the shop. Elizabeth laughed and agreed to show her around the next day.

After dinner, Elizabeth went out to the stillroom for a bit of quiet and to check on a few potions that were busy infusing. She sat down in the armchair in the corner with a sigh. Aunt Gloria popped in beside her.

"You've been busy, Lizzie Grace. I'm glad that things are going so well for you."

"Thanks, Aunt Glo. Me, too. I guess I'm feeling a little overwhelmed at the moment, though. Everything seems to be happening so quickly."

"It is. Don't worry. You have friends and family around you to support you and help you figure it all out. We'll make it work."

"I know. Thank you. Argh."

"Baby steps, Lizzie Grace. Tackle one small thing at a time. You'll get there."

Elizabeth sighed again.

"I was thinking about your case, Aunt Glo. And about Mathilda and John. What exactly were all of you doing back then that someone would still be so mad at you so much later?"

"I really don't know, Lizzie Grace. A group of us worked together for the Supernatural Oversight Council for a couple of years. We went undercover, did research, that kind of thing. We were rarely in the limelight. We were all young and thought it would be fun. We had no idea what being undercover was really like or the things we would see. We were young and stupid."

"Did you apply for the job?"

"No, the Council came to us. Apparently, we all had skills that the Council had taken note of. My skill at potions, John's as a Shifter who could shift into whatever animal form he liked. Others were excellent at glamours. We had a couple of high ritual Witches, an Air Mage, a Fire Mage, and a Techno-Mage. John and the Techno-Mage worked together a lot. They were like brothers. There was an Aes Sídhe, a Brownie, a Pixie, and several other Shifters. We were all pretty close. We were like the arcane troubleshooters of the Council. The Air Mage was married—she was a little older than the rest of us. They mostly used her for scrying on the wind. She had a couple of small children. I guess she had been working for the Council for a few years before our group was formed. Her name was Alice. We all looked up to her." Aunt Gloria's gaze faded into the distance as she remembered.

"What happened to Alice? Is she still alive?"

Aunt Gloria shook her head.

"Alice died two years after I joined the group. Oddly enough, her death had nothing to do with her work for the Council. Her husband was devastated. He packed up his kids and moved them to Oregon, I think. Back to wherever he was from."

"Was he a Witch too?"

"No, Wolf Shifter. It was an odd match, but it worked for them."

"Were they bonded?"

"No, just very much in love," Aunt Gloria smiled and shook her head.

"How did Alice die?"

"Cancer. She had been feeling tired for a while but thought nothing of it. Put it down to being a mother of young children plus working for the Council. One night she lay down to sleep and didn't get up again. Her husband had a Healer scan the body. That's when we found out that she'd been sick."

"Did any of your cases end badly? Or cause a lot of trouble for anyone?"

"I'm sure they did, but nothing that was so bad it would warrant a forty-year vendetta."

"I really think that we should check on the other members of that group, Aunt Glo. Were you still in contact with any of the others?"

"One or two. Their information is in my address book in the house."

"Do you think you could have a look around the Spirit Realm and see if any of them have passed on and might be willing to talk to you? Maybe start with John since we know he's dead."

"I'll see what I can do, Lizzie Grace."

"Thanks, Aunt Glo. Let's see what we can find."

13

Elizabeth decided she needed a tablet to keep track of all of her projects. She asked her sister Lucy, who sent her to a Techno-Mage named Garrett in the next paranormal Haven over, Still's Falls. The Techno-Mages had made tremendous leaps in the last six months in modifying modern technology so that Witches and other magicals could use it. Elizabeth came back with a brand new, state-of-the-art tablet that weighed less than a pound and was powered by magic. Apparently, it could do just about everything except walk by itself or the dishes. Garrett had shown her how to use the calendar app to schedule her life, as well as how to connect to both the paranormal and the mundane internets. The tablet came with a nifty stylus that could double as a wand if needed. It had tiny blue and purple crystals embedded in it. The whole thing was a work of Techno-Magical art. Like Calvin and Clara, Garrett had given Elizabeth an excellent deal in return for the occasional high-end potions. The deal included maintenance and troubleshooting, for which Elizabeth was extremely grateful.

Garrett had set Elizabeth up with a notetaking software that Elizabeth was planning to use to keep track of ideas for the shop and tasks she wanted to complete. She also used it to start a folder on Aunt Gloria's merry group of friends.

Elizabeth added the names of everyone in the group, starting a file for each name, then creating a master list containing all their names and whether they were alive or dead. So far, she only had data on the members of the group who lived locally. Elizabeth searched the desk in Aunt Gloria's office for the address book her aunt had mentioned. She found it in the upper right-hand drawer.

Aunt Gloria had been a very organized Witch, and her address book reflected that. All her contacts were arranged alphabetically by last name. Elizabeth looked up Mathilda and John. There was a little star by their names. Elizabeth looked through the little book, searching for more stars. She found fifteen.

"Aunt Glo!"

"Yes, Lizzie Grace?"

"Are these names with the stars the ones from your group?"

"Yes, that's right."

Aunt Gloria came to look over Elizabeth's shoulder at the book. Elizabeth had made a list of the starred names as she found them.

"Hmm. Ok. Well, George Finlay is dead. He was the Techno-Mage. John's friend. He was shot, actually. George became a cop after the group broke up. He stayed on the Council's payroll as a liaison with the human police force. He was killed in a gang shoot-out in New York. His wife Amy wasn't part of the group—they met later. I didn't know her very well."

Aunt Gloria read down the list as Elizabeth made a note on her tablet.

"Alice passed, as I told you. Carl, the Fire Mage, he's still working for the Council, I think. The two half-Sidhe Illusionists were sisters, Mayenne and Sabine. I think they returned to France. The three High Magic Witches, Loraine, Dora, and Michelle, I'm not sure what happened to them. They were very close, closer than sisters, almost. They did everything together. They stayed a little apart from the rest of the group. They were friendly but not close to everyone else. They were outstanding at long-range spells and hexes, or ones that had to last a while. They could do extremely complex spell-weavings when they worked together."

"Do you remember where they were from?"

"Maryland, I think? I think Loraine had ties to New Orleans—they spent time down there every once in a while." Aunt Gloria looked at the list again.

"Lorien, the Aes Sidhe, I think he went home, too. I'm not sure where his family was from. Madelynn, the Brownie, has a restaurant in Silver Falls. Sharalee, the Pixie, owns a shop in Oregon, I think. She and Madelynn stay in touch. The other three Shifters, Lukas, Elise, and Sean, came from a pack in the Midwest. I think they stayed with the Council as enforcers."

"Thanks, Aunt Glo. I'll call the ones I can reach now."

Elizabeth looked at the clock. It was after three in the afternoon in the North East. Which meant it was lunchtime on the West Coast. She decided to start with the members of the group on the East Coast.

She tried the number for Carl, the Fire Mage, first. A man's voice answered in Spanish.

"May I speak to Carl Humphries, please?"

"No, no Carl here. This is my number."

"Oh, I'm sorry. Thank you for your time."

Elizabeth called Madelynn next. The phone went to voicemail. She left a message, stating that she was Gloria's niece and asking the Brownie to call at her earliest convenience.

The numbers for Lukas and Elise had been crossed out, so she tried Sean next.

"Hello?" A deep, masculine voice answered.

"Hello, my name is Elizabeth Sloan. I'm Gloria Sloan's niece. I'm looking for Sean Flynn?"

"This is Sean. What can I do for you, Elizabeth? How is Gloria? It's been a while since I've spoken to her."

"My Aunt passed away several months ago. That's why I'm calling, actually. Aunt Glo is here with me in spirit form, and we've noticed a pattern of strange deaths affecting members of your group of friends from back when you all worked for the Council together. I'm trying to get in touch with anyone else in the group that I can, looking for more information. And trying to warn people, if I can."

"You said a pattern. Who else is dead?"

"John Monroe. Mathilda held on, with Gloria's help, for her children, but she will be passing in two months when her daughter's child is born."

"What evidence do you have that Gloria and John's deaths were not natural?"

"Gloria was poisoned, and John was electrocuted. He was working on a house with his son. The power was off. The bolt came out of nowhere. George Finlay was shot in the line of duty—I haven't linked his death to this yet. But something just seems off, and Aunt Gloria agrees with me. Frankly, I'm glad to find that you're still alive, Mr. Flynn. Are you still in touch with Lukas and Elise? My aunt said the three of you were close."

"We are. We're cousins. Lukas and Elise are still enforcers for the Council. I took over as Alpha of our Pack several years ago. My father was Alpha before me." Sean Flynn paused. "I'll get in touch with Lukas and Elise. We'll start calling the other members of the group that we are still in contact with. Who else have you spoken to so far?"

"I left a message for Madelynn, but that's it. I was going to try Sharalee next. I don't have information for Lorien, the High Magic Witches, or the Illusionists. Aunt Gloria thought that Mayenne and Sabine returned to France."

"They did. Elise is still in touch with them. I'll have her call them and get back to you. Is this a good number for you?"

"Yes. Thank you, Mr. Flynn. I really appreciate your help. Oh, who was your contact at the Council? Do you think we could reach out to them, too? If someone has it out for your group, it seems like the leader would be an excellent target."

"The handler of our group was Sarah Faraday. She was a tough woman but fair. A real straight shooter. She passed away about fifteen years ago. She drowned in a boating accident."

"Another accidental death? Mr. Flynn, that adds to my theory. Can you think of anyone else we should contact? Was there anyone else in your group, or close to your group, that might be a target?"

"Lukas was seeing a girl, a Fire Witch. Samantha Rhodes. They broke up not too long before the group did, and she moved home to Raleigh. She was around for most of our time together. She helped on a few missions as a consultant. Several other Council operatives functioned as support for our team. Dylan, a Techno-Mage who supported George and got him supplies and things. Roger Falcone, who handled our logistics. Rosie Boyd, who handled us for Sarah. Rosie was Sarah's assistant. Those were the people we mainly worked with. We occasionally worked with other teams when we needed backup or when a mission was more extensive than we could handle on our own."

"Do you have contact information for any of them?"

"I don't, but Elise and Lukas might. I'll ask them to get in touch."

"Thank you, Mr. Flynn."

"Thank you, Elizabeth, for getting in touch and bringing this to my attention. I will tell Elise to call you as soon as she has answers. And I will get in touch with Lorien. I'll let you know what he says. Please give Gloria my best."

Sean Flynn hung up. Elizabeth put down the phone slowly. She looked up at Aunt Gloria, who was hovering nearby. Gloria shook her head.

"I didn't know that Sarah was dead. This is turning out to be worse than I thought. I wonder who else is gone?"

MADELYNN CALLED BACK AT SEVEN THAT EVENING. ELIZABETH AND the children had just finished dinner. Maddie was in the sitting room playing with Oreo, and Josh was on the patio out back. He was working on a sculpture under the fairy lights strung around the outside of the seating space. His Faery Dog Familiar, Connor, slept by his feet.

"Hello, I'm returning a call from Elizabeth Sloan? This is Madelynn, Gloria's friend."

"Hi, Madelynn. Thank you so much for calling back."

"Of course, my pleasure. You said you had an important question for me?"

Elizabeth filled the other woman in on her suspicions and what she had learned from Sean Flynn.

"My goodness." Madelynn was quiet for a moment. When she spoke again, her voice was stern.

"Sean said he would have Elise call you when she had more information about the others?"

"Yes, he did."

"Good. Please let me know what they find. I will call Sharalee myself. We talk at least once a week. I'll call her as soon as I hang up here." Madelynn took a breath.

"Elizabeth, I don't know if Gloria told you, but our group was very close. I considered the members part of my family. I felt it when those who passed moved on but believed the stories of accidental death and death on the job. I haven't used the family bond much other than to check in over the years. I knew that everyone had to go their own ways, like a child leaving home. But we are still tied. I can feel the bond still active in everyone except Sabine, Dora, and Michelle. Lorien went into the hills so that bond feels a little different, but I know he's alive. I will contact him and tell him to stay where he is. If someone is after us, Lorien is safer at home in Faery. It worries me that these deaths are so widely spaced. Someone is playing a long game. That suggests that they are not sane. And that they are very good planners. I will also get in touch with everyone else. And I will find Loraine and ask her what happened to Dora and Michelle. I felt them pass at the same time, but I don't know how they died. I know they were in the South, somewhere. Loraine is still in that area. I will try her family in New Orleans. She always liked it there."

"Thank you, Madelynn. Please let me know what you find out as soon as you can. Oh, does your bond extend to the support staff? Rosie, Dylan, and Roger? Or to Samantha Rhodes?"

"Samantha, yes. And Rosie. Not to the other two. I never liked them very much. Dylan was very good at what he did, but I just didn't trust him for some reason. Roger was a hard person to get to know. He functioned very well at planning and organization, but he was socially awkward. Roger preferred to set everything up from afar. He would relay anything he had for us through Rosie."

"Are you still in touch with Rosie?"

"Yes. I'll call her now, after Sharalee."

"Thank you, Madelynn."

"You're welcome, Elizabeth. Maybe I'll pop over for a visit if that's alright with you. I didn't visit Gloria enough when she was alive. I would like to take the opportunity to see her while I can before she moves on."

"That would be lovely. Aunt Gloria would love to see you. There are a lot of Brownies here in Fairweather Falls. We have one who lives with us, and one of my best friends is one too. You would be welcome here."

"Thank you, my dear. I'll call you as soon as I hear from Sharalee, Rosie, and Loraine."

Elizabeth hung up again.

"Well, I guess we play a waiting game, now. I'm glad that Sean and Madelynn are taking the lead in contacting everyone else," Aunt Gloria said. "The others will take it much more seriously, coming from them. Not that they wouldn't take it seriously coming from you, dear." Aunt Gloria smiled at Elizabeth.

"I understand, Aunt Glo. I guess I've done what I can. And now, we wait."

14

Elizabeth thought about telling Jonah about Aunt Gloria's friends but decided she should have more information first. So the next day, while she waited for everyone to get back to her, she focused on potions and the store.

Elizabeth spent the morning in the stillroom, then headed over to the shop after lunch. A warm tingle filled her body when she stepped through the door. The shop was happy to see her.

Elizabeth patted the door frame as she walked in.

"I'm glad to see you, too," she told the store.

Elizabeth wandered around the shop, looking at the current book selections. She made notes of where there were holes in the inventory and went looking for Mr. Jackson's ordering information. She found an old-school Rolodex on a shelf under the cash register. Looking through it, Elizabeth made notes on her tablet, transferring contact information for book suppliers and certain customers that had accounts or had made regular purchases. She called the suppliers and told them the store would be open again, placing several orders as she did so. She was especially excited to receive the order from the Fae book supplier. The Fae books had been her favorites as a child. She could look at the beautiful illuminations for hours. The Fae hid many elements in their artwork, so there was always something new to see. You could stare at an illustration for hours and still not find everything contained within.

As she was getting off the phone with the Fae book supplier, Andomiel, there was a knock at the door. Elizabeth opened it to find Calvin and a young girl standing on the sidewalk in front of the shop.

"Hello, darling. I found this young woman standing out here looking nervous. I think she's here about apprenticing, isn't that right, sweetheart?" The flamboyant Kitsune smiled at the young girl, who nodded.

"Come in, both of you," Elizabeth said. She stood aside as they filed into the store. Another girl hurried up as Elizabeth was closing the door.

"Hi! Are you Ms. Sloan? My name is Claire. I heard you were looking for apprentices for your potion-making business. I'm an Earth Witch. I was going to leave this in the mailbox, but I'd love to talk to you if you have the time?"

Elizabeth smiled at the girl. She certainly had fire.

"Come on in. I have one other person here now about the apprenticeship. We might as well all talk together at the same time."

Claire followed Calvin and the other girl into the store. Elizabeth looked around, then, seeing no one else approaching, closed the door. She was turning around when another knock sounded behind her. Turning back, Elizabeth saw a young man of about sixteen standing on the step.

"Hi, can I help you?" Elizabeth asked.

"I'm here about the apprenticeship? Are you Ms. Sloan?"

"Yes, I am. Come in. I have two other interested parties here at the moment."

The young man stepped into the store. Elizabeth felt a warm tingle up her spine. The store liked this young man.

"Why don't we all go into the back? There are tables there in the cafe section. Calvin, do you want to look around, or is there something I can help you with?"

"Oh, I was just dropping by to see how you were doing. I'll listen in if that's all right with you," Calvin answered.

"Sure."

Elizabeth led everyone into the potions and cafe area in the back room. She sat them at one of the round tables in the cafe section.

"How did you all hear about the apprenticeship?" Elizabeth asked.

"My mother told me," the more outspoken of the two girls said. "We have a Brownie at our house, and she told my mother. She thought it would be an excellent opportunity for me. I want my own shop, eventually. It would be good for me to learn not only potion making but how to run a business as well."

"How old are you? Where are you in school?"

"I'm seventeen. I'm a junior. I'm going to go to Hellebore Academy after high school to train as a Potions Master."

"That sounds like a good plan. How about you?" Elizabeth said to the quieter girl.

"My mother told me about it," the slightly younger girl all but whispered. "Meg told her about it at the market."

"And what are your plans after school? What grade are you in? And what's your name?"

"My name is Maia. I'm a sophomore. I'm fifteen. I'm not really sure what I want to do after school. I am an Earth Witch, but I have a strong second Gift in Water. I like working with plants. I like to draw and paint, too. I'd love to find a way to combine the two."

"That sounds like a wonderful idea. And you?"

Elizabeth turned to the young man.

"My name is Michael Kennedy. I'm sixteen. I'm a junior too. I'm an Earth Mage. My parents are Air Mages and aren't sure what to do with me. The teachers at school thought it might be a good idea for me to work with you and learn more about my Earth Gifts. I like mixing things and seeing what happens. I have a deep connection to dirt and stone, too. I don't have a really clear idea of where my interests lie."

"Ok. Do you all understand how an apprenticeship works? You would learn potions making under me, then also help out in the shop. I would not pay you a wage, but you would receive a stipend every month. As your potions skills progress, you would be able to sell your own lines here in the shop, under your own brand, and keep seventy percent of all sales of those products. Do you all live locally?"

All three young people nodded.

"That makes it easier. Ok. Let me show you around. If you think this is the right fit for you, we can give it a three-month trial period. At the end of that time, if you want to continue, we will make the arrangement permanent. When you are ready to leave for school, or whatever you decide to do next, I will give you a recommendation. How does that sound? Remember, an apprenticeship is about learning from a master in your chosen trade. This will require work on your part. But it could really prepare you for a wonderful career and give you a great start in the world."

The three young people looked at each other, then turned back to Elizabeth.

"We'll do it," Claire said, answering for all of them. The other two nodded.

"Well, that's your staffing sorted out," Calvin replied. "Now we just need to find you a fabulous store manager, so you can focus on your potions and teaching this lot."

"I guess that's the next step. Let's work on getting these three set up first, though. I wonder if the shop could create a stillroom upstairs next to the office for us to learn in?"

The shop rumbled a little bit. All three teens stared at Elizabeth, eyes wide.

She grinned.

"Oh, I forgot to mention. The store is sentient. She needs to be treated with respect. If she likes you, you can ask her for help, and she will provide it. If she doesn't, she can make your time here difficult. She already likes you, Michael. Why don't you all introduce yourselves to her properly? Just place your hands against a wall or doorway and introduce yourselves like you would to any other person."

"This is going to be fun," Calvin said, watching the three teens as they all found a wall and placed their hands on it. Michael smiled, Maia looked surprised, and Claire grinned.

"I think you're going to have your hands full with this lot," the Kitsune continued. "It's going to be a wild ride. And you'll all be better for it. Now, we must discuss uniforms for the shop. Something elegant yet easy to move in. I love your look, darling. Maybe we can stick with the time period and outfit the children in the same style." Calvin cast an eye over the three teens.

"Bring them over to my shop when you're done here. We'll get them sorted out." Calvin swept from the room, leaving Elizabeth staring bemusedly after him. She hadn't even thought about uniforms or a dress code for the shop. What else had she forgotten?

Calvin did indeed sort out a uniform for the shop. He found long walking skirts for the girls, with white blouses trimmed with lace and matching jackets, in deep hunter green. He provided brown pants and a green jacket for Michael, under which went a white button-down shirt and waistcoat. The waistcoat had flowers and leaves embroidered on it in gold.

"We look amazing!" Claire stated as the three apprentices stared at themselves in the mirrors at Vix. Michael was grinning. Maia stared at her reflection as if trying to memorize every detail. She looked around at the others. "Can I take a picture? I want to draw us. I think I can make a logo out of this."

Claire took her phone out of her bag and snapped pictures of them all. "Here, what's your number? I'll send them to you." Maia and Claire exchanged numbers. "Here, take mine too. I want to show my Grandparents. They'll love this," Michael said. Claire added his number and sent him the images.

"You know, Maia," Elizabeth said. "My friend Robin is a graphic designer. She was going to design the logos and branding materials for the store. I like your idea, though. I think it has real potential. Would you mind discussing it with Robin? I'm sure the two of you could work together."

Maia stared at Elizabeth. "Really? You'd let me do that?"

"Of course. You will be learning all the aspects of running a business while you're with me. You may as well get started on the branding and marketing now. And like I said, I like your idea. I'll call Robin and have her set up a time with you. Ok?"

Maia nodded, her eyes wide.

❧

Elizabeth had spent a few minutes going over schedules with her apprentices, then sent them home with instructions to have their parents call her that evening. She thanked Calvin, then started the walk back home. As she walked, her head filled with ideas for her apprentices and the shop. Completely involved in her thoughts, it took Elizabeth a moment to notice when a car slowed to a crawl beside to her.

"Oh! Jonah. I'm sorry, my head was in the clouds," Elizabeth felt her cheeks flush.

Jonah smiled up at her.

"I was wondering how long it was going to take you to realize I was here," he joked.

Elizabeth blushed.

"So anyway, Liz. I heard you were looking for a store manager to help out with the shop? I have a cousin back home who would love to work with you. She's actually my cousin Sinéad's daughter; do you remember Sinéad?"

Elizabeth nodded. Sinéad was several years older than Jonah and had already been married when Elizabeth knew her before.

"Yeah, so Morgan was born the year I met you. She's twenty-eight now and an accomplished Earth Mage. Morgan has a strong second Gift in Air, of all things. She loves to bake and cook and could easily run the cafe part of the shop blindfolded. She's actually a bit of a Kitchen Witch. Morgan's been looking for a change recently and maybe the chance to get away from family for a bit. Sinéad's been trying to force her to marry and settle down recently, and I think Morgan's just about had it."

"I was going to have Meg handle the baked goods for the cafe," Elizabeth said.

"Maybe they could work together? I'm sure Morgan would love Meg."

"I guess I can talk to Meg about it. Maybe we can work something out. Is there a way to meet Morgan? Can she come over for an interview? She has to meet the shop, and that has to be done in person."

Jonah looked confused.

"The shop is sentient," Elizabeth told him.

Jonah blinked.

"Ok, then. I can invite Morgan over for the weekend—would that work?"

"That'd be great. Thank you, Jonah."

"Thank you. Morgan's a good kid. I think you'll like her," he paused. "Can I give you a lift the rest of the way home?"

"Sure, thanks," Elizabeth climbed into the cruiser and buckled in. They drove in silence the rest of the way back to the cottage. It was a companionable silence. Neither Elizabeth nor Jonah felt the need to break it until they pulled up into the driveway before the house. Elizabeth turned to Jonah to thank him.

"Liz, I'm really glad you came home. Do you think you might like to go out to dinner with me sometime? I'd like the chance to get to know you better as the person you are now."

Elizabeth blinked. She hadn't dated at all since Jared had died two years ago. She opened her mouth to decline.

"I'd like that," came out instead, surprising both of them.

Elizabeth blinked.

Jonah smiled.

"Great. Say, Friday night? We can stay in town if you want to stay close to your kids. Then maybe next time we can take the portal to somewhere else?"

"Thank you. That sounds great," Elizabeth hesitated. "Jonah, I haven't dated at all since Jared died. I think the only reason I'm agreeing to this is because I know you. Please don't be offended if things don't go well."

"Don't worry about it, Lizzie Grace. I know you, too. We'll be fine." Jonah smiled and backed the car down the drive. He waved as he drove away.

Elizabeth stared after him for a moment.

"It's good to see you getting out, Lizzie Grace," Aunt Gloria said, materializing beside her.

Elizabeth turned to look at her Aunt.

"Am I doing the right thing, Aunt Glo?"

"Of course you are, darling girl. I have often thought that some people come together solely to produce children together, not because they are fated mates or meant to stay together for the rest of their lives. I think that was the case with you and Jared. You couldn't really fully be yourself with him. Eventually, it would have destroyed whatever love you had for him. In a way, the fire did you a favor. Now you will remember him with love. Jonah knows you as you truly are. He's a Witch, too, and you can be your whole self with him. A relationship with Jonah has the potential to truly grow and flourish."

"I don't know if I want a relationship right now, though. I have so much going on. The kids coming into their Gifts, the shop. New apprentices. Getting used to being home. Where am I going to find the energy for a relationship on top of all that?"

"Don't worry about it, Lizzie Grace. Fate always finds a way." Aunt Gloria smiled and disappeared.

15

That evening the phone rang as Mary was setting dinner on the table. Elizabeth answered.

"Sloane residence, how may I help you?"

"Elizabeth, it's Madelynn. I have some information for you. I would prefer to share it with you in person. I think your instincts are spot-on. Something is definitely very, very wrong. Would it be possible to visit, say, tomorrow morning?"

"Of course. Come whenever you like. And Madelynn... thank you. Thank you for believing me and for looking into this."

"Thank you, Elizabeth, for bringing it to my attention. I will see you in the morning. Take care."

"You too. See you tomorrow."

Elizabeth set the handset back on its charger and turned to Mary.

"We will be having a visitor tomorrow, Mary. I don't know how long she will be staying. She's a Brownie, a friend of Aunt Glo's."

"That's wonderful; I'll get a room ready for her. It will be nice to meet another of my kind. My experience is mostly limited to those who live around Fairweather Falls."

"Thank you, Mary. Kids! Dinner!"

❧

Madelynn arrived just after breakfast. She was small, like most Brownies, with long, wavy dark hair and a comforting air about her. Gloria had called Madelynn the heart of their group, and it was easy to see why. She fairly radiated comfort and love.

Madelynn hugged Elizabeth as they met on the front porch.

"It's so nice to finally meet you in person, Lizzy Grace. Gloria was so proud of you for following your heart and making your own way. She was sad that you chose to live in the human world, but she understood. I'm sure she's glad you came home."

"I am, Maddie; you're right about that," Aunt Gloria materialized next to her friend. Madelynn turned with a smile.

"Gloria! I'm so glad that I get this chance to see you again before you go home for good."

"Me too, Maddie. I'm sorry it's under these circumstances, though."

Madelynn frowned and nodded.

"Let's go inside, and you can tell us what you've found, Madelynn," Elizabeth said. "Did you bring any bags? Mary set a room up for you in case you wanted to stay for a while."

"That's very kind, Elizabeth, thank you. Let's see how the day goes. If you don't mind, I would like to set up a conference call with the others, so we can all share what we've found."

"Were you able to get in touch with Loraine and Sharalee, then?"

"I was, and I called Sean as well."

Elizabeth led the way into the sitting room. Madelynn had a backpack over one shoulder. She set it on the ground and took out a laptop. Placing it on the coffee table, she opened a video conferencing program and started a call. Taking out a phone, she sent a brief text. Soon the others were joining the conference. When the last person had joined, Madelynn cleared her throat.

"Hello, everyone. Thank you all for making the time to get together like this. Gloria's niece, Elizabeth, has noticed a disturbing pattern in accidental—and not so accidental—deaths among our little group of friends. Sean and I have spoken to you all, so you know what we've found. Let's report to Elizabeth and Gloria, who is here with us in spirit form before passing on. Sean, will you start?"

Sean nodded.

"Thank you, Madelynn. Elizabeth called me the other day and explained her concerns. I called Lorien, Lukas, and Elise. Lorien is safe in Faerie. He sends his best wishes to everyone. He told me that the last time he was in the human world was for Sarah's funeral fifteen years ago. He told me that at that time, he had felt there was something strange about her death. He felt as if someone was watching him at the funeral and observed a car following him when he left. Nothing else happened, so he wrote it off and has been focused on his life in Faerie since then. He is very disturbed to know that so many of us are now dead or dying. He agrees that there is something wrong and will lend us any help he can from Faerie. If needed, he will return to the human realm to help with our investigation."

Sean paused for a moment.

"I also spoke to Lukas and Elise." The other two Shifters nodded. They were on screen together. Looking at them, it was easy to see the family resemblance.

"Sean asked me to call Mayenne and Sabine," Elise said. "Mayenne is well. Sabine," Elise stopped and took a breath. "Sabine is dead. She was on holiday with her husband in Greece two summers ago and got food poisoning. She always had a delicate immune system, if you remember. Whatever she ate, it killed her."

"Wait, two years ago?" Elizabeth broke in. "Does it seem to anyone else as if these deaths are accelerating? At first, they were far apart. Gloria wasn't even aware that Sarah had died. Why didn't anyone tell her? Now, suddenly, within the last few years, John, Gloria, and Sabine are all dead? Two by poisoning?"

"More than that," Madelynn spoke up. "Loraine tells me that Dora and Michelle were killed in a car accident two years ago. They were taking a trip to Austin to see a friend's band perform. Their car went off the road during a rainstorm on the way home."

Loraine nodded. She had curly reddish-brown hair that fell around her shoulders. Tortoiseshell glasses in a cat-eye shape accentuated her eyes.

"It's true. I didn't go because my daughter's children were sick, so I stayed home to help her. Her husband was killed in the line of duty overseas, and she is raising five kids alone. Well, with me, of course. Dora and Michelle had families, too. Their loss is devastating to our Coven."

Loraine, Dora, and Michelle were High Magic Witches who devoted their time to studying spell craft and ritual. High Magic Witches tended to follow the old ways of staying in Covens. They usually lived in Coven-run towns and didn't mix very much with other supernaturals. They hired out their spellcrafting services for a stiff price.

"So eight out of twenty-two people are dead. That is not a good ratio," Lukas said.

"Has anyone heard from Carl?" Sean asked. Everyone shook their heads.

"I lost touch with him after he left the service," Lukas said.

"Why did he leave? I thought working for the Council was his life," Aunt Gloria asked.

"Carl was injured on a mission. The man he was partnered with went rogue, and the mission went sour. Carl was disillusioned after that. Especially after losing the closeness of our group. He healed, physically, but mentally, Carl had doubts. He took some time off and just never came back," Elise said.

"I think someone needs to see if they can find out where Carl is now," Sean said.

Lukas nodded.

"I've already started looking. I'll let you know as soon as I find him."

"What about the support team? Samantha, Dylan, Roger, and Rosie?" Elizabeth asked.

"Samantha was an old girlfriend, not really a part of the team," Lukas said.

"But she was there a lot, Lukas," Gloria said. "She spent almost all of our downtime with us. She may have seen something, or.... I think we should check on her, too."

"I can tell you that Carl, Samantha, and Rosie are alive," Madelynn said. "I can't tell you where they are. The number I had for Samantha has been disconnected. I found Rosie, though."

Rosie nodded.

"I kept in touch with everyone for a little while. Gloria, I didn't know that you never received my message about Sarah's death. I sent out notifications to everyone in the group. When you didn't respond, I just thought you were still mad at Sarah for her reaction when you left the team. I misjudged you, and I'm sorry for that."

"It's ok, Rosie. I forgave Sarah a long time ago. Her whole life was the Council, was running our team. She had put a lot of work into us. I know she was hoping the team would stay together for longer than it did. I definitely never received a notice of her death, however. How did you send it?"

"I sent it by Sprite and by email. Like usual. Over our secure servers."

Gloria looked perplexed.

"Then it should have reached me. I don't know why it wouldn't have."

"Did you send those notices to everyone, Rosie?" Sean asked.

"Of course."

Now everyone looked confused.

"Are you seriously telling me that no one else got those notices, either?" Elizabeth asked.

"We knew because we were still working for the Council," Elise said. "We told Sean. She wasn't killed in the line of duty, so it would have been her family's responsibility to let everyone know. It never occurred to me to check with everyone else in the group. I mentioned it to Carl-he was still with the Council then. And I think I told Mayenne."

"I told Lorien," Sean said. "But I've been horrible about staying in touch with everyone else since taking over as Alpha of our Pack. And it was so long ago. It never occurred to me that not everyone knew. I didn't know that Rosie had sent out notices."

Rosie looked troubled.

"Guys, I've been sending you all messages for years. Are you telling me that you're not receiving any of them? None at all? I mean, I wondered why I never heard back, but I just thought everyone was busy with their lives and had moved on."

"Rosie, why didn't you mention to me that you had sent out these messages?" Madelynn asked.

Rosie looked confused.

"I don't know. I...."

"Rosie, I think you should check with the Sprites that are supposed to carry your messages. Check if you actually did send them. And if you did, find out if they were delivered to the people they were addressed to," Aunt Gloria said.

Rosie nodded.

"I know that I am more isolated from everyone, living on the West Coast," Sharalee said. "It seems that those dead are mostly on the East Coast and, in Sabine's case, in Europe. Maybe whoever is behind this is based on the East Coast?"

"But they were able to travel to reach Sabine if her death is a part of this," Elise pointed out.

"It's too much of a coincidence if it's not," Sean said.

"I don't believe in coincidences," Madelynn stated.

The group was quiet.

"I think we have a real problem here," Sean said. "It looks like Elizabeth and Gloria are right. Someone is out to get everyone from our team. We need to find Samantha, Dylan, Roger, and Carl and make sure they are ok. Samantha and Carl are alive somewhere, but Maddie never did trust Dylan, so he's not a part of her bond. And Roger was always too squirrelly. He never really gave any of us a chance to bond with him. Still, he was fabulous at what he did. He should be fairly easy to find."

"He's a computer genius. If he doesn't want to be found, he won't be," Lukas said.

"We'll find him," Loraine said. "I'll have the Coven work on locator spells for them. Gloria, how is Mathilda?"

"She's hanging in until her first grandchild is born. Then she will let go. Frankly, I'm amazed that she's made it this long. I know it's only because of her powerful love for her children and her younger daughter needing her so much that she has made it for this long."

"Do you think she would mind a visit? I'm so sorry I didn't know about John. And I would like a chance to talk to you again, Gloria, before you go."

"We'd love to see you, Lori. Come when you can. Mathilda has almost two months. And I plan on staying for as long as I can."

"Thank you, Glo. As soon as I have an answer on those locator spells, I'll come up for a visit."

"Do you think it would be wiser for you all to stay separate? Make it harder for whoever is behind this to get to you?" Elizabeth asked.

"It doesn't seem to have made a difference to them so far," Madelynn said.

"I'm going to come in too," Sharalee said. "I'm suddenly feeling very isolated and alone out here by myself."

"You can stay with me, Sharalee. I'll reinforce the wards on my house and the restaurant," Madelynn said.

"Let's all meet at Gloria's in three days," Sean said. "My Beta can take care of the Pack for a bit. Hopefully, by then, we'll have a better idea of what is going on."

MADELYNN DECIDED TO STAY WITH ELIZABETH AND GLORIA UNTIL the meeting. Sharalee would join them that evening. The following day, Gloria, Madelynn, and Sharalee went to pay a visit to Mathilda.

Elizabeth turned her attention back to the shop. She had decided that each apprentice would spend one day a week in the stillroom with her and two days in the shop. Monday would be Maia in the stillroom, Wednesday Michael and Friday Claire. As she had hired the kids on Wednesday and still needed to talk with their parents, she decided to start their apprenticeships the following Monday. That gave her time to meet Morgan and be a part of the meeting on Saturday with all Aunt Gloria's team members.

Morgan arrived on Friday morning. Jonah brought her to the store just before lunch. The young Witch had long red hair and green eyes that twinkled with merriment. Her hair was pulled back in a braid to keep it out of her eyes. Little curls had escaped from the braid, framing her face.

"Liz, this is my cousin Morgan, Sinéad's daughter. Morgan Louise, this is Elizabeth Sloan. She owns the shop and cafe."

"It's nice to meet you, Ms. Sloan," Morgan said, holding out her hand.

"Thank you for coming, Morgan. It's nice to meet you, too," Elizabeth said. "Please call me Liz. What did Jonah tell you about the store?"

"Well, he didn't tell me what it's called, and I didn't see a sign over the door. Does it have a name? I know it's a bookstore cafe, right?"

"It's never had a name. It's always just been the bookstore. I am adding the cafe and a potions apothecary in the back. Oh, and Morgan? If you are going to be working here, you should know, the store is sentient. She can play tricks sometimes, and if she doesn't like you, she'll make that known."

Morgan grinned.

"That's excellent. Cool. Well, I don't know what Jonah told you about me. I love to cook and bake. I can totally make food for the cafe. I helped to run the bakery back home. I need to get away from my mother before she drives me crazy. Anything I don't know, I am very willing to learn."

"That's good to know. I have someone already contracted for the pastries and baked goods, but I would love to have you talk to her. Maybe the two of you can work something out together? Her name is Meg—she's a Brownie. She has a stall out in the marketplace. I've known her my whole life. Since she already has her own business, maybe the two of you can work out some sort of deal, dividing the baked goods between the two of you. Or maybe you can do some soups and savories while Meg sticks to the sweets. What I really need is someone who can run the shop and help oversee the apprentices while they are here, so I can focus on the potions and apothecary end of the business. And the books. Though, I may ask for your help in ordering and receiving those as well. We'll see. I actually love ordering the books myself."

"I can do that," Morgan said. "I managed the kids who worked the counter at the bakery back home."

"Good. Well, why don't you find a patch of wall and introduce yourself to the shop? If she likes you, we'll give it a go and see how it works out for all of us. Do you have somewhere to stay in town?"

"She can stay with me until she finds a place of her own," Jonah said.

"No offense, cousin, but I think we would kill each other in days, if not hours," Morgan said wryly. She turned to Elizabeth.

"Jonah's one of my more... serious-minded... cousins. I'm a little bit more of a free spirit. With an excellent work ethic, though." She grinned.

"There's an apartment over the shop," Elizabeth grinned back. "I'm using part of it as an office, but if the shop likes you, I'm sure she can set you up in the rest of it. We can make it part of your benefits package. Free room and board. You can eat in the cafe, especially since you will be making most of the food."

"That's amazing! Thank you, Liz!" Morgan hurried to the nearest wall and laid her hand flat against it. A warm tingle ran up Elizabeth's spine. The shop liked Morgan.

"Ok. The shop likes you. Let's give this a go. The kids are starting their apprenticeships on Monday. Can you be ready to start then as well?"

"Yes, I can. I had already given two weeks' notice to the bakery. If this hadn't worked out, I was planning to hit the road and start driving. I would have come here first, then figured out where to go next. I would have gone to every Haven with a bakery to find a job if I had to. This is perfect. I am so glad this worked out!"

"Why don't we go get some lunch?" Jonah asked, standing from the chair he had been sitting in as the ladies talked.

"That's a good idea. Just one more thing. Shop, would you like a name?" Elizabeth asked. That same warm feeling ran up her spine, this time with a touch of excitement.

"Something that reflects the worlds of wonder I found here in your books when I was a child, but also covers the potions and cafe...."

"Garden of Wonders? Earthly Delights?" Morgan suggested.

"Let's brainstorm over lunch," Elizabeth suggested. "Shop, if you have any ideas, I would love to hear them." A slight tremble ran through Elizabeth's feet as if the shop was laughing.

Suddenly, a young woman materialized in front of them. She had long, wavy dark brown hair, tanned skin, and large, almond-shaped brown eyes.

"My name is Samara," she said, smiling. "It's been a long time since anyone has thought to give me a name. Jackson knew who I was, so he never bothered to name the shop. I've been the Spirit of the Shop since it was first formed, many, many long years ago. I'm glad that you are expanding the shop again. I will enjoy having so many wonderful people around. You made wonderful choices, Elizabeth, in your apprentices."

Elizabeth blinked. Then she smiled.

"It's nice to meet you, Samara. I think I may have seen you when I was little. Thank you for introducing yourself to us."

"You did see me. I read you stories when you were tiny. Your mother would leave you in the shop with me while she ran her errands elsewhere. It's good to have you back."

"What about Samara's Garden?" Jonah suggested. "Garden of knowledge, good food and potions?"

Samara beamed at him.

"I like this one, Lizzie Grace. You can keep him," the House Spirit said.

Elizabeth and Morgan grinned while Jonah blushed.

✤ 16 ✤

After getting to know Morgan better over lunch, Elizabeth decided she liked the young woman very much. She suggested they head over to Meg's stall when they finished eating.

Meg smiled and came out of her tent as they approached.

"Elizabeth! And Jonah. How are you on this beautiful day? And who is this lovely young woman?"

"Hi, Meg. This is my cousin, Morgan Louise. She's going to manage the shop for Liz," Jonah said.

"It's very nice to meet you, Morgan. Here, choose a treat." She led the little group over to her tent. Cakes and pastries of all kinds were laid out on the table in front of the tent. Morgan's eyes widened as she took in the spread.

Meg grinned and handed Elizabeth and Jonah each a cupcake. Chocolate with chocolate and a cherry for Jonah, and vanilla with chocolate frosting and sprinkles for Elizabeth.

"There's lots of love baked into every bite," Meg told them with a smile.

"Thank you, Meg. Morgan likes to bake, too. She helped to run a bakery in Dale's End before coming here. I thought that the two of you should meet. Maybe you can work together on choosing the menus for the cafe? I know you were going to provide all the baked goods, but I thought it might be good to have simple fair like quiches, soups, and sandwiches too. Maybe coordinated with whatever the baked goods there are for the day? We could have one featured baked good and create the food for the day to compliment that item? Since you both like to bake, I thought I would leave it all up to you. After all, we all stand to gain from this arrangement."

"That's a wonderful thought, Lizzie Grace! Morgan, when you get settled in, let's talk. Where will you be living? Maybe we can get to know each other better over baking."

"Liz is giving me the apartment over the shop. Samara is going to add whatever I want. I guess we'll need a commercial kitchen—though that would probably be better off the cafe on the first floor. But I would love to have a full kitchen to myself too? Do you think that would be ok, Liz?"

"I think you should ask Samara for whatever you want. In regards to the cafe, ask for whatever you think best. That part belongs to you and Meg."

Meg looked at Elizabeth.

"Who is Samara, Lizzie Grace?"

"It turns out the shop is sentient. There is a House Spirit named Samara inhabiting it. She's been there since it was first formed. She says it was a long time ago. And that she used to babysit me for Mom when I was little."

Meg blinked.

"Well, that explains a lot. I'm happy to know that you will be well taken care of. I wonder why I never realized she was there before."

"I don't think she comes out very often. Though she said she likes the apprentices I've taken on, so maybe she'll make herself known more now? Anyway, she's great. We met her today before lunch."

"I would like to meet her, too," Meg said.

"Why don't you come over when you're done here, and I'll introduce you?" Morgan offered. "We can look at the cafe space and decide what we want for the kitchen. And maybe you can help me with the apartment upstairs?"

"I would like that very much. I should be finished here around three today, I think. Does that work for you?"

"That would be great."

"Elizabeth, do you think I could store some of my goods for the market here in your coolers in the cafe? It would mean that I could bring more and not have to worry about them going off."

"Sure, Meg. You can do whatever you like. You are helping me out by selling your amazing baked goods in the cafe. And I love you. You're family. You could also do some of your baking in the cafe kitchen if you like."

"Thank you, Lizzie Grace. That's very kind of you. I think I will bake at home still, but I do appreciate the use of the coolers."

"Of course."

They said their goodbyes and walked back towards the shop as Meg turned to help another customer. A small family was eagerly looking over the table of deliciousness. The child's eyes were wide as she looked at all of the scrumptious options.

Elizabeth opened the door to the shop and let them in. She walked over to the counter at the back of the bookstore and reached under the cash register. Opening a drawer, Elizabeth took out a set of spare keys. Reaching over the counter, she handed them to Morgan.

"These are the keys to the front and back doors and the back gate. You should be perfectly safe here, especially with Samara here to protect you. Why don't you spend some time getting your apartment set up? Talk with Meg and Samara about the kitchens. I will check in with you tomorrow. I have another meeting tomorrow about something not shop-related, so I'm not sure I'll get into town. But I want to hear what you come up with. Then on Monday, I'll meet you here to open around eight in the morning. How does that sound? I think we should start early on the first day. I'll have the kids come in around nine. During the school year, they'll be on afternoon shifts, but for now, they can work full days." Realizing that Morgan wouldn't have any food in the apartment yet, she said, "Why don't you and Jonah come over for dinner tonight? Mary loves to cook for larger groups. There is usually more than enough food. Mary is the Brownie that has adopted us. She's Meg's niece. You'll like her. She's a lot like Meg. Actually, I think I'll invite Meg, too. Then we can go over everything tonight after dinner. I think that would be better for me. Tomorrow could get complicated."

Jonah raised an eyebrow at her.

"I'll explain later. We might need your help soon, anyway."

"That sounds great, Liz. Morgan, you good with that plan?"

Morgan nodded. She was smiling.

"Thank you both so much for this. I can't believe how well this is working out. I really appreciate all that you are doing for me, Liz. Thank you so much for giving me this chance."

"Of course. I'm glad to have you. I'm going to do a bit of shopping. I'll see you tonight."

Jonah hugged Morgan and said goodbye as well. He followed Elizabeth out of the store.

"Want some company while you shop?"

"Sure. That would be nice."

They walked through the market in silence for a few minutes. Liz picked up some cookies from Meg, some flowers and honey from one small organic farmer, and some seasonal vegetables from another. Then she headed towards The Flower's Daughter.

"So, what is it you might need my help with?" Jonah asked.

Liz sighed.

"I wasn't going to mention anything yet. But it does seem like the right time now. You know that Aunt Gloria was poisoned, and there were no clues to build a case on?"

Jonah nodded.

"Aunt Gloria used to be part of a team of investigators for the Council when she was younger. Of the twenty-two people in her team, including support personnel, eight are dead or missing. The deaths look like accidents or like things that happened in the line of duty. But it's a really high death rate when you look at the deceased as members of the same team. The deaths started around the time the team broke up and were widely spaced out so that they were never connected before this. Then, there have been at least five deaths in the group in the last two years: a car crash, an electrocution, and two poisonings. Two of the group members died in the car crash. Aunt Gloria is worried about the rest of the group members and had me get in touch with them all. We met over video chat yesterday. They are all coming into town tomorrow to meet in person. They all agree that someone is out to get the members of their team."

"Do they have any idea why?"

"Not a clue. And it's possible that the two earlier deaths were just accidents, except that the death notices that the team leader's assistant sent out never reached the other members. It looks like they were never sent at all, even though Rosie swears she did. She's checking with the Fire Sprite service the group used to use."

"I wonder why the deaths are spaced so far apart. That seems strange," Jonah said. "Maybe they thought the chance of getting caught would be lower if they were more spread out? The group really has no idea why they are being targeted?"

Elizabeth shook her head.

"None. They haven't even worked together in over thirty years. One runs a restaurant, one an apothecary; three were High Magic Witches, one's a clan Alpha. Three members of the group still worked for the Council, though one of those has gone off the grid. Madelynn, the Brownie with the restaurant, says he's still alive, but she doesn't know where. Apparently, the team was really close, and she adopted them all as her family. She can feel if they are alive or dead and the general direction of where they are. If she concentrates, she can tell if they are ok or if there is something wrong. She's working on finding the two missing people she still has a connection to. There are another two that she never liked, so she didn't include them in the bond. Lukas and Elise, who are enforcers for the Council, are looking into finding those two."

"Why do you need my help? I mean, of course, I am happy to help. But if this was a Council team, then surely the Council has jurisdiction."

"I think it would be a good idea to have the mundane police involved as well, just in case. And you are the police representative here. I mean, I know you're a Witch, and our peacekeepers here are really a liaison team with the mundane police. But that gives you insight into both sides, paranormal and mundane. You've had their training as well and have access to their ways of doing things. We may need those as we learn more."

"Like I said, I am happy to help." Jonah looked at The Flower's Daughter.

"Did you want to go in here?"

"Yes—mom's birthday is next week. I wanted to talk to Clara about a present." Liz slapped her forehead. "I completely forgot to tell Morgan to go see Calvin for her uniform. I'll have to remember to tell her tonight."

"Why don't you go see Clara, and I'll go take Morgan over to Vix. I'll see you at your house later for dinner?"

Elizabeth thanked him, then turned to enter the clothing store.

THE BELL OVER THE DOOR CHIMED AS ELIZABETH ENTERED THE Flower's Daughter. Clara came through an entryway in the back wall, smiling.

"Elizabeth! How lovely to see you. How is Mags working out as Maddie's teacher?"

"Mags is fabulous. Maddie adores her. I truly appreciate all that she is doing for my daughter."

Clara smiled even more widely.

"My brother is happy to have Mags out of his hair and engaged in something useful. A bored Mags is a mischievous Mags. She causes no end of trouble when she's bored. So I appreciate you taking her on."

"Well, it works out well for all of us then. My mother's birthday is next week, Clara. I was hoping you might help me find her the perfect gift."

Clara took charge at once. Nora, like most of Elizabeth's family, was an Earth Witch. Her talents lay in green growing things, with a second Gift in animal communication. She volunteered at the Familiar Sanctuary regularly when she wasn't tending her gardens. She sold her herbs to local restaurants and herbalists. They were of excellent quality and fetched a high price. Elizabeth used some of them in her potions work as well. She needed to get her own gardens in order so she could grow all she needed herself. That was another task for the apprentices to help with. Their help would ensure that it happened much more quickly than if Elizabeth were trying to find the time to do it all on her own.

They looked at clothing, shoes, bags, and hats. Clara laid aside several items that Elizabeth thought might be possibilities. Nothing was jumping out and screaming 'buy me!' at her yet, though.

They made their way over to the jewelry case by the cash register. Fae metalwork was exquisite. Right away, Elizabeth saw an absolutely gorgeous rainbow moonstone and labradorite necklace that would be perfect. It had delicate drop earrings that matched, with the beautiful blue stone on the bottom with the white on top.

"Clara, that's it. That necklace set is perfect."

Clara smiled and took it out of the case.

"This is a beautiful set. My niece Róisín made them. She is young yet. This is the first time I have sold her work in the shop."

"Well, she certainly has talent. My mother will love this."

"I will tell my niece that you said so. She will be happy to hear it." Clara placed the jewelry in a green velvet box and tied it with a matching ribbon. She handed the gift to Elizabeth. Elizabeth paid her and started to say goodbye. She caught herself and turned back.

"Clara, do you know an Aes Sidhe named Lorien? I'm not sure where in Faerie he lives."

"I do know Lorien. He is my cousin on my mother's side. How do you know of him?"

"He was friends with Aunt Gloria. They worked together on a team for the Council."

Clara nodded.

"I remember that, now. He never speaks about his time then. I had the impression that the things they did were secret."

"They were an investigative team. Clara, someone is killing off members of that team. There have been five deaths in the last two years. Lorien knows, we told him, but just in case, maybe you can check in on him? The team is meeting at my house tomorrow. I don't know if Lorien is coming—I think they told him to stay in Faerie where he is safer."

"I will check in with him. If you don't mind, I would like to come to this meeting. Lorien is family. If he chooses to stay in Faerie, I can report back to him. I think he will come, though. Lorien is not one to stand by when there is something to be done."

"We'd love to have you. Maybe you'll be able to see a pattern we've missed. At the moment, no one has any clue who is doing this or why."

17

Elizabeth left The Flower's Daughter, delighted with both her purchase and the conversation. Saturday morning, members of the former Council team started arriving just after nine. Mary was still cleaning up the kitchen from breakfast. She paused and set out tea and snacks in the sitting room.

Mags had taken Maddie out to play in the forest. Magnus had Joshua working in the studio he had created for them out behind the house. Half was dedicated to stone carving, and half to blacksmithing. It seemed that Joshua had a talent for both. Joshua's body had begun to fill out from all the physical labor Magnus had him doing. Elizabeth found herself smirking when she thought about Joshua's impact on the girls in school in the fall.

Lukas and Elise arrived first. Mary had added rooms to the house for everyone. She took them upstairs and got them settled. The doorbell ran again as they were vanishing up the stairs. Elizabeth opened the door to find a tall man with striking brown eyes and broad shoulders standing on the doorstep. He had a commanding air about him, a force of power that radiated out from him like an energy field.

"Elizabeth? I am Sean Flynn. Have Elise and Lukas arrived yet?"

"Please, come in. They just arrived. Mary took them upstairs to get settled. They'll be down again in a minute."

Elizabeth led Sean into the sitting room. Aunt Gloria was standing in the center of the room.

"Gloria! I am so sorry I can't hug you. I apologize for not staying in touch more often."

"It's good to see you, Sean. I apologize too. None of us were that great about staying in touch with everyone. Life has a way of getting away from you, sometimes. I am happy that you're here now, though, and I get to see you again before I move on."

Elise and Lukas came down the stairs. Elise hugged her cousin. Then Sean and Lukas clasped arms and did the bro hug thing. The three Shifters sat down.

Madelynn and Sharalee had been out in the gardens. They came in through the kitchen and found the others in the sitting room. The Shifters stood up again, giving hugs all around.

The doorbell rang again. This time when Elizabeth opened the door, she found two Aes Sídhe standing in front of her. Clara introduced her cousin Lorien.

"Lor! We told you to stay in Faerie!" Sean exclaimed as they entered the room.

"Like I could stay away when the rest of you were in danger," the tall, white-haired Fae said. More hugs were passed around. Lorien introduced Clara to the other team members.

The doorbell rang again. Jonah stood on the doorstep, holding a large bag of Meg's baking. He kissed Elizabeth's cheek as he passed her into the house. Behind Jonah came Caz, supporting his mother, Mathilda. Elise hurried over and hugged the other Shifter gently.

"Tilly, we were so sorry to hear about John. He was a good man and a strong Shifter. Sit here with me." She led Mathilda over to the couch and sank down beside her. Mathilda rested her head on Elise's shoulder and began to cry.

Caz looked uncomfortable. Sean moved to stand before him.

"I am Sean Flynn, Alpha of the Dancing Moon Wolf Clan."

"Casey Monroe. Everyone calls me Caz. I'm Mathilda and John's son." Caz bowed his head before the stronger Shifter.

Sean put his hand on Caz's shoulder.

"I'm very sorry for your loss, son. If you ever need anything, let me know. John was a good friend and the best team member. We will sing his name to the moon. As we will Tilly's when the time comes."

Caz teared up.

"Thank you, Sir. If I could ask, Sir, I have two sisters. One is married and expecting her first child. The other is much younger. I'm worried about raising her on my own. She's only fifteen. We have friends, but we've never lived in a Pack. My parents came here to be near Gloria. Would it be possible for my sister to visit your Pack? I know we're a different bloodline, as Free Shifters, but I think it might really help her."

"Of course, son. Why don't you all come? Whenever you're ready. Our hearts and homes are open to you."

"Thank you, Sir."

Mathilda had been watching through her tears from the couch.

"Thank you, Sean."

"Of course, Tilly. Anything for you. You know that."

Mathilda smiled back tremulously. Elise continued to stroke her hair.

The doorbell rang again. This time there was a woman in full robes on the other side. Her robes were a deep burgundy color. Around her neck, she wore an elaborate pendant set with a large, blood-red ruby. She had pulled her long brown hair into a tight braid down her back.

"Elizabeth. I am Loraine LaRue. Goddess' Blessing on your house."

"Thank you, Loraine. Goddess' Blessing to you. Please come in."

Loraine entered the house and headed straight for Mathilda and Elise. Then she stood and hugged Madelynn and Sharalee before turning to everyone else.

"I'm sorry I have been out of touch for so long. It's good to see you all."

The doorbell rang again. A woman with wildly curly brown hair pulled up into a twist stood on the other side. She wore long, light blue robes and a silver moonstone pendant.

"Elizabeth, I am Mayenne. A blessing on your house."

"A blessing to you, too. Please come in."

As Elizabeth was closing the door, another woman appeared in front of her. This one was smaller and slightly rounder than the elegant Illusionist.

"Hello, Elizabeth. I'm Rosie Boyd. Thank you for having me. Are the others here yet?"

"Yes, everyone is inside. I think you're the last, for now. Please, come in."

Rosie entered the sitting room, which was now filled to bursting, and said her hellos.

Mary expanded the room and added more comfy chairs.

Soon everyone was seated. Sean took charge.

"I am glad to see everyone here. I wish it were under better circumstances. Before we get started, let's take a moment of silence to remember those we have lost."

Everyone bowed their heads. After a moment, Sean stood up.

"ROSIE, WOULD YOU START US OFF, PLEASE? WHAT DID YOU FIND OUT about the messages you sent us?"

Rosie stood, looking troubled.

"I don't know what's happening. The Sprites say I never gave them messages to send. But I remember doing it! So very clearly. I remember sending official death notices, too. But there are no logs of those notices, either. The only thing I can think of is that someone must have altered my memories or bewitched me, but I don't know how that could be possible. No one knew who I was. I was support staff. Most people thought I was an administrative assistant at a law office in the mortal world. Only someone who knew about our team, someone at the Council, could have gotten close enough to me to do this. And they never would. I don't understand."

Everyone frowned.

"Rosie, forgive me for asking, but you seem mortal to me. What are you, exactly? How did you come to be working for the Council?" Elizabeth asked.

Rosie smiled.

"Sarah recruited me. I'm half-dryad, so my only real Gift is a connection to nature and turning into a tree. My father was human. I was working as a hairstylist, straight out of beauty school. Sarah was one of my clients. She told me I impressed her with what an organized mind I had and asked me what my dreams were. I told her I didn't really know. I enjoyed doing hair and working at a job that allowed me to talk to people all day and help them to be happy. But I wanted to travel and wasn't sure I wanted to be a stylist forever. Sarah visited once every three months or so for about a year. Sometimes she came in more than that if she wanted something different, like a special occasion do. After a year, Sarah offered me the position as her assistant, working for the Council. She told me I would get to travel with her and be a part of a team that was actively helping others, making a real difference. She said she was building a team that she hoped would become more like a family and would be together for life. My parents had passed away early, and I was pretty much on my own. The thought of being a part of a team like that was irresistible to me. I said yes right away."

"And what was Sarah?"

Everyone looked at each other.

"Do you know, I never saw her use magic?" Elise said slowly.

"I could feel her power, and there was a lot of it, but I never saw her use it, either," Madelynn said.

"She was not Aes Sídhe," Lorien said slowly. "But she did have ties to Faery. I could feel it on her."

Everyone looked at Rosie.

"I only saw her use magic once," Rosie said. "And it wasn't really magic. Nothing flashy, I mean. Once, before the team was fully formed, we were going on a recruiting trip. We were looking for High Magic Witches. It wasn't you, Loraine. There was another Witch she was interested in as well. She didn't expect you to demand your sisters come with you. She thought she would have to find three separate Witches willing to work together. Anyway, when we got close to the house of the Witch she was after, she suddenly froze. Her face turned hard, and it looked like she was fighting something. For a moment, her face looked like it was made of bone. She was driving, and her fists gripped the wheel so tightly I thought she would leave marks. A wind started to rise in the car. Then, she swore, and everything went back to normal. She turned the car around and drove away. I asked her why we weren't going after the Witch, and Sarah said the Witch was dead. I asked her how she knew, and she said she just did."

"Could Sarah have been a Bean Sídhe?" Elizabeth asked.

"Or a Reaper?" Mathilda asked in a low voice.

"If Sarah were a Bean Sídhe, she would have started wailing. She wouldn't have been able to control it like that. She would have had to be impossibly strong."

"She was strong. I could feel it," Lorien said.

"But what was a Bean Sídhe doing working for the Council as a Team Leader?" Sean asked. "I thought most of them went back home to the Fae Realm?"

"They did," Lorien answered. "Still, there are always some in a race that choose to make their own way. It is possible. I would say that it's much more likely than if she were a Reaper. Reapers usually do tend to be the solitary creatures they are said to be. And while Sarah usually had Rosie do most of the work, I saw Sarah in enough social situations that I would think it unlikely she was a Reaper. "

"But, if she was a Bean Sídhe, she couldn't have been killed in a boating accident. The only way they can die is to pass on their powers to their daughters. And Sarah had no children," Gloria said.

"Then what happened to Sarah? Where is she?" Sharalee asked. "Why hasn't she been in touch with any of us? Why would she let us think she was dead?"

"Maybe she was trying to protect us? Maybe she knew something was wrong?" Madelynn said.

"I don't think she would have stayed away from us for so long. And when the deaths started adding up, I don't think she would have left us alone. She would have come to help. Sarah saw patterns better than most of us. It's one reason she was so good at her job and how she knew which ones of us to recruit to her team. She would have tried to keep us safe."

"Has anyone spoken to Sarah's family since her death? Lukas asked.

Everyone shook their heads.

"I think we need to get in touch with Sarah's family," Sean said.

"Rosie, do you have their contact information?"

Rosie shook her head again.

"Sarah handled all contact with her family herself. I saw a picture of her with a man that I assumed was her husband. But that was the only photo I ever saw. They never called her through the Council offices."

Sean looked at Lukas and Elise.

"We'll look into it. I wish we had Roger's skills on this. He could find anyone," Elise said.

Sean looked at Loraine.

"Lori, were you able to find Dylan, Roger, or Samantha?"

Loraine nodded.

"Dylan, the little creep, is dead. He got into trouble with a crime network in Chicago, a Fae-led one. They killed him for owing money and not following orders."

Sean frowned.

"Dylan was a creep, but he would never have gotten into bed with people like that. He was too self-righteous. Dylan wanted to work his way up to being the Techno-Mage on a team of his own. How could he have gotten involved with organized crime? Are you sure of that story, Loraine?"

Loraine frowned.

"We traced him to Chicago. I had some sisters from a Coven there look into it for me. That's the information they were able to get on him."

"What was he doing in Chicago?" Elizabeth asked.

"I don't know."

Lukas sighed. "We'll look into that, too." Elise patted his shoulder.

"Has anyone considered that Sarah could be behind this for some reason?" Elizabeth asked. "Or Dylan? Or any of the ones that we haven't found yet?"

Everyone else shook their heads.

"No way," Sean said. "There really is no way. Part of our orientation into the team was to swear a blood oath to protect each other and all members of the team. Geases were placed on us so we couldn't be turned. They were very, very strong."

"Did anyone actually see Sarah take these oaths?"

Everyone nodded.

"We all took them together," Loraine said. "It was a powerful ceremony. The High Priestess of the Council presided over it. It was ironclad."

"Did the support team participate, too?"

Everyone nodded.

"And there is no way these bonds could have been broken?"

"There is always a way. But it would not have been easy. It probably would have been dangerous to the person the oath and geases were being removed from," Loraine replied.

"So it's more likely that it was someone on the outside of the team, but close enough to know who the members were. A romantic partner, family member, or someone else in the Council?"

"Loraine, were you able to find Samantha?" Sean asked.

Loraine smiled.

"I was. Samantha is living in Savannah, teaching at an art college there. She's thriving. She's married and has three children. Her husband is an Earth Witch, and their children are all strong in their own Gifts. Two of them are Fire Witches , and the middle one is an Earth Witch. They are adorable. I video conferenced with Sam before I came up here. She sends her love to everyone. She had no idea what was happening and asked me to let her know if there was anything she could do to help."

"Are you sure she wasn't playing you?" Elise asked.

Loraine nodded.

"As sure as I can be without truth spelling her. I would have to be there with her to do that."

"I suggest that someone needs to go pay Samantha a visit," Sean said. "Loraine, would you be willing to do that since you already have re-established contact with her?"

Loraine nodded.

"Thank you. What about Roger? Were you able to find him?"

Loraine shook her head.

"I got a general reading on him, but nothing more than that. He's alive, somewhere in the Northern Midwest states, I think, but that's as close as I got."

"Ok. Thank you. We'll have to find a way to draw him out. I don't think Roger would ever betray us, but having his skills right now would be immensely helpful. I would still like to find him. Does anyone know any other Techno-Mages whose focus is information through the internet?"

Everyone shook their heads.

"I know there are others working for the Council," Lukas said. "I haven't worked directly with them. I guess I can ask if one of them would help us find Roger."

"How is what Roger did different from what George and Dylan could do?" Elizabeth asked.

"George and Dylan worked directly with devices and electronics, enhancing them with magic, turning them into something more than what they had been designed for," Madelynn said. "Roger's Gift was different. He could literally find anything that was ever on the web, anything with an electronic data signature, anywhere. It made it really hard for him to be around other people. I always thought that Roger might be a little on the spectrum, too. He had really a hard time in social situations and preferred to do as much of his work as he could from home whenever possible."

"So, could we put a message out on the internet that we are looking for Roger? Would he see it?"

"Only if he were consciously looking for information about whichever of us sent it. Or monitoring anything with his own name in it."

"Which he very much might do," Sharalee said. "I remember him as being slightly paranoid about things."

"It's worth a try," Elizabeth said. She reached for her tablet.

"What would be the best way to do this?"

"Send me an email to my Pack email telling me that Gloria is asking about Roger and hoping he is safe. Use the phrase, 'she heard about the forest fire that took out the family hunting cabins, and that eight of them were totally destroyed.' That will let him know that eight of the team are down, and we're concerned for his well-being. If he's listening, he'll find us."

"Unless he's too paranoid to come forward, and this just makes him hide even more," Sharalee said.

18

Elizabeth sent the email to Sean's Pack email.

Sean looked at Lukas.

"Were you able to find Carl?"

Lukas nodded. He frowned.

"Carl really isn't doing well. He's drinking and living by himself in a run-down house on the coast of Connecticut. Whatever his partner did before he went dark really did a number on Carl. He doesn't have faith in anything anymore. He was sad to hear of the deaths in the team but felt that there was nothing he could do to help. He doesn't even use his magic anymore. He's a wreck."

Madelynn frowned.

"I'll sort him out. I'll pay him a visit as soon as we're done here."

Sean nodded.

"So, what we've learned here, really, is that the support staff are all alive, but there are eight dead members of the actual field investigation team. One of those members might not actually be dead but is definitely missing. It is highly improbable that anyone actually on the team is behind any of this because of the oaths taken and the geases placed on all of you. Is that about it?" Elizabeth summarized.

Everyone nodded.

"What about Alice? The Air Witch who died before the team broke up? You said she died from cancer, not from anything related to the team, right, Aunt Glo?" Elizabeth looked at Aunt Gloria.

Aunt Gloria nodded.

"If it's possible that family members could be involved in some way, that opens up whole new avenues of investigation. You said that Alice had a husband and children. Would any of them be likely to do something like this if they blamed the team for Alice's death?"

Sean shook his head.

"Alice really did die of cancer. She was a wonderful woman and a fabulous Air Mage. She could fly if she wanted to. Even carry one person with her if she needed to. She was like the big sister, or the mother, of our team. We were all devastated when she passed. We never did find another Air Mage to replace her."

"Did anyone else have any significant others or family members that might hold a grudge for any reason?"

Everyone shook their heads.

"Well, someone does. We'll just have to figure out who. And no one can think of anyone else who worked for the Council who might have a grudge against your team for any reason?"

More head shaking.

Elizabeth sighed.

After the meeting, Madelynn and Sharalee portaled down to Connecticut to see Carl. They would return to Fairweather Falls after they spoke with him. Loraine called Samantha and arranged a visit, then left to return to the South. Lukas and Elise returned to the Council. Sean turned to Mathilda before he returned to his Pack. He sank to his knees before her, where she was seated on the couch.

"Tilly, I meant what I said earlier. You and your children are welcome in our Pack at any time. To visit, or to stay, if you like. I will happily take on your children as Pack members if you wish it. Or if they ever wish it in the future."

Mathilda smiled up at him.

"Thank you, Sean. That means a lot to me. I am so glad that I got a chance to see you again before I left." She reached out and laid her hand on his cheek.

Sean leaned forward and kissed her forehead, then stood.

"Thank you for hosting this meeting, Elizabeth. I will stay in touch. Please let me know if you and Gloria figure out anything else." He turned to Aunt Gloria.

"Glo, I am very glad I had this chance to see you again. I am sorry it's taken so long. And that it was under these circumstances."

Gloria blew the Alpha a kiss.

Sean smiled and waved as he left the house.

"I will stay in Fairweather Falls for a while, I think," Lorien said. "I will visit with my cousin. I would prefer to be on hand in the event that anything is discovered." He bowed to Elizabeth and Gloria. Clara smiled at them and followed him out.

Caz stood and helped his mother up.

"Thank you, Gloria and Elizabeth. I am grateful to have this chance to see everyone again before I go. I need to go home and rest now. I'll see you both soon," Mathilda said as her son led her to the door.

Mayenne stood as well.

"I will return to France. Please, keep me informed of any new developments. If I think of anything, I will be in touch. Thank you for inviting me." And Mayenne, too, left.

Rosie remained on the couch. Her hands were clenched in her lap.

"Rosie? What will you do, now?" Aunt Gloria asked.

"I don't know, Gloria. I don't know anything anymore. What other things that I think I remember aren't real? How much of my life is a lie?" Tears were rolling down the woman's face.

Elizabeth looked at Gloria, then back at the distraught woman before her.

"Rosie, would you like to stay here with us for a while? Let's see if we can figure this out. You're welcome to stay for as long as you like."

Rosie nodded.

"Thank you. I appreciate it. I don't know what to think anymore."

Mary came in from the kitchen and led Rosie upstairs to get her settled.

Aunt Gloria turned to Elizabeth.

"Lizzie Grace, I think we need a strong Mind Healer to look at Rosie. She's right. There could be a lot more wrong than she knows. If someone has been messing with her memories and her mind for so long, there could be permanent damage. I want to make sure she'll be ok. And if there are any other altered memories, I think we need to know what they are."

Elizabeth nodded.

"Do you know any good Mind Healers, Aunt Glo?"

Gloria shook her head.

"I've never needed one. I know there are some that work for the Council. Let's ask Elise to find us one."

Elizabeth sent a quick email to Elise. As she finished, her inbox pinged with an incoming message.

The fire was devastating. A memorial garden is being planted. Interesting things are being unearthed. I'll visit soon.

R-

"Aunt Glo!" Elizabeth exclaimed. Gloria poofed back in.

"Roger replied. He's coming to see us."

Elizabeth's stomach rumbled. Not knowing when Roger would arrive, she decided to have lunch, then spend some time in the stillroom. There was a potion she had meant to try for lucid dreaming, and she wanted to research potions to bring back lost memories, just in case they couldn't find a Mind Healer to help Rosie.

Elizabeth was deep into her potions books when Maddie came bursting through the stillroom door.

"Mom! Look what I learned!" Maddie had a small potted plant in her hand. As Elizabeth watched, the plant grew, putting out leaves and flowers until it was too big for its pot. Elizabeth caught it as Maddie dropped it, the plant growing too big for her to hold.

"That's amazing, Maddie! Let's get this planted. It's a very pretty rose bush. Where do you think it would like to be?"

Mags was grinning from outside the door. The three planted the rose bush along the side of the house.

"Maybe you can have your own garden here, Maddie," Elizabeth suggested.

"That would be cool! Thanks, Mom!" Maddie ran off to choose some seeds from the garden shed.

"Mags, Clara's cousin Lorien is here for a visit," Elizabeth told the young woman.

Mags grinned.

"I like Lorien. He's fun when he wants to be. He has some amazing stories from when he was in the human realm. He hasn't left home in a long time, though. Why's he here?"

Elizabeth gave Mags the cliff notes version.

"Huh. Well, I'm glad he's here. We'll have some fun. He can help with Maddie's training, too. He can help her with Oreo and flying. He's strongest in Air, and he's great with familiars and Fae creatures. I guess he's staying with Clara?"

Elizabeth nodded. "Yes, that's what he said."

"Cool. Maddie and I will head over there next."

ELIZABETH SPENT SOME TIME WITH MADDIE, HELPING TO GET HER garden in. Then she went back to the stillroom. She was deep in thought over her books, notes and ingredients all around her, when a nervous cough at the door startled her.

Elizabeth jumped and looked up. A thin, dark-haired man was standing at the door to the stillroom. He had tortoiseshell glasses over blue eyes and was dressed like a hipster in skinny jeans and a black turtleneck sweater that surely was much too hot for the current weather.

"Can I help you?" Elizabeth asked.

"I think maybe I can help you," the man said. "I intercepted your email to Sean—that was his idea, I assume? He knew I'd be watching for anything with my name in it."

"Roger?"

"Yes, Roger Falcone. And you're Elizabeth Sloan, Gloria's niece. I researched you before I came here. I looked into everyone. You're right; there's been too much death. Have you figured out who's behind it yet?"

Roger stared at Elizabeth, then looked away. He seemed to have a hard time making eye contact for very long. His hands were twisting his sweater unconsciously.

"No. We were hoping that you would be able to help us. Because of the blood vows and geases, we are almost sure whoever it is can't be a member of the team or the support team. But someone has been messing with Rosie's mind for years, and it almost has to be someone who works for the Council. We hoped that you could use your skills to look into everyone who might have had an issue with your team and also the circumstances surrounding all the deaths the team has experienced—starting with Alice. Everyone else thinks her death was truly cancer, but I think it needs to be counted as the first suspicious death in the team. Though, now that I'm thinking about it," Elizabeth cocked her head to one side, "Rosie said there was a Witch Sarah wanted to recruit to the team who died as Sarah was going to talk to her, as the team was just beginning to form. Maybe we should start there. That death is associated with Sarah, and therefore the team." She shook her head.

"And that's the other thing. No one knows what Sarah was, but based on Rosie's memories, we've come to the conclusion that she was probably a Bean Sídhe. Which means her death was faked. Either Sarah is in hiding, or someone is holding her captive and has been for fifteen years. The others are fairly certain she is being held. They feel she would have reached out when the other deaths happened. But no one has heard from her in fifteen years."

Roger blinked.

"I can look into that for you. I've started already, actually. I've found a few things. I started with Carl because I wanted to know what was so bad he would leave the Council. And John. Can I tell you what I've found?"

"Please. Let's go inside. Mary, the Brownie that lives with us, will make us some tea, if that's ok with you. It will be quiet. I have children, but they are out with their teachers and will be gone until dinnertime."

Roger looked nervous but allowed Elizabeth to lead him into the house.

She got him settled as Mary placed a plate of cookies on the table in front of the new guest. Then she put the kettle on for tea.

"Now, what did you find?"

19

Roger pulled a tablet out of the bag that was slung across his body. He set it up on the table. Its case folded into a supportive triangle, allowing the tablet to stand upright at an angle so that everyone could see it.

"I started with Carl, as I said. Carl was an excellent Fire Mage. He was absolutely great at controlling his element. After the team disbanded, Carl chose to stay on with the Council. He was assigned a partner, an Earth Mage named Patrick Coonerty. Things went along fairly smoothly for a couple of years. They were close, as partners, but not like family, as our team had been." Roger paused and took off his glasses, polishing them on the tail of his shirt.

"About two years after Carl started working with Patrick, Carl started filing reports that he thought there was a mole or a double agent within the Council. Captures that they were sent on went south, or the individual they were after had vanished before they got there. Even when they went in suddenly, with no warning. Carl suspected it was someone in his division and reported to the supervisor directly over him. The reports were never passed up the chain. They were actually destroyed, but since he sent them electronically, I found them. Maybe he knew I would if I were ever to go looking."

"Anyway, Carl grew increasingly more suspicious. He filed a report about a year later with the head of the division directly. About three weeks later, Carl's partner turned on him during a raid. Carl was injured, and his partner disappeared. While Carl was on medical leave, his sister and her family received written threats that vanished after reading. Carl reported those to the Council, too. This time, to someone even higher up the food chain. An investigation was started, and several people were stripped of their status and incarcerated. Carl's entire division underwent a complete overhaul. It turned out that the head of the division had been dirty for years. They offered Carl the position of department head after that, but he declined. He left the Council and retired to Connecticut, where he's been at the bottom of a bottle ever since."

"Could this person, the former head of Carl's division, have anything to do with what's happening now?"

Roger shook his head.

"Doubtful. His division didn't really have too much crossover with our team. I'll keep looking, though." Roger took a sip of tea.

"So, Sarah. I looked into the files she had on all the people she was recruiting to the team. I found that Witch that died. It was reported as a High Magic ritual gone bad. An explosion killed her. The team that investigated said there was nothing left of her house."

"And you're sure Sarah's Witch died in that explosion?"

"Someone did. There's no reason to suspect it wasn't her. No one has seen or heard from her since. Her coven was devastated and held full services for her. Her family stayed with the coven. Her daughter is a participating member now. She's in her late fifties. I am looking into her as well."

Roger ate a cookie. Elizabeth had to sit on her hands to remind herself to be patient as he ate. The Techno-Mage took another sip of tea and went on.

"You were right about Sarah. She was working for the Council for years before she formed our little team. Years. Like, since the founding of the Council. The current version, set up five hundred years ago. Before that, there are no records of her. Of course, there are very few records from back then that have been digitized, so I may have missed some. Sarah's files were encrypted and highly classified. It took a little bit of work to get into them. It was an acceptable way to spend an afternoon. So thank you for that."

Roger took another sip of tea. He appeared to be getting more nervous. He was drinking more, and his hands were in constant motion. Elizabeth suspected that there was more than just being an introvert going on here. She wondered if Roger had ADHD or was on the spectrum, as Madelynn and Rosie had suspected.

"So, Sarah was a Bean Sídhe, like you thought. Or, half, anyway. The other half was never determined. Sarah came into her powers fairly young. She began working for the Council when she was around one hundred and fifty years old. Sarah never married, so the person who passed himself off as her husband was lying. It looks like he was Sarah's partner for a while, a low-level Witch with an Earth Gift in Stone. He worked for a contractor as a stonemason. He vanished not long after Sarah was reported dead. I've found no electronic trace of him since then. It's like he ceased to exist. Which either means he's dead, or he went through the Veil to another realm."

"Could he have been fake, to begin with? What if he just went on to become someone else?"

"I would have found him through facial recognition, anyway. If he was here on Earth, there is no way he could have hidden from me."

Elizabeth thought for a moment.

"Do you think Sarah was taken to another realm?"

Roger shrugged.

"It's possible. She's not here. And she would have been almost impossible to kill. So, unless they found a way to do that, the chances that she was taken to another realm are high."

"I wonder if it has anything to do with the deaths in the team at all, then."

"It would be an enormous coincidence if it didn't, and I don't believe in those," Roger said.

"Good point."

They were quiet for a moment. Mary started to make dinner preparations. Roger stood abruptly.

"I should be going. I'll keep looking into everyone. I'll let you know when I've got anything else."

"You're welcome to stay. Madelynn, Sharalee, Mathilda and Lorien are in town. They would like to see you. They were truly worried about you. And if Sarah was truly taken to another realm, Lorien would be the one to track her."

Roger paused, then shook his head.

"I don't want to intrude. I should go."

"We have plenty of space. Our house is sentient. Her name is Eleanor. She would happily provide you a room to whatever specifications you like. Even make it dark and soundproof if that would help you."

Roger glanced at Elizabeth.

"I never told anyone about my diagnosis. Didn't want it to color their perceptions of me. I know they thought I was odd, but that's ok. I… need a lot of space and time to myself. I get overwhelmed too easily to be around people for too long."

"I understand. If you stay, you can work from here. Eleanor will make the perfect room for you. I would feel a lot safer if I knew where you were."

Roger smiled.

"No one's found me at my house for years. I think I am probably safer there."

"They weren't really looking. This way, you have all of us to protect you. And you could be a part of the team again, as much or as little as you like. I promise the kids won't bother you. Josh is almost sixteen. He's an Earth Mage and has only recently had his Gifts unlocked. He spends all of his time with his mentor, Magnus. They have their own studio and smithy out back. Maddie is eight. She's an Elemental Mage. She and her mentor, Mags, are usually out roaming the land. Mags is Lorien's cousin. Another cousin, Clara, lives here in town, too. Lorien is staying with her."

"It's been a long time since I've been around other people on a regular basis," Roger hesitated.

"You might like it. And you can stay in your room whenever you need to. No one will bother you. Please, just consider it?"

Aunt Gloria popped into view.

"We would love to have you, Roger. I'm sorry that we didn't make it more obvious what an immensely important part of the team you were before. None of us quite understood you, and I apologize for not making more of an effort to try."

Roger had startled when Gloria appeared. He stared at her for a moment. She smiled at him.

Roger nodded.

"Thank you, Gloria. I'm sorry I wasn't more upfront about the way my brain works and what I needed back then." He took a deep breath. "I'll stay for a little while. Thank you, both. It would be nice to see everyone again. In small doses." He smiled briefly.

"Good," Aunt Gloria said.

Mary used her magic to double what she was making for dinner. In her not-so-humble expert opinion, the man needed a few good meals in him.

Elizabeth introduced Roger to everyone at dinner. The Techno-Mage made it through dinner, then took dessert with him to the room that Eleanor had prepared for him. After he left, Elizabeth made sure that Maddie understood that Roger needed a lot of time to himself and that she wasn't to disturb him when he was in his room.

The next morning, Elizabeth and the children went over to Nora and Elliot's for brunch. It thrilled the older couple to have all of their grandchildren living in the same place at last. Lucy's children were twelve, ten, and eight. Marc, the oldest, looked up to Josh and badgered him with questions about his training with Magnus. Marc was an Earth Witch like his mother. Louisa was the middle child at ten. Maddie was thrilled to have a girl cousin, and the two of them became fast friends despite the age difference. Louisa was an Air Mage like her father, Thomas. Timothy, the youngest at eight, was a Water Mage like his paternal grandmother. He was the first Water Mage in Elizabeth's family for several generations. Tim was an easygoing child — until something really got him angry. He had a sturdy sense of justice. He tended to lash out with his Gifts when he was upset. Lucy and Thomas were working very hard to help Timothy use his Gifts responsibly.

After brunch, the children went outside while the adults sat on the porch and talked.

"How is everything going with the shop?" Nora asked Elizabeth.

"It's going extremely well," Elizabeth smiled. "The apprentices and Morgan start tomorrow. I think they're all going to work very well together. One of the apprentices is quite the artist. I am going to have her work with Robin on the branding for the shop. Maybe Sandra can work with them as well. I'm thinking about asking Sandra to give Maddie art lessons. Maybe Maia would like to be a part of that too."

"That's a great idea. It sounds like you're giving these kids more than just a standard apprenticeship. You're taking an interest in them as people and allowing them to expand their interests and talents in a practical way. That's the mark of a true teacher, honey. Well done," Elliot said.

"What about the other two?" Lucy asked. "And the manager? Morgan?"

"Claire is a force of nature. She wants her own shop someday. She's excited about learning everything about running a potions business. I think she is going to be an incredible addition to the shop team. Michael is still trying to find his focus. I might ask Magnus to work with him a bit. Michael is only a few months older than Joshua. It might be good for them to learn together." Elizabeth paused.

"Morgan is outstanding. I am delighted that Jonah suggested her for the job and also that I could help her out. I think she'll get along very well with the kids and will do an excellent job running the shop. She already has some fabulous ideas and gets along well with Meg. The two of them are going to run an empire out of the cafe, I'm sure." Elizabeth grinned.

"Are you sure you have room for all of this in the shop?" Nora asked.

Elizabeth grinned again.

"So, there's something I haven't told you yet about the shop." She looked around at her parents, sister, and brother-in-law. They all looked back at her in surprise.

"The shop is sentient. It's inhabited by a House Spirit named Samara. She's been with the shop since it was first opened. She's beautiful and very cool. She and Morgan are going to work very well together. And she approved Morgan and all the apprentices. She likes them and is happy to be working with them. Though, I guess you knew about Samara, Mom? She says she used to babysit me in the shop when I was tiny."

Nora laughed.

"She did. I'd forgotten that. I wonder how I could have forgotten. Samara is lovely. I'm glad that she's working with you and that you are all getting along so well. That's wonderful, sweetheart."

"Is there anything else going on that you want to tell us about, Sis?" Lucy asked with a twinkle in her eye. "Something to do with a tall, dark police officer, maybe?"

Nora turned excitedly to Elizabeth.

Elizabeth blushed.

"Jonah asked me out to dinner. He wants to get to know me as the adults we are now."

"That's wonderful, Elizabeth!" Nora said. "Where will you go? When are you going?"

"We were going to try to keep it quiet for a bit until we saw if it would work out. I guess that's impossible now," Elizabeth glared at Lucy, who shrugged and grinned.

"Don't be silly, sweetheart. And don't worry about it. No one will think any worse of you for it. Jonah is quite the catch. I always thought he was just waiting for you to come to your senses and come home. It's so nice to know I was right!" Nora looked very pleased with herself.

Elizabeth sighed. She would have to warn Jonah that the whole town would know that he'd asked her out by tonight.

"Look, guys, there's something else I wanted to talk to you about," Elizabeth said. "Mom, you might want a cup of tea for this."

Nora looked worried.

"Just tell me, Elizabeth. You're not sick, are you? Because we'll get the best Healers to take care of you if you are. There are several good ones who owe me for my herbs over the years."

Elizabeth shook her head.

"No, Mom. I'm fine." Elizabeth looked at Nora, then at everyone else.

"Aunt Gloria is still here, in Spirit Form. She's been with me since my first day back. She says she's come to see you, Mom, but you haven't allowed yourself to see her yet. She misses you and would really like to talk to you."

Nora froze.

Elliot patted her shoulder.

"It's true, honey. Gloria popped in to see me several days ago. She loves you very much and is just waiting for the time when you're ready to see her again."

Tears rolled down Nora's face. Gloria was Nora's older sister, older by three years. Nora had looked up to her sister her whole life.

"Mom, Aunt Gloria used to work for the Supernatural Oversight Council when she was younger, before I was born. She was part of a special investigative team. There were twenty-three people associated with that team. Of those twenty-three, eight have died under strange circumstances in the last fifteen years. One died while the team was still in existence. They thought it was cancer. Now, with everything else going on, we're not so sure. Aunt Glo and I have been in touch with everyone on the team, and we're looking into the deaths and the team itself. Mathilda and John were part of the team too. That's why they moved here to Fairweather Falls; to be closer to Aunt Gloria after the team disbanded. Several of Aunt Gloria's friends will be staying with us for a while. Madelynn, Sharalee, and Roger. Madelynn and Sharalee are staying to help Mathilda until her time comes in a couple of months and also to help us look into this mess. Roger is a Techno-Mage. He can see anything that has ever been transmitted electronically. He's helping with research. Roger's also somewhat ADHD or on the spectrum a bit and needs a lot of space and quiet. Eleanore has made a special room for him. So when you see him, don't be offended if he seems rude or leaves suddenly. His brain just works a bit differently. Ok?"

The other adults stared at her for a moment.

"Well, that's certainly a story," Thomas said. "Have you told Jonah? Maybe the police can help?"

"We included him in a team meeting yesterday. There's probably not a lot the mundane police can do at this point. This seems to be solely a paranormal issue. But we thought it would be wise to include him, just in case. It also looks like there might have been someone from the Council involved in the deaths. Someone has been altering the memory of the team admin for years, and it had to be someone with insider knowledge. We're looking for a good Mind Healer to come have a look at her and figure out how much of her memory is true." Elizabeth paused.

"I feel really sorry for Rosie. She doesn't know how much of what she remembers about her life is true or how much was made up. She's single, and her parents died a long time ago. She would have been an easy target. She's worried that things might have happened that she has no memories of. I'm hoping that we can get a Mind Healer here as soon as possible." She looked around at the others. "Does anyone know a good one?"

"I do," Thomas said. "I know a great one. He's Fae and works for the Council. He's completely incorruptible. He also works for the Fae Council. I can get in touch with him if you like?"

"I'm not sure having someone who works for the Council involved is a good idea," Elizabeth said. "Let me ask Aunt Gloria's friends and get back to you. Thank you, Tom. I appreciate your help. I very well might ask you to contact him for me. What's his name? Maybe Aunt Gloria's friends know him already."

"Ciaran MacNamara. He's Fae nobility, Aes Sídhe. He spends most of his time either in Faery or in California. He's part of a new adventure happening there. The local Academy has expanded to accept students from the Fae, Dragons, Phoenyxes, and Merfolk. His sister is in partnership with the Casey Witches in developing and breeding Fae plants for the Earth Realm."

"Oh, how wonderful!" Nora exclaimed. Elliot looked interested too.

"I've met Brendan and Celine Casey, of course," Nora said. "I get a lot of my new seeds and starts from Brendan. Elizabeth, if the Caseys trust this Mind Healer, then you can absolutely trust him."

"Thank you, Mom."

"Liz, Ciaran is a fully trained level five Fae Mind Mage. He works with his brother-in-law, Nathaniel Brooks, level three. They are the best, and as I said, completely incorruptible."

"Thank you. I'll ask Lorien and Clara if they know him. Lorien is the Aes Sídhe member of Aunt Glo's team. He's Clara's cousin and is staying with her while we sort this out. I'll stop by and see them this afternoon."

20

Elizabeth rode her bike into town after leaving her parents' house. She planned to stop in to see Clara and Lorien, then check in with Morgan at the shop.

Clara kept The Flower's Daughter open for short hours on Sundays during the summer. During the winter, the store was closed on Sundays and Mondays. Clara was just opening up when Elizabeth rolled up to the shop at one.

"Hello, Elizabeth! It's a beautiful day. Have you come to shop?"

"Hi, Clara. No, I was hoping to talk to Lorien for a moment, if he's here?"

"Good day, Elizabeth," Lorien replied, coming up behind his cousin. "How can I be of assistance? Have you learned anything new?"

"I have; several things. Can we talk inside?"

"Of course," Clara said and stepped back to allow Elizabeth to walk past her into the store.

Elizabeth leaned against the counter and looked at the tall Aes Sídhe.

"So, first of all, Carl helped to uncover a large level of corruption in the Council. That's why he left. He was completely disillusioned by the whole thing. And Sarah was a Bean Sídhe, at least five hundred years old."

Lorien smiled.

"You found Roger, didn't you?"

Elizabeth grinned.

"He replied to the email that Sean had me send. Roger is currently staying at my house while researching everyone involved with the team. Oh, and Lorien? He would like to see everyone, but Roger needs a lot of space and quiet. His brain works a little differently from other people's. It's not that he's being rude; he just gets overwhelmed very easily when there are a lot of people around. Or when he has to talk to someone for a longer period of time. But he does care about the members of the team, and he is looking forward to seeing you all."

Lorien bowed to Elizabeth.

"Thank you, Elizabeth. I will visit whenever Roger is comfortable seeing me. Please tell him that I appreciate his coming to help us solve this puzzle."

"I will. So, in addition, I want to find a Mind Healer for Rosie. She's in a really bad way. She's terrified that nothing she remembers is true and that she may have done things she doesn't remember. My brother-in-law suggested a Fae Mind Mage by the name of Ciaran MacNamara. Do you know him?"

Clara and Lorien looked at each other and grinned.

"Of course we know him. We're distantly related. Ciaran is absolutely the best person to look into this and to help Rosie. And we can trust him to keep this quiet, even from the Council, until we are ready to bring everything to light. I will call him right away." Lorien turned and went into the back of the shop, where Clara kept a large mirror for communications. He returned a few minutes later.

"Ciaran and Nathaniel are coming. They are not needed anywhere else right now. In fact, Ciaran is getting ready to be handfasted to his Bonded soon. I think he would enjoy a break from the preparations. Fae handfastings are very complicated things."

Someone cleared their throat at the shop door.

Elizabeth turned to see two tall Aes Sídhe males, one fair, one dark.

"Thank you for coming, Ciaran, Nathaniel," Lorien said, striding over to hug both men. He led them over to Elizabeth.

"Gentlemen, this is Elizabeth Sloan, Potions Master and Earth Witch. And you know my cousin Clara."

The two newcomers bowed to the women.

"It's lovely to meet you," Elizabeth said. "Thank you for coming to help Rosie. She's in a lot of distress."

"Of course. We're glad to be able to help," the blond Fae, Ciaran, replied. Nathaniel smiled.

"Rosie is at my house. She mostly stays in her room or the garden. If you like, we can go back there now?"

"That would be wonderful. I would not want to leave the poor woman in distress for any longer than necessary," Nathaniel said.

"I rode my bike over, but we can walk back if you like?"

"I will teleport us there," Ciaran offered.

Elizabeth said goodbye to Clara and Lorien, who promised to visit soon. She walked outside with the two Aes Sídhe.

"Hang onto your bike, and think of home," Ciaran said. He put his hand on her shoulder. Nathaniel put his hand on Ciaran's shoulder. In a blink, they were back at the house.

Elizabeth led them into the kitchen.

"Mary, where is Rosie right now?"

"She's outside on the patio. She saw Roger a little while ago. It went well. She has some tea and cookies; shall I make you some as well?"

"That would be lovely, thank you," Ciaran said.

Mary smiled and turned to put the kettle on.

"You are blessed indeed to have one of the Brùnaidh looking after your house," Nathaniel said to Elizabeth as they stepped outside.

"I know. Mary's Aunt Meg is one of my favorite people on the planet. When we returned home this summer, Mary arrived and said that she was now in charge. It's heaven having her here."

Rosie looked up as the three stepped out onto the patio.

"Rosie, this is Ciaran MacNamara and Nathaniel Brooke. They are Fae Mind Mages. Lorien and my family vouch for them. They are here to see if they can help you with your memories."

Rosie started to shake. A tear slipped down her cheek.

"I'm so scared of what we might find," she whispered. "But it's better to know than to be wondering and worrying like this. Please, help me."

Ciaran knelt on the ground in front of Rosie.

"Nathaniel and I will take turns searching through your mind to see if we can figure out what has been done to you, ok? I will go first, then Nathaniel. This way, we will be doubly sure that we haven't missed anything. We'll start when you're ready."

"I'm ready," Rosie whispered.

Ciaran placed his hands on Rosie's head and closed his eyes. From the outside, it looked as if he were just standing there, doing nothing. But if you looked at his eyes, you could see they were moving quickly under his closed lids, as if watching something very closely.

After about ten minutes, Ciaran took his hands from Rosie's head and stood up. He looked infinitely sad. He sat down next to Rosie and held her hand.

"Rosie, I'm afraid you were right. Someone has been messing with your head for a very long time now. I would say for most of your life. How long has it been since the team broke up?"

"Over forty years now," Rosie whispered.

"And how long were you with the team before that?"

"From the beginning. The team was together for fifteen years before it broke up."

"So you've been associated with the team for around fifty-five years, is that right?"

Rosie nodded.

Aunt Gloria popped into view next to Rosie.

"Rosie was the glue in the support staff that held us all together. She came with Sarah when we were all recruited and handled all paperwork and administrative duties. I'm not really sure what Sarah actually did after recruiting us. She would pop in for motivational talks and mission reviews, but Rosie did all the actual work. It was Rosie we went to if we had questions or problems. Rosie handed out assignments and made sure we got paid. All reports were handed in to Rosie. And it was Rosie who made sure that birthdays and significant days in our lives were celebrated and given as days off whenever possible. Rosie took care of us, Alice would listen to us gripe, and Madelynn linked us all as a family. Rosie and Alice were our parents, and Maddie our big sister. We couldn't have done what we did without them."

Ciaran nodded.

"Rosie, from what I've found here, I think your mind has been altered by two separate people, the first one starting at a very young age. Probably ten years or so before you met Sarah, or maybe even earlier. The second one shows traces going back to the early years of the team. Maybe two to five years in? It's hard to say, exactly. I am going to ask you to let me try again, only this time I want you to tell me what you remember about your life as I'm working. Start as far back as you can remember. This may take a while, depending on what I find. Let me know when you are ready to begin."

Rosie had paled even further as Ciaran spoke. She hesitated, then nodded.

"I'm ready."

Ciaran moved to stand behind her this time and placed his hands back on her head.

"Go ahead, Rosie," Nathaniel said once Ciaran was in place.

Rosie talked about her childhood, growing up with her Dryad mother and human father. She'd had an idyllic childhood. They had lived near her mother's tree in a rural area of upstate New York. Her father was a park ranger and looked after the local forests. Then, when Rosie was in her senior year of high school, her father was shot by an out-of-season hunter. He died on the way to the hospital. Rosie's mother was devastated. Her tree got sick and gradually died. Rosie's mother died with it. Rosie finished school and became a hairstylist. She told Ciaran about meeting Sarah, joining her in her recruitment efforts, and working for the Council. She took them through the years of the team, then the years afterward. The half-Dryad recounted everything exactly as she remembered it. When she was done, Ciaran stepped back and sighed.

"Rosie, almost all of your memories have been altered. As I said, I believe there were two separate people at fault here. I would like Nathaniel to see what he thinks. Then we'll talk about the next steps. Ok?"

Rosie nodded.

Nathaniel knelt in front of Rosie and laid his hands on her head. When he pulled back, he frowned.

"I believe Ciaran is right. I sense two different energy traces in your mind, Rosie. I get the feeling that one is not malicious, though. Your memories were altered, but... I have nothing concrete to go on, just a gut feeling. The second one, the later one, that one is completely malicious and self-serving."

Rosie looked confused.

"How could it not be malicious? How could someone mess with my mind and not be evil?"

"They could have thought they were protecting you in some way," Aunt Gloria said.

"We'll find out when we remove the altered memories," Ciaran said. "Your genuine memories are still there. They are just hidden. We will find them and bring them to light."

Ciaran looked at Elizabeth and Aunt Gloria.

"I think Rosie has had enough for today. I would like to begin the work of retrieving her true memories tomorrow, if possible. Nathaniel and I will stay in town if you could recommend a good inn."

"You can stay with us. Mary made our house, Eleanor, sentient. I'm not entirely sure how it works. She didn't invite a spirit to inhabit the house. It was like she gave the house its own spirit. Anyway, Eleanor can make rooms for you. Just tell her what you would like."

"That's very kind of you," Nathaniel said. "Please, let us know how we can help you while we are here."

"I appreciate the offer. Maybe you could talk to Mary about that."

Elizabeth looked at Rosie.

"Rosie, Sweetheart. Would you like to take a rest? This is a lot to handle. I know I would like to hide away and process by myself for a while if it were me."

"Thank you, Elizabeth. I think I would like a rest. Thank you."

Rosie stood and made her way into the house. Aunt Gloria went with her to make sure she was ok.

Elizabeth looked back at the Aes Sídhe before her.

"What does this mean for Rosie? What will getting her memories back do for her?"

"We can't really know until it's done. But I would think she will feel whole, maybe for the first time ever. I think Rosie has most likely been living with anxiety her whole life and not known why. This should help take care of that. It will give her a chance to find out who she really is and come to terms with anything she may have done under the manipulations of whoever was messing with her mind. It will help her get to know herself better, which is something we should all strive to do."

"So you think it's a good idea to go through with this."

"Yes, I do. It won't be easy for Rosie, but I can tell she has a strong network of people who care about her here. And that makes all the difference."

Elizabeth stood.

"Well, come inside, and let's talk to Mary and Eleanor about rooms for you and anything Mary might like help with. Oh, and I should tell you. The team's support Techno-Mage is staying with us. His mind works a little differently than other people's, and he needs a lot of space and quiet. Eleanor made him a special room that he stays in most of the time. If you do see him, take it easy with him. And don't be put off by his attitude. He's not being rude. He's just trying to protect himself."

The Fae nodded.

Elizabeth led the way into the kitchen.

"Mary, Ciaran and Nathaniel will be staying with us for a while. We'd like to ask Eleanor to make rooms for them. They would also like to know if there is any way they can help you while they are here."

Mary's eyes twinkled.

"There are some plants and herbs from Faery that I would dearly like to be able to cook with," the grinning Brownie said.

“My mate is an herbalist and Potions Master,” Nathaniel said. “She can get anything you might like. She is working with Brendan Casey in Valerian’s Cove to bring many of those plants into the Earth realm and hybridize them to thrive here. Please, give me your list. It will be our pleasure to provide them for you.”

Mary rubbed her hands together in glee and reached for a pen.

21

On Monday morning, Elizabeth left Ciaran and Nathaniel with Rosie, overseen by Aunt Gloria.

Elizabeth made her way into town on her bike to meet with Morgan at the shop at eight. The apprentices would show up around nine.

Morgan was waiting in the bookstore at the front of the shop when Elizabeth arrived.

"Good morning!" The enthusiastic young woman said as Elizabeth walked in.

"Good morning," Elizabeth smiled. "How was your first weekend in your new apartment? Did you get settled in?"

"I did, thank you. Jonah helped me get what I needed from home and ran interference with my parents too. My mom's not happy, but my father made her let me go. He understood my need to spread my wings a bit."

"That's good. I'm happy for you." Elizabeth paused. "So, are you ready to dive into everything Samara's Garden?"

"Yes!"

Samara materialized in front of them, and the three women spent the next hour going over ordering books and gifts for the bookshop, working the register, and Morgan and Meg's plans for the cafe. By the time the kids arrived for their first shifts, Elizabeth was even happier that she had given Morgan a try. The woman had terrific ideas for the shop. Elizabeth was excited to see how they would all work out.

The three teens all arrived on their bikes at nine. Claire led the way inside, talking a mile-a-minute.

"Good morning," Elizabeth said. "Thank you all for being on time. Now, normally, Claire would be with me at the stillroom on my land on Monday, but since this is our first day together, let's all start here getting to know the shop. Then, this afternoon, I'll take Claire to the stillroom and let Michael and Maia work with Morgan. Ok? Let's get started."

They spent several hours getting the kids up to speed on everything. Elizabeth had some boxes of potions ready to be set out, and Morgan had some recipes that she wanted everyone to try as possibilities for the cafe. She fed them all lunch. Elizabeth approached Maia as the youngest apprentice was unpacking a box of calming potions in the apothecary section.

"Maia, have you talked to Robin about your ideas for the logo and branding yet?"

"Yes, I talked to her yesterday for a bit. We're going to get together this week. Thank you, Elizabeth. I never thought my designs would be taken seriously."

"You're most welcome," Elizabeth said. "Actually, I had another thought as well. I have another friend, Sandra, who was an excellent artist in school. I'm not sure how much art she's been doing lately, but I was going to ask her to give my daughter art lessons. Maybe the three of you could all work together? You could all help each other. I'm sure there are things that each of you are good at that the others could learn."

Maia's eyes lit up.

"That sounds great! I would love that."

"Good. I'll talk to Sandra and Maddie's teacher Mags later today. If everyone is good with it, I'll send everyone each other's contact info."

Maia glowed.

After lunch, Elizabeth took Claire home with her to the stillroom.

This was the first time that Elizabeth had shown the stillroom off to someone new, and she felt an intense sense of pride as the young woman walked in, a look of wonder on her face.

"Wow, this is amazing!" Claire said. "This is nothing like our potions classroom at school. This is sooo much better!"

Claire walked around looking at the shelves and counters, the various apparatuses and tools Elizabeth used in her trade.

Elizabeth let her browse for a moment, then called her over to the table.

"Ok, so this is where we will work on Mondays. Why don't you tell me what you have learned in school and where your interests lie? What excites you the most about potions? Are you most into healing? Cosmetics? Magical helpers?"

"What do you mean, magical helpers?"

"Potions that are spells in and of themselves. Like potion bombs with different effects, those are good for combat. The Council uses a lot of those. I haven't made any of those in a long time. Aunt Gloria and I mainly focused on healing potions, with a few cosmetics thrown in."

Claire thought about it for a moment.

"I think cosmetics and some healing? Like, healing cosmetics, if that makes sense? Like, if someone is sick, they should still be able to look their best, you know? And maybe the potion could heal as well?"

"That's an excellent idea," Elizabeth said. "Why don't we start there, then. We'll start with lotions and salves, as they are easily adapted to include healing herbs. Then we'll go from there. Do you have good herbal resource books? Ones that properly list the medicinal and magical correspondences of all the herbs?"

Claire nodded. She listed off the titles. Two were school course books, which Elizabeth felt were too dry and didn't carry enough real-world information. She wandered over to the bookshelf she kept her resource materials on. Humming to herself, she pulled out three books.

"Here, take these home and look at them tonight. I would suggest buying your own copies of all three. They are extremely thorough and complete. You will most likely find yourself making notes in the margins as you experiment with the herbs. You will find your own understanding of them. Some will work exactly as stated, while some may work differently for you. For that matter," Elizabeth paused, "You should have your own recipe book that you record everything you do in. I would keep two-one for while you work and one for writing finished recipes in. That way, your finished book is neat and clean, while you can make all the notes you like in your working book. You can use a regular notebook for the working book, but I would get something substantial for your finished recipes. You put a lot of work into them, and that book should be special."

Elizabeth pulled her recipe book from the shelf to show Claire, then Aunt Gloria's.

Claire nodded.

"Can I get a finished book from the bookstore?" She asked.

"Sure. That's a great idea. I should keep some on hand, anyway. Good idea, Claire. Tomorrow on your shop shift, look through the catalogs and find some you like. Have the others do the same. I'll order the top ten. And some workbooks, too."

Elizabeth handed a scratch pad to Claire along with a pen, then turned her recipe book to the page for a calendula salve for chapped or irritated skin. "Let's start here."

❧

After a full day of work, Elizabeth was tired. She was beyond happy with how the day had gone. Claire had proven to be an enthusiastic learner, full of questions and good ideas. Elizabeth was looking forward to working with the other two apprentices and seeing where their interests lay. Which reminded her—she needed to ask Magnus if he would consider working with Michael along with Josh.

Elizabeth walked into the kitchen to find Mary and Nathaniel cooking together, while a fair-haired Aes Sídhe woman held an infant at the counter. Wonderful smells were coming from whatever it was that Mary was stirring on the stove.

"Elizabeth, please let me introduce my mate, Siofra MacNamara-Brooke, and our daughter, Dervla Eimear MacNamara-Brooke. Siofra decided to bring Mary her herbs herself." Nathaniel smiled at the beautiful Fae woman, who blew him a kiss and smiled back.

"It's very nice to meet you," Elizabeth said.

"You, too. Thank you for keeping my husband busy. And my brother, too. They get antsy if they don't have a puzzle to solve. And I am glad we can help Rosie. She's lovely, and no one deserves what she's going through."

Dervla reached for Elizabeth to pick her up. Elizabeth looked at Siofra, who nodded. Elizabeth picked up the young Fae and slung her onto her hip.

"How are you, pretty girl? Are you having a good day?" The infant smiled up at her. Someone had clearly fed her a cookie. There were crumbs all over her face and dress. The little girl had curly brown hair and bright blue eyes, just like her father's. Elizabeth kissed her forehead and smiled back at her.

"You're hired," Siofra said. "She usually takes longer to decide if she likes someone. She liked you right away. That means you are a very good person. We're glad to know you. Beware, we hit up everyone she likes for babysitting when we need a night out. We can portal everywhere, so it doesn't matter where in the realms they are."

Elizabeth grinned back.

"Any time. Mine are eight and almost sixteen now, so it's been a while since I've had a baby to play with. Have you met my two yet?"

Siofra shook her head.

"Well, they should be home soon for dinner. Hopefully, their mentors will eat with us tonight. I believe one of them is related to you, Siofra? The Lady Mags is Maddie's mentor."

Siofra's eyes twinkled, and she laughed.

"They finally found something to keep her busy, did they? I bet her father is thrilled. He was beginning to despair. Oh, I hope she does stay for dinner. I haven't seen Mags in forever. I'm not sure she's ever met Dervla. Nathaniel and I have settled in Valerian's Cove and don't go back to Faery very often anymore. We're too busy, what with the nursery, the Academy, and everything else going on."

"Thomas mentioned something about that. What exactly are you all doing out there?"

Siofra and Nathaniel proceeded to tell the story of the Casey Witches of Valerian's Cove and their connections to Dragons, Phoenyxes, and Fae. They talked about the Academy and the new Fae potions classes that Siofra was teaching.

"I wonder if we could convince the Academy in Boston to expand like that? I think it would do everyone around here a world of good," Elizabeth said. "We tend to get too stuck in our ways around here unless we break free and leave."

"We started the expansion because of the Caseys and their children's remarkable new Gifts. One is Witch, Dragon, and Phoenyx, one is Witch, Phoenyx, and Techno-Mage, one is a Witch and Fae Earth Mage, and one is a Witch and a Fae Illusionist. The Earth Mage and the Illusionist both have strong Dragon Spirits, too, but they haven't Shifted yet."

Elizabeth blinked.

"Wow. That's a lot of power for young children to hold. My two are both Mages, too, but we're straight Witch in our family."

"But your daughter at least must be powerful if Mags is teaching her."

"She is. So is my son. He's an Earth Mage. His teacher is a Gnome named Magnus. Maddie is an Elemental Mage."

"Magnus! Oh, I haven't seen him in ages! So this is where he settled! Oh, it will be so good to see him again!" Siofra's eyes had lit up, and she was smiling brightly.

Just then, the back door opened, and Josh came in. Magnus rode on his shoulder.

"Siofra! My angel, what are you doing here?" The Gnome cried. He leaped off Joshua's shoulder and landed on the table in front of the Fae woman.

"Nathaniel came to help Rosie, and I decided to pop in for a visit! I had no idea you were here! Oh, Magnus! It's been too long."

Nathaniel was watching his wife with a smile. Elizabeth looked at him inquiringly.

"Magnus was one of Siofra's earliest teachers in Earth magic. Siofra is a Fae Earth Mage. Her focus is in plants rather than stone, but Magnus is the one who taught her to love the Earth in all its forms.

They stayed in communication for years but lost touch a few years ago when things started getting busy for us."

The back door opened again, and Maddie flew in—literally. She landed next to Elizabeth.

"Who's the baby, Mom?"

Mags came in on two feet behind her.

"Siofra! What are you doing here? Is Ciaran here? Is this your kid? Hand her over, Elizabeth. Auntie Mags wants a go." Mags grabbed Dervla, who laughed and patted Mags' cheek.

Siofra explained again what she was doing there. Nathaniel said hi to Magnus and Mags, then Ciaran came in with Madelynn and Sharalee, a somewhat disheveled man shuffling through the door behind them. The man looked ill. He was too thin. His face was haggard, his bloodshot eyes downcast. Clearly, this was Carl, the Fire Mage. Madelynn must have decided to bring him home.

Ciaran exclaimed at seeing Magnus and Mags, and the reunion continued. The teachers agreed to stay for dinner. Magnus called his wife and had her bring the kids over as well.

Everyone moved out onto the patio. Mags had taught Maddie how to shrink herself, and now she was running around in the garden with the Gnome children. Oreo flew overhead, monitoring the action.

"Magnus, before I forget," Elizabeth said, "One of my apprentices is an Earth Mage. His parents are not and don't know what to do with him. His teachers at school have helped, but he doesn't know where his true affinities lie, and he's Josh's age. Would you consider working with him as well as Josh a few days a week? I think it would be good for the boys to work together."

"I'd be happy to. Let me know what the young man's schedule is with you, and we will work around that."

"I appreciate it, Magnus. I think he has a lot of potential. And it will be good for Josh to make a new friend his age."

❧ 22 ❧

Feeling very proud of herself for getting her apprentices all sorted out, Elizabeth decided to see if her friends would like to have a girl's night out. She called Robin, Sarah, and Sandra. They agreed to meet Wednesday night at the diner.

Tuesday was the first day the apprentices started their full summer schedule. Michael would be with Elizabeth for potions, while Maia would be in the store in the morning and Claire in the afternoon. Michael would work with Josh and Magnus on Monday afternoons and Wednesday and Saturday mornings. For now, this schedule seemed to suit everyone. When school started again in the fall, things would have to change, as the apprentices would be unable to work until after school. They might have to hire a daytime person to help Morgan in the shop, depending on how busy it got. Scratch that; they definitely would. Someone would have to run the cafe while someone else ran the rest of the store. Oh well. A task for another day. They still had over a month until they had to figure that out.

Wednesday evening came quickly. Elizabeth found herself excited to spend time with her friends. She had been so busy since coming home that she hadn't made enough time to see them. She walked into the diner and waived at her sister Lucy, who was working behind the counter. Lucy owned the diner, having bought it from the previous owners when they retired. Technically, the diner had its own name, Leah's Kitchen. But everyone had just called it 'the diner' for years, and it'd stuck.

Robin was already seated in a booth toward the back when Elizabeth walked in. She waived to make sure that Elizabeth saw her.

"This feels like when we were kids," Elizabeth said.

"I know, right? How many days did we spend in here, after school, and on weekends?" Robin had a chocolate milkshake in front of her, with whipped cream and sprinkles. She took a long sip through the wide, compostable straw.

Sarah and Sandra walked in as Elizabeth sat down. Robin waved again, and the other two made their way over.

Sarah slid in next to Robin and Sandra next to Elizabeth.

Lucy's server, Caitlyn, brought them all menus. The three newcomers ordered their own shakes, then looked at each other.

Suddenly, they all burst out laughing.

"I feel like I'm in school again. Are we going to complain about Mrs. Doyle or Principle Schumann?" Sarah joked.

Sandra blushed at the mention of her mother, then laughed with the rest of them.

"What's been going on, Liz? You've been so busy since you've been back that we've hardly seen you since we got Sandra settled in at the farm," Robin said.

Elizabeth told them all about the shop.

"Oh, Sandra, that reminds me. Do you still draw? I remember you being great at it in school. My daughter Maddie loves to draw, and so does one of my new apprentices, Maia. I was hoping that maybe you could draw with them a couple of days a week? Sort of like a drawing club, and you could all learn from and support each other?"

Sandra blinked.

"I haven't really drawn much in years," she answered. "Mother thought it was a waste of time."

"That's criminal; you were really good," Robin said. "Maia's got talent too. She's going to help with the logo and branding for the shop and the apothecary products. I think a drawing club is an awesome idea. I might join too."

Sandra smiled.

"It would be nice to draw again on a regular basis. Maybe this could be the kick I need."

"Ooh, let's go art supply shopping tomorrow!" Robin exclaimed.

Elizabeth and Sarah rolled their eyes. They all knew how Robin got in an art supply store. It took hours to get her out again.

"Maybe Maddie could go with you?" Elizabeth suggested. "Maia has the shop in the afternoon. I don't know what she'll be doing in the morning."

"It could be a great first meeting of the club, to all go supply shopping together. Maybe we could pick a theme and buy supplies based on that," Sandra said. She was sounding more animated than Elizabeth had seen her since being back.

Sarah looked at Elizabeth and smiled. Elizabeth smiled back. It was good to see Sandra excited about something.

Talk turned to Elizabeth and Robin's kids, then Elizabeth took a breath and told her friends about Aunt Gloria's past and the mystery surrounding the deaths on her team.

"I always thought there was something strange about John's death," Robin said.

Sarah nodded.

"I had a weird feeling about it, too."

"It's definitely weird that so many of the team are dead and that the deaths were so close together. And you really have no idea who could be behind it?" Sandra asked.

Elizabeth shook her head.

"Ciaran and Nathaniel, the Aes Sídhe helping Rosie, are going super slowly unraveling her memories. They just finished with her childhood today. They are going to start on her time with the team tomorrow. The leader's name was Sarah, too. She was supposed to have died fifteen years ago, but if we're right and she was a Bean Sídhe, then that's impossible."

"What did they find about Rosie's childhood?" Sarah asked.

"It's so sad. A lot of it is as Rosie remembered. Her mother was a

Dryad. She married a man who was a park ranger that took care of the woods. Rosie thought he was mortal. It turns out he was a Bear Shifter. He was supposed to take over as the Alpha of his Sleuth, but he married Rosie's mom instead. Rosie thought he was shot to death by an out-of-season hunter. Apparently, what actually happened was that another member of the Sleuth challenged him for Alpha when it became clear that he had no intention of taking over from his father. Rosie's father died in the fight."

"Wait, so Rosie is half Shifter, half Dryad? How does that work?"

"We're going to find out. Apparently, Rosie's Shifter side was bound when she was an infant. Her father didn't want her to have anything to do with his Sleuth. I guess they were very traditional and hide-bound and didn't treat their women very well. Plus, as a half-breed, Rosie would have been looked down on and mistreated, anyway. So he had a Witch bind her Bear inside her. Rosie never knew. And the same Witch apparently was the one to hide these early memories at Rosie's mother's urging. Ciaran is looking for the Witch to break the binding and a Bear Shifter who can teach Rosie about her Shifter side."

"Does Rosie have a tree, like a Dryad?" Robin asked.

Elizabeth shook her head.

"She always thought she was a magical dud. She has a connection to nature and to the forest that is deeper than most people's, but has never felt tied to a tree. Her mother never planted one for her. Her mother was a Quaking Aspen Dryad. I suppose that if Rosie wanted to try, she could nurture a seedling and see if she could bond with it. But it might make traveling uncomfortable. I think she would want to be safely settled in a place before trying that."

"So she may be more Shifter than Dryad, then," Sandra said.

Elizabeth shrugged.

"Ben will help Rosie learn about her Shifter side," Robin stated. "And I am happy to talk all things Dryad with her."

"Thanks, Rob. That'd be great," Elizabeth said.

Caitlyn came over to check on the table. The women all reached for their wallets.

"Lucy says it's on the house, as Elizabeth's first girl's night out back home," Caitlyn told them.

They all looked over at Lucy and waived. She grinned back.

"So will you tell us what the Mind Mages find out about who was controlling Rosie while she was a part of the team?" Robin asked.

"Of course. I'm counting on you guys to catch anything I miss. We work better together."

"Damn straight we do!" Robin said, and everyone laughed.

THURSDAY MORNING EARLY, ELIZABETH SAT ON THE PATIO WITH Rosie and Aunt Gloria, waiting for Ciaran to begin the next stage of uncovering Rosie's memories. Madelynn and Sharalee sat nearby. Carl was in his room, as was Roger. Roger had continued to dig for information on Sarah Faraday and on every member of the team, looking for anything that could have prompted the killing spree. So far, he had found nothing. Alice's medical records checked out. Her family was all accounted for. None of her family had been missing or on vacation during the times of the murders. It looked like they were all in the clear. It seemed as if Alice's death really was a coincidence. Still, Roger kept digging.

A lot of hope was riding on Ciaran and Nathaniel's efforts over the next few days.

Madelynn moved to sit next to Rosie and took her hand.

"Are you ready, Rosie?" Ciaran asked.

Rosie nodded.

Ciaran again slid into Rosie's mind. The Mage looked at her memories of meeting Sarah, of becoming a part of the team. He looked at the death of the High Magic Witch. He looked into the recruiting of the other team members. Wherever he found a memory that had been tampered with, he dug more deeply and found the accurate memory beneath it, freeing them so Rosie could access them. When he was done there, he stopped and retreated.

Rosie was crying again.

"I think we can stop there for today," Ciaran said softly. Rosie nodded again.

"What did you find?" Madelynn asked.

Rosie leaned into the Brownie, still crying.

"The memory altering started with the first recruiting project, the Witch that was murdered," Ciaran said. "Before, Rosie remembered the house exploding before they reached it. Now, it's clear that the house exploded just as they pulled up to it and that they were chased away from it. Sarah protected them and got them safely away. It seems that Sarah may have been only half Bean Sídhe. She used Fae magic to protect them and get them away. Shortly afterward, an Aes Sídhe man came to the office to see Sarah. They got into a fight, then the man left. As he left, he stopped and modified Rosie's memory."

"Why? What did this man look like?" Elizabeth asked.

"He had dark hair and bright blue eyes. He was very slender. The strange thing was that he looked somewhat like Sarah. Perhaps he was a relative?"

"But why would he change Rosie's memory?"

"Maybe he didn't want anyone to know he had been there?"

Rosie raised her head from Madelynn's shoulder.

"Sarah never spoke of him, and I never saw him again."

"Is there any way to find out who this man was?" Elizabeth asked.

"We can make an image of his face and see if anyone recognizes him," Sharalee said.

"Know any good artists?" Madelynn asked.

"I know three. They're all on a shopping trip together right now. But they'll be back by lunchtime. Maia has a shift at the shop. I'd rather not get Maddie involved. I'll ask Sandra if she'll do it when they drop Maddie and Mags back off here."

Sandra agreed to draw the man's face. Ciaran cast the image onto a bowl of water, and Sandra got to work. After a while, she sat back, satisfied. She held out her drawing pad for Ciaran to take. He had her make a slight adjustment to the man's expression, then nodded. He turned the pad so that everyone else could see it.

"Does anyone recognize this man?"

Everyone started at the drawing. The man's eyes were cold, his mouth tight. His cheekbones were sharp under his skin. His long dark hair was pulled back off his face.

Madelynn cocked her head to the side.

"He looks familiar, somehow. I feel like I've seen him somewhere before, but I couldn't tell you where."

Ciaran looked at Madelynn.

"Would you mind if I looked into your memories? Maybe I can see."

Madelynn nodded. Ciaran placed his hands on her head.

After a moment, he pulled back.

"You're right; you did see him briefly. He came to visit Sarah another time. You saw him leaving. You were coming up from the side of the building, and he was so angry when he left that I don't think he registered you were there. Which probably saved you from having him mess with your mind as well."

"So this man, who looked somewhat like Sarah, visited her several times at the team offices," Madelynn said.

"Then there should be other records of him. He would have had to cross the wards to get in. Sarah must have given him permission and the location of our headquarters. Otherwise, he couldn't have gotten in."

"Not necessarily," Nathaniel said. "If he was closely enough related to Sarah, he might have been able to portal directly to where she was. Regardless of wardings. It's an Aes Sídhe thing."

"How close would he have had to be?" Elizabeth asked.

"Father or brother most likely."

"But Lorien said that Sarah wasn't Aes Sídhe."

"Maybe she hid that side of her self?" Nathaniel suggested.

"You can do that?"

"Yes, though it must have been draining for her to do it for so long."

"I think it's time we give this sketch to Roger and see what he can come up with," Aunt Gloria said. Elizabeth took the drawing and went inside. She climbed the stairs to Roger's room and knocked on the door. After a moment, Roger opened it.

"I'm sorry to bother you, Roger," Elizabeth said. "We have an image of the man who was messing with Rosie's mind and were hoping you might be able to use it to find him. He visited Sarah several times that we are aware of so far at the team headquarters. Ciaran said if he was closely enough related to Sarah, he could have used that link to portal in."

Roger took the drawing and looked at it.

"This is very good. Who drew this?"

"My friend, Sandra. She's an Earth Witch, but art has always been her true Gift."

Roger was still looking at the drawing.

"Give me a few minutes. I'll come down when I'm done."

Roger closed the door in Elizabeth's face.

She stared for a moment, surprised. Roger rarely came downstairs. And now he was volunteering?

She made her way back to the waiting group on the patio.

"Roger is looking into it. He liked your drawing, Sandra."

Sandra blushed.

Mary brought out iced tea and cookies while they waited. After about fifteen minutes, Roger came out the back door.

"Ok. So, there are several possibilities for this man. Two live in the Earth Realm. One is harder to track down. He's popped up from time to time, done a few deals in the Earth Realm for resources and other business ventures. Mostly in real estate. There's not a lot about him online. His name appears to be Daffydd Neil. Or David Neil. Not sure. He's used both. My guess is that he stays mostly in Faerie."

"I know of Daffydd MacNeil," Ciaran said. He was frowning.

"Daffydd MacNeil is an Unseelie Sídhe. He's midway up the rankings in the court. He's a hard man. Very old-fashioned. He has a son and a brother-in-law. His wife died giving birth to his son. His son is very like him. The brother-in-law is not. He's a good man. I will contact him at once."

Ciaran strode into the house to find a mirror. He was back with another Fae almost immediately.

"Everyone, this is Connor O'Brien. Connor's sister, Gráinne, was married to Daffydd."

"I told her not to marry him. But father insisted. She died a year later, bearing Daffydd's heir." Connor looked grim.

"I have stayed in my nephew's life as much as possible, but Daffydd never trusted me. Luckily, he was never around much when Phillip was younger. So I was able to visit fairly often. Ciaran tells me you have questions about Daffydd?"

Ciaran filled the other Fae in.

"I see. I was not aware that Daffydd had any other children, but he would have kept her a secret if she were a half-breed. And if she were powerful, he would have wanted to control her. He has no sisters, so she must have been his daughter."

"Could he have kidnapped her, do you think?" Madelynn asked.

"If she didn't bend to his will, then yes, I could see him doing that to get what he wanted. I think Philip could answer more of these questions for you. If you don't mind, I will ask him to join us."

"Are you sure that's safe? If his father is so controlling, what's to say Philip isn't involved in this? And that he won't go running back to his father?"

Connor shook his head.

"Philip hates his father. There are rumors that my sister did not die from birthing him. Rather, Daffydd had her killed as soon as she delivered his heir. Apparently, an intelligent wife was a liability to Daffydd. There were rumors that she had seen something she shouldn't have. Also, Daffydd has not been the best of fathers to Philip. Whereas I have tried to be the best uncle I could, and made sure that Philip knew that his mother's family loved him, and showed him as much as I could what that means in a healthy family."

"But when I met him, Philip impressed me as being very like his father," Ciaran said.

Connor shook his head.

"Philip played the game for as long as he had to. As soon as he was old enough to leave his father's house, he came to me."

Everyone looked at each other. Finally, Madelynn nodded.

Connor focused for a moment, then suddenly, another Fae male was standing before them. He looked very much like his father, yet his eyes were kind, and the planes of his face not quite so harsh.

"Uncle," the newcomer bowed to Connor. "My Lord MacNamara. How can I be of service?"

"Philip, we think your father has done something very wrong here in the Earth Realm. He may be behind several deaths, all connected back to one person. We suspect that that person is Daffydd's hidden daughter."

Philip froze. He stared around the group.

"That bastard. That's what he's up to." He shook his head.

"I always thought it odd that Father never remarried, especially when it became clear that I would refuse to follow in his footsteps. If he had another child waiting in the wings, that would make sense. Yet it sounds like this child is not bending to his will, either, if he is killing those close to her. It sounds as if he is using their deaths to manipulate her."

"I believe you may be right," Ciaran said. "This woman is half Bean Sídhe. She disappeared about fifteen years ago. Her death was faked in this realm. Daffydd has been messing with the mind of her assistant for at least forty years. We are uncovering those hidden memories now. So far, the consistent thing is Daffydd's visits to this woman. Can you think of any place he could be keeping her?"

"He would have to be keeping her somewhere close, where he could get to her easily. If he's kept her alive this long, there is something he wants from her. Do you know what other Gifts she might have besides the Foretelling? Does she have Fae Gifts?"

"We know she can cast shields and some defensive spells. I am hoping that we will learn more once we recover more of Rosie's memories."

"That wouldn't be enough to interest him. There must be something else." Philip frowned, then straightened.

"I will see what I can find out back in Faerie. It has been a long time since I visited my father's lands, but I still have connections there. I will reach out and let you know what I find."

Ciaran nodded to the younger Fae, who vanished.

"Philip will make it his mission to find her if he can," Connor said. "He is a good man, and the idea that he might have a sibling will drive him to protect her. He spent a lot of time with our family after he left his father. His father didn't find it worthwhile to come after him while he was with us. We are a much larger family and have a higher standing in the Courts. Plus, he knew that Philip would never do what he wanted easily. It wasn't worth the effort. We were able to help Philip recover from his father and become the person he is today."

"So this whole thing is about Sarah?" Rosie asked.

"It looks like it. Do you still want to recover the rest of your memories?" Ciaran asked.

Rosie nodded.

"Good. Then we will carry on tomorrow. For now, rest, and let's everyone focus on happier things for the rest of the day. Tomorrow we'll begin again."

23

Thursday was Claire's day in the stillroom again, so after Phillip left, Elizabeth went to get ready for a day with her eager apprentice. Claire arrived just as she was unlocking the stillroom door.

"Good morning, Liz! Making that calendula salve was fun. What are we doing today? Can we do a dry skin lotion? My mother asked if I would bring her some."

"Sure, that's easy. We can mix shea butter, coconut oil, and jojoba. Is it just dry skin, or is there anything else bothering your mom?"

"Just the dry skin. She says no matter how much water she drinks, her skin is dry."

"Hmm. Ok. Is there anything else bothering your mom right now?"

"No, I mean, just normal mom stuff. My brother is being a dick, but that's nothing new. He's fifteen and going through a phase. He's an Earth Witch, too, but not very strong. He's always been jealous of me, no matter what anyone says or does. He's never happy. He's gone all goth lately. It's driving my mom crazy."

Elizabeth smiled.

"Let's include a spell for balancing energies and a spell for calming.

Does she have any sensitivities to certain smells? We can add lavender oil to the lotion to help her relax."

"No, she loves lavender. That would be great. Thanks, Liz!"

They spent the next hour working on the lotion. The lotion itself didn't take too long to make, but Elizabeth wanted to see if Claire could come up with the spells independently and infuse them into the lotion herself.

"Make sure you focus on exactly the result you want. You are infusing the spell, and the lotion, with your will," the Potions Master told her apprentice.

Claire thought really hard for a few moments, her mouth turned down in a frown. She bit the end of her pencil while she thought.

"Ok. So, does it have to be two spells, or can I combine them into one?"

"Balance can be calming. But you are looking at two separate things here. You want to balance the energies in your mother's body while helping her to calm her mind. Each will affect the other, but it is best to create a separate spell for each purpose in this instance."

Claire nodded and began to write. She stopped, looked at what she had written, crossed a few things out, and added a few others. Finally, she was ready. She looked up at Elizabeth.

"Ok. Now, you are going to say your spells, one at a time. Hold the jar of lotion in your hands. Imagine the energy of the spell infusing through the whole jar of lotion. I see colors, so for me, it's easy to imagine the color of the spell infusing whatever I'm working on. You will find the way that works best for you."

Claire took a breath and began. She started with the spell for balance.

"My mother's skin is dry and tough
Balance her energies, so she has enough
Water to moisten, Earth for strength,
Fire for passion and Air at length."

. . .

Claire closed her eyes and imagined light blue energy infusing through the lotion. After a moment, she opened her eyes.

"I couldn't come up with a better rhyme for strength. Do you think it will work?"

"As long as you were keeping your mind on the result you wanted, it should be ok. We do the best we can. Try the calming spell, now."

Claire closed her eyes again and took another deep breath.

"My mother's mind is full of worry.
Bring her some calm in a hurry."

"Short and to the point. I like it," Elizabeth grinned. Claire smiled. She had seen a yellow light infuse the lotion this time. Like warm sunlight on a winter's day, streaming in the window, that you just wanted to curl up and fall asleep in.

"You can take that home and give it to your mom. Tell her to try just a little bit first, to see if it works, and make sure there are no adverse reactions. If all goes well, she can use it whenever she needs."

"Thank you! She'll be so happy."

Claire put the jar in her bag, then turned back to Elizabeth.

"Will we be doing any more advanced stuff? I've done things like this in class before. Not large scale, of course, but the Potions teacher at school is pretty good. Though he does have to follow the school curriculum and teach everyone, so he doesn't have a lot of time to help me get ahead. He lets me do my own thing sometimes."

"I need to see what you've learned so far and what your skills are. Let's take it slow for the first few weeks; then, we'll move on to harder things. My teaching style is most likely very different from your school teacher's, too, so you may learn new things from me, even if we are going over things that you've learned before."

Claire nodded. They got back to work.

On Friday, Michael had potions while Claire and Maia were at the store. Elizabeth had arranged for Magnus to bring Josh to meet Michael towards the end of the day to see if the boys could work well together.

Michael had a good head for potions. He was calm and exceedingly careful in his measurements and technique. The salve that he turned out, one for burns, was adequate but lacked the same vibrancy and power as Claire's. Elizabeth suspected that while Michael liked herbs, his natural talents might rest in another form of Earth magic.

Josh knocked on the door around three Friday afternoon.

Michael was just finishing putting a salve for cuts and bruises, containing oils infused with yarrow and plantain, into jars. He startled when he heard the knock, dropping the jar in his hand. Luckily, it landed on the old oak table and stayed in one piece.

Elizabeth opened the door and invited Josh and his teacher inside.

"Michael, this is my son, Joshua, and his Mentor, Magnus. Magnus is teaching Joshua about stone and metalworking with Earth magic. Josh is an Earth Mage too."

Magnus was sitting on Joshua's shoulder. He looked at Michael, his head on one side.

"What are you interested in, young man? When you are not practicing magic or doing your schoolwork, what do you do?"

"I like to read. I usually find somewhere to read in the woods. I find a tree or a nice rock to lean against. I lose track of time sometimes. I've gotten in trouble for coming home late."

Magnus looked at Elizabeth.

"He has a lot of energy built up. It's making him tired. He doesn't know how to release it properly. Some of it's draining when he sits on the Earth. But he needs a more creative outlet for it. It would do him good to be more active. On the days he is in the stillroom with you, I will take him after lunch, in addition to my regular time with him. Does that work for you?"

"Yes. I think you're right, Magnus. I think Michael would be happier working with you in metals and stone. He should still spend some time with me here to have a balanced idea of the scope of Earth Magic. Josh, you should spend some time here with me, too. Maybe you can work with me here at the same time as Michael, then Magnus will take both of you together afterward? It's good to know even the basic salves and compounds, in case you need to make them someday."

Magnus nodded.

"Will I work for you, too, Mr. Magnus?" Michael asked. "I won't have a lot of time left. I mean, I'm willing to do whatever you need. I am really grateful for the opportunity to learn from you both."

Elizabeth and Magnus looked at each other.

"How about you give me ten percent of the sales of anything you make and sell in the shop for the duration of our work together," the Gnome said to the young Earth Mage. "That way, we won't have to rework your schedule anymore. You need time to relax and have fun, too, you know."

"I can do that. Thank you."

MICHAEL CLEANED UP FROM THE DAY'S WORK, THEN MAGNUS TOOK the boys off to the smithy. Elizabeth locked up the stillroom and headed back to the house. She was thinking about what potions she wanted to carry in the shop and what the apprentices could help her make. Claire might be able to help with more of the advanced potions. Despite what Claire had told Elizabeth about the potions teacher at the local school, Elizabeth was beginning to suspect that the young man was not nearly as skilled as he could have been. Claire was so bright and could be learning so much more. Elizabeth was grateful that the girl had found her way to the shop.

Rosie was sitting in the kitchen with Mary, watching as the Brownie began preparations for the evening's meal.

"How did it go today, Rosie?" Elizabeth asked as she sat on a stool at the end of the island. She grabbed a cookie from the plate set in the middle.

"It was amazing! Ciaran and Nathaniel are very good at what they do. I remember everything, now. That Daffydd, he tried to stop Sarah from forming the team. He wanted her to return to Faery and work with him. When she wouldn't leave the Council, he seemed to back off for a bit. Then, just before Sarah vanished, Daffydd came back. I guess he felt he'd waited long enough. He changed my memories around the last month of Sarah's life and her death. He made me think I'd sent out the notices when I hadn't. Sarah had stayed at the Council after the team broke up. She ran a few other teams for a while, none as close as we had been, though. She was very good at her job."

"You mean you were," Madelynn said, coming in and snagging a cookie for herself. She looked at Mary.

"If you ever want a change, you can come work for me in my restaurant," she joked.

Mary smiled. "My place is here. But that's very kind of you to say."

Madelynn grinned.

"What did he change about the last month of Sarah's life?" Elizabeth asked.

"He made me think she was married and that the person who reported her death was her husband. Even though I knew Sarah never dated."

"And no one ever questioned it?"

"Sarah was very private. She never talked about her home life. She took the whole work/life separation thing very seriously. We all learned not to ask her about it after a while."

"If I had a homicidal psychopath for a father, I'd want to hide it, too," Elizabeth said.

"Was there anything important that you remembered?"

Rosie shook her head.

"It seems to be mostly his visits and the misinformation around her death."

"Well, I'm glad you have your memories back. I was kind of hoping there would be more, though. We still don't have very much to go on."

"I know. I'm sorry about that," Rosie said.

Madelynn swallowed a bite of cookie.

"What could he possibly want Sarah for that is so important that he would do this, that he would kill to convince her to do it?"

Madelynn asked the question again after dinner when the team gathered again by video conference. Mayenne was absent, as it was too early in the morning in France. Elise would report to her later.

"That's an excellent question," Sean said. "I think that the young man, Philip, has a point. Sarah must have a Gift that Daffydd wants to exploit in some way. Is there any way we can find out what that Gift is?"

"Sarah never used magic where anyone could see her unless she was defending herself or someone else. And I never saw anything other than basic defensive magic," Rosie said. She was feeling like a failure for not being able to provide more helpful information.

"You never saw her exhibit the Foretelling? Not even when Alice died?" Elizabeth asked.

Rosie shook her head.

"Sarah was out of town when Alice died. She was supposed to be at an S.O.C. conference in Europe."

"She didn't take you with her?"

"She left me to run the team. She came back as soon as she heard what had happened."

"So you had a way to communicate with her?"

"We used mirrors."

"And you never saw anything in the mirror that might help?" Sean asked.

Rosie shook her head again.

"Now that we know Sarah is alive, has anyone tried to reach her through the mirrors?" Elizabeth asked.

Everyone looked at each other, then shook their heads. The members of the team all seemed thoroughly embarrassed.

"It didn't even occur to me," Elise said. "Some Enforcer I am."

Madelynn went over to the mirror on the back wall of the sitting room. She placed her hand on the frame and focused. After a moment, she shook her head, turning back to the group watching her.

"I suggest that we keep trying," Sean said. "Even if Daffydd is keeping her away from mirrors, unless he's keeping her somewhere and not letting her out, she'll come into range of a mirror, eventually. Meanwhile, we'll check in with Connor every day. Hopefully, Philip will find something. Lukas, were you able to find anything more in Sarah's files at the S.O.C?"

Lukas shook his head.

"I looked at every trace of information about her that has ever been online," Roger said. He was standing near the door to the stairs, leaning against the wall. "There was nothing new. Sarah was very good at covering her tracks. She really didn't want people knowing very much about her."

"Can we look into her family's histories, on both sides, and see if we can figure out her Gifts that way?" Loraine asked.

"That's a good idea. Connor would be the best person to look into that," Lorien said. "I will ask him."

"Well, I guess that's our next step," Sean said. He looked around the room, eyes settling on Carl, who was hunched over, arms resting on his knees. Carl hadn't talked much since Madelynn and Sharalee had dragged him back with them.

"Loraine, make sure Samantha and her family are protected. The rest of us, increase your personal wards and the wards and protections around your families, homes, and businesses. I am going to have our local Witches add extra protections to my Pack lands. Maddie, can you protect Tilly and her family?"

Madelynn nodded.

"We will all protect Mathilda and her family," Aunt Gloria said. Elizabeth nodded.

"I will add extra protections to the land here and have my parents strengthen theirs as well. Oh, and Lucy's family too." Elizabeth said. "If he can't reach one of you directly, he may go for other members of your families. I'm making sure mine is protected."

"He may not strike again. He may have pushed Sarah over the edge, killing so many of us," Loraine said. "Sarah would never back down, but she would do her best to protect us. Maybe we should be looking for Daffydd's corpse."

"I think Sarah would have come home if that were the case," Rosie said. "She would have come back to apologize for the deaths, and to make it right, as much as possible. Not that it's at all possible, but she would want to see the rest of us and set the record straight."

There was a moment of quiet.

"Well, I have Pack business to attend to before I can sleep," Sean said. "Lor, let us know what you hear from Connor. Lori, make sure that Samantha is protected. Everyone else, stay safe. We'll talk again in a few days."

24

Elizabeth's first date with Jonah had gone well. They discovered that they still enjoyed each other's company and had made plans to do it again the following week. Elizabeth still wasn't sure she wanted another relationship just yet, but it was nice to go out with an old friend. At least she already knew he was a good person.

Elizabeth's week was filled with potion making with her apprentices and work on the shop. Morgan was carrying most of the work for the shop, so Elizabeth could focus on the apprentices and building up stock for the apothecary part of Samara's Garden.

Philip had not found Sarah yet. He had spoken to his contacts on his father's estate. They told him she had been there in the past but had been moved five years ago, just as the deaths started up again. Daffydd was rarely at the estate now, and no one knew where he was spending most of his time. He had not been seen at Court for months.

"Which makes me think things are not going his way right now," Connor said with a grim smile as he talked with Lorien through the mirror one night. "Daffydd was always one to make sure he was seen at Court, making alliances and working to further his own interests. He has let most of those alliances go over the last year. No one is admitting to having seen him recently. I have informed Their Majesties of what is going on. Ciaran backed me up, so they know I'm not just trying to cause trouble. Her Majesty the Queen is furious that Daffydd might have been holding Sarah prisoner for so long and has ordered her own investigation. If nothing turns up soon, she may call in the Guardians. The Court has an alliance with them now. With the Dragons, and the Phoenyxes as well."

Lorien blinked.

"I have been tucked away in my corner of Faerie for too long. Apparently, I have missed a few things," the tall Aes Sídhe said.

Connor smiled.

"An alliance has been formed between Faerie, the Earth Realm supernaturals, the Merfolk, the Dragons, and the Phoenyxes, all because of a family of Witches on the West Coast. The Caseys. A child of their line is the new wielder of the Sword of Fire. What have you been up to that you've missed all of this, man? It's been the talk of both Courts for months now. Both Courts are part of the alliance. The Caseys and their friends saved children from both Courts, and now the Courts are indebted to them forever."

"I remember hearing that the Royal Children were found. I was in the middle of building a home for a friend and wasn't paying much attention to anything else. I shall have to catch up," Lorien said. "If the Guardians get involved, Daffydd best hope he is never found. Otherwise, a Dragon might eat him for lunch."

"He'd give them indigestion," Connor said. He made a face. Then he grinned. "Seeing one eat him would please me, however. I wonder if I can offer my services to them in finding him in return for being there when they catch him."

ELIZABETH RESTED HER BIKE AGAINST THE SIDE OF THE HOUSE AND let herself into her mother's kitchen.

Nora turned from the stove to hug her eldest daughter.

"Hello, Sweetheart! It's so nice to see you. How is everything going with the shop?"

"The shop is doing great. It's ready to open. We're going to have a little opening celebration this weekend. Do you think anyone will come?"

Nora rolled her eyes.

"Elizabeth, *of course,* people will come. The whole *town* will come. It's been too long since we've had our own bookstore and apothecary. Gloria sold her potions out of the stillroom. It will be a blessing to be able to get them in town now. And *everyone* wants to see what you've done with the store. How are you advertising the opening?"

"We just put a sign in the window," Elizabeth said. She was feeling a little foolish. She had forgotten the draw of something new in a small town, living away from home for so long.

"Don't worry; I'll take care of it. Has Morgan planned a menu for the opening yet? I would suggest plenty of free samples, as well as your regular menu items. Maybe you should have free potion samples, too? Of some of the more generic ones, of course. And maybe a raffle in the bookstore. Have a couple, or several, prize baskets people can choose to spend their raffle tickets on. Make part of the proceeds of the raffle go to a good cause. The Familiar Sanctuary, maybe."

Elizabeth stared at her mother.

"You're really good at this, Mom. Do you want a job as our marketing manager?" She grinned.

"I'd be delighted to help plan special events for the shop," Nora replied. "At the very least, you should have holiday specials. Maybe make the staff's birthdays into special events, too. Celebrations are always good for business."

Elizabeth shook her head, smiling.

"Well, welcome to the team," she reached out and shook her mother's hands.

Nora grinned.

"I'll expect ten percent of all profits on the celebration days," she told her daughter.

Elizabeth rolled her eyes and agreed.

"So, Mom, there was another reason I came to see you. I was wondering what you thought of our school's current teachers. I've noticed that my apprentices are way behind where they should be in even basic herbal knowledge and preparation skills. It says something for Claire's enthusiasm and draw to plants that she's as far along as she is. The other two, it's like they're starting from scratch. I know our school is a public high school, but they do offer electives so the kids can get more experience in their Gifts, or at least, they used to. I mean, what's going on? I'm worried about Maddie and Josh starting school there in the fall."

Nora sighed and sat down at the table, across from her daughter.

"Our local school has gone through several principles since you left—some better than others. The current principal is more about keeping up with the mortal world than making sure magical children get the training they need in their Gifts. He says that should be the parent's job. That they can choose to attend a magical college afterward to learn more about being magical. Never mind that by doing so, he's not preparing the students to get into or attend a magical college or university. Many of our children in the last ten years have ended up studying on their own, taking extra classes somewhere else, or going to mortal schools and trying to fit in. It's not ideal, but the principal is the mayor's brother-in-law and shows no sign of wanting to leave his position."

"So he gets away with hiring substandard teachers?" Elizabeth couldn't believe what she was hearing.

"The potions teacher is his nephew on his side of the family. His sister's child. He was floundering until his mother got him the job here. And because he's family, the principal won't fire him, even though many in town have complained."

"Are the other teachers as bad?"

"Some of the teachers have been there for many years and are very good at their jobs. It's the ones hired since Principal Jones took over that are less than ideal."

Elizabeth sat back in her chair.

"Mom, I can't have Maddie and Josh getting a substandard education, especially with how strong their Gifts are. This makes me doubly glad that Mags and Magnus have taken them on as students."

"I know. I was very relieved when you told me," Nora agreed.

"This isn't fair to our children," Elizabeth said.

"I know, Sweetheart. Lucy's children are in the same boat. Marc gets extra teaching from us, and Lucy has arranged extra help for Louisa and Timothy as well. Many of the parents have banded together to teach the children what they can. But it's not ideal."

"I just moved us home. I don't want to move again to find the children a better school." Elizabeth's mind was going a mile a minute.

"Has anyone tried organizing the parents? Drawn up a petition?"

"It's been done. Nothing ever happens."

"And no one's appealed to the Supernatural Oversight Council? Or the Witch's Council? Or the Shifter Council?"

"The individual Councils have said they will look into it, but they are moving very slowly. And since the children are still getting an education, enough to get them into at least some third-level schools and training programs, it's not really on their radar. Especially since they know that the families who care are doing their best to make sure to get their children the training they need outside of the school."

"But they shouldn't have to!" Elizabeth exclaimed.

"I know, dear. I agree with you."

"Didn't Thomas say that there was a new Academy in California that taught everyone, regardless of race? Are the children that go there getting the training they need?"

"Yes, I believe they are, but you're not thinking of moving there, Elizabeth? You've only just come home! The town needs their Potion Master, and your family needs you."

"I was wondering what we'd have to do to get the Academy to set up a branch here," Elizabeth said.

Nora tilted her head to the side.

"You know, that's not a bad idea. We're not the only local paranormal school with issues. And there isn't a good Academy around here. The nearest branch is in Massachusetts, and most families don't want to send their children so far away. Especially the younger ones."

"I'd like to know more about the Academy in Valerian's Cove," Elizabeth said.

"Ask Thomas or that nice Aes Sídhe that was here to help Rosie. He has connections to that area, doesn't he?"

As soon as Elizabeth got home that evening, she called Siofra through the mirror. She remembered that Siofra and Nathaniel had moved to Valerian's Cove because of Siofra's project with Brendan Casey of Casey's Nurseries.

Siofra answered immediately.

"Hi, Elizabeth! You just caught me at the right time. Dervla is sleeping. That's the only time I really have to speak to people without interruption. What can I do for you?"

"I was hoping that you could tell me more about the Academy in Valerian's Cove? My brother-in-law, Thomas, was telling me a little about it. That it had expanded to take in more magical beings. I am becoming increasingly worried about our school here and am looking at all the options."

"What's wrong with the school in Fairweather Falls?"

"The principle's focus is on academics over magic, and the children are leaving unprepared for living in the paranormal world. Many of them don't get into further paranormal education. This isn't a mortal school, where reducing the arts curriculum is horrible but isn't usually life-threatening. This is magic. Without the proper training that the school is supposed to supply, things could go horribly wrong."

Siofra blinked.

"Even the mundane public school here in Valerian's Cove is better than that. We care too much about our children to not give them the best training we can. And now that the Academy is open to all magicals, not just those who can pay the Academy fees, it's getting even better. They are even accepting mortal students now. They see it as important that everyone learn together, saying that everyone has something to offer, which is completely true. And the more we work together from a young age, the better off we all will be. Some choose the local public schools, and that's fine. Everyone still gets the training they need. Hasn't anyone done anything to try to change things in your school?"

"My mother says they have, but the principal is the mayor's brother-in-law, and nothing gets done. And the Councils are dragging their heels about getting involved because the kids are getting some education, and their parents are doing their best to make up the difference. So it's not seen as a real problem."

Siofra shook her head.

"Our children's education is a concern to everyone. Are you thinking of sending your children here? We would look after them. They would be among good people. If you wanted to move here yourself, we would be thrilled to have you."

Elizabeth shook her head.

"I just moved us here. I don't want to move again. I was wondering what it would take for us to get a branch of the Academy like the Valerian's Cove Academy here."

Siofra was quiet for a moment.

"I know that Brendan Casey and Maria Hemenway, the Academy Headmistress here, were thinking about expanding. Other branches of the Academy have been interested in what we are doing here and have started to alter their curriculums as well. Where is the nearest Academy to you?"

"It's several hours away. Most people don't want to send their children so far away, especially the younger ones."

"Then it sounds like it would be good to have a branch of the Academy near Fairweather Falls. Do you think there would be enough interest in the area to support it?"

"There are a lot of Havens around here. And we have a portal here. So people could come from further away. Though I guess the same could be said for our children going to the Academy in Boston, but, as I said, few here want to send their children down south."

"Have you approached the S.O.C. about the problem yet? They would have to approve a new branch of the Academy."

"Not yet. I've only just begun looking into this."

"Ok. Let me talk to Brendan and Maria here, and maybe Aldona. Aldona is the Crown Princess of the Fire Mountain Dragon Clan. I know she helped get the S.O.C. to approve the curriculum change with the current Academy here. Maybe they can give you a copy of the plan they came up with to get things started."

"I appreciate it, Siofra."

"Of course. Also, why don't you talk to people in Fairweather Falls and see what kind of support you can get for the idea of a branch of the Academy in your town."

Elizabeth agreed and signed off. She had a lot of thinking to do. The opening of Samara's Garden would be the perfect time and place to sound out the townsfolk about their feelings on the school.

25

Friday night, Jonah took Elizabeth to a lovely restaurant in Silver Falls, two Havens over. They went through the portal, arriving on the town green under a canopy of trees. The little grove sat in the center of the town square, protecting the portal. The portal system was still relatively new, the Dragons who ran it still expanding their reach. Most Havens had them by now.

The restaurant Jonah had chosen was called the Silver Birch, and it was beautiful. There were plants everywhere, with soft lighting, including fairy lights strung all along the patio that hosted outdoor dining year-round. Even in winter in Maine. Magic was wonderful. A dome of magic covered the deck, keeping it the perfect temperature in every season. A snowstorm could happen outside the dome while diners enjoyed their food and watched from the warmth and safety inside.

The hostess led Jonah and Elizabeth to a table at the patio's edge, next to a beautiful garden. The restaurant was at the edge of town and sat on a quarter-acre of its own land. Gardens had been carefully tended all around it.

A server brought them menus and a breadbasket, then left them, promising to return to take their order.

Elizabeth looked over the menu with rising excitement.

"This is amazing! There are so many things! Oh, wow. Look at that pasta primavera! There are Fae vegetables in there!"

Jonah smiled at her. He was watching her more than paying attention to his own menu.

"This is Madelynn's restaurant. Since she's in Fairweather Falls until the current situation is figured out, her niece, Shelley, is in charge here. Madelynn thought you might like it. She suggested I bring you here."

"I do like it very much. If this is Madelynn's place, then I'm sure the food is fabulous. What are you going to get?"

They ordered their food, then sat back to wait.

"No news yet on finding Sarah?" Jonah asked.

Elizabeth shook her head.

"Not yet. It's a good thing I have so much else going on, or I'd be worrying about it all the time."

She filled Jonah in on the situation with the school and her hopes for a branch of the Academy in Fairweather Falls.

"I think that's a brilliant idea," Jonah said. "I know I've heard a lot of parents complain about the current school and wish the Academy had a branch nearby. How can I help you?"

"I need to get an idea of the kind of support the idea could have in town. It would be an enormous change for everyone. There would be more people in town, meaning more traffic. But our children would get the best magical education they could get. I'm hoping to talk to people at the opening tomorrow."

"I'll help," Jonah said. "Do you have an interest sheet parents could sign? Something to collect names and show support?"

"That's a great idea. I'll make one up tonight."

"Why not ask Robin to do it? She could make it look all official."

"I'll call her as soon as I get home."

"Take a minute and call her now. It might be late by the time you get home."

Elizabeth grinned at her date and stepped outside for a few minutes. When she returned, the food was on the table.

"I see the old trick of leaving the table to hurry the food up still works," she grinned.

Jonah grinned back.

"Robin will have something ready by the opening tomorrow. That was a great idea, Jonah. She's excited, too. She says she'll be the first person to sign, and she'll make her husband sign too. And her parents. Her children attend the local school, and she's part of the parent group trying to take up the slack."

"I wonder why no one has ever asked the Academy to open a branch here before," Jonah said.

"I think they have, but I don't know why it never happened. Anyway, I hope it works this time. I really don't want to send my children to Boston or Valerian's Cove. Even with the portal. I want to keep them at home for as long as possible."

ROBIN BROUGHT THE PETITION WITH HER THE FOLLOWING DAY, along with several clipboards and jars of pens. True to her word, every adult in Robin's family had signed already.

"Sheila and Don will be here later this morning. They said they would sign then," Robin said, speaking of her husband's parents.

At ten, Elizabeth opened the door to the shop. There was already a line of people waiting outside to come in. Soon Samara's Garden was packed, people browsing the books and the apothecary and filling the tables in the cafe. Morgan, Meg, and the apprentices, who were all in the shop that day for the special opening, were all running about helping customers while Elizabeth operated the register and talked to those coming in.

Nora appeared next to Elizabeth around lunchtime. She had a mug of tea and a cookie in her hand.

"Well, this is certainly a success. Morgan has had to refill the trays of samples several times already in the cafe. How is the raffle going?"

Elizabeth nodded to the jars holding tickets on the table to the right of the register. There were five baskets filled with goods from the shop set out. The jars were already overflowing with tickets.

"You really made this an awesome event, Mom. Thank you."

Robin popped up in front of the register.

"I just filled another clipboard! I think every adult here and many of the teenagers, who probably just came for the free food, have signed the statement of interest. Several people have offered to do whatever they can to help make it a reality. They really want a branch of the Academy here. Everyone is fed up with nothing getting done about the public school."

A short, brown-haired young man with glasses snorted as he overheard what Robin was saying.

He turned and left the store, stuffing a cookie into his mouth as he went.

"That's the potions teacher," Robin told Elizabeth. Elizabeth stared after the man as he passed in front of the window towards the market.

By the end of the day, all the samples were gone, the cafe was empty of food, and they had sold out of many of the potions in the apothecary. Even the bookstore had seen an overwhelming number of sales. Elizabeth collapsed into a chair in the cafe after locking the doors. Morgan and the apprentices were seated around her. They were all exhausted. Maia looked ready to drop. Her head was on her arms on the table in front of her. Elizabeth wondered if the young girl had actually fallen asleep.

"I think that was an outstanding first day," Elizabeth told her staff. "I'm happy that tomorrow is Sunday, and we have a late start. I'll need to spend a lot of time in the stillroom to replenish the stock. Already."

"I'm glad I had enough food to get through the day," Morgan said. She smiled at Meg, who had stayed to help the entire day through. "I couldn't have done it without you, Meg. You're a blessing to us all."

"I had fun, Sweetheart. This was a wonderful day. I'm glad it went so well. Congratulations, everyone."

"Maia, since you missed your day in the stillroom today, if you want to come by tomorrow, I would love your help," Elizabeth said.

Maia raised her head.

"Can I spend all of my time in the stillroom with you? I don't think I'm cut out for customer service. I kept freezing when people asked me questions, even when I knew the answer."

Elizabeth looked hard at her youngest apprentice. Maia was a much more quiet person than the other two. She was also younger. And she did have a touch for the potions.

"I think we can work it out. I would have to hire more help for the mornings when you guys go back to school in the fall, anyway. I think it would do you good to work in the store at least one day a week, but you can work with me the other days. That means that there will be three of us in the stillroom on the other days. We'll get a lot more done. And it looks like we are going to need it." She paused.

"How did the rest of you feel about the day?"

"I loved it!" Claire exclaimed. "I'm exhausted, but it was so much fun! I can pick up Maia's store shifts on Tuesday and Friday. I would enjoy working more in the store. If that would help?"

"That might work. Michael, how do you feel about all of this?"

"It was fun. I'm exhausted, too, but it's a good tired, you know? Most people were really nice about everything. I got a lot of compliments on our uniforms and the food. I can take full days Thursday if that helps."

Morgan looked up.

"I think we'll have to hire another full-time person anyway, Liz. I was rushed off my feet in the cafe. We need someone making more food in the back and someone floating between all the sections helping out. I want to bake and be the manager, but I'm not sure even I can handle it all. We need more help."

"Well, it's good we know it now. Ok. Morgan, you're still manager. You need to be able to go out front when needed. Maybe you do most of the food prep in the early morning with whoever we hire for the cafe, and then they stay in the kitchen making whatever is needed during the day to your recipes. We'll have the apprentice of the day man the register for the cafe and apothecary, and you can be out front in the bookstore. Or the other way around, whichever works out best. Try it both ways for a week and see what suits everyone. We may need to hire two extra people. One to help in the kitchen, and another counter or salesperson. Running a shop is more work than I thought!" Elizabeth smiled. She got back smiles all around in return.

⁂ 26 ⁂

Elizabeth had brunch with her family Sunday morning at her parents' house, then left the kids there while she headed home to get to work brewing more potions. Maia would be over around one o'clock to help.

As she was heading around the back of the house, her phone rang. She took it out of her pocket, blessing all Techno-Mages as she did so.

"Hey Rob, what's up?"

"Oh my gosh, Elizabeth, you must be so happy with how yesterday went! The store was packed all day! I bet you made a ton of sales."

Elizabeth smiled.

"Yeah, we did. I'm going to have to hire two more assistants and spend more time in the stillroom. One of my apprentices will be with me full time making potions. She discovered she really doesn't like customer service or being around people so much. But she's got a real talent for potions-making, so I'll keep her here with me."

"That's so great. You're awesome at figuring out what people need and how to make things work out. Guess what? We got over *three thousand* signatures yesterday on the petition! Can you believe it? I didn't even realize we had that many people in town! Some must have come from the other Havens. This is so cool! I think we have a real chance of getting the Supernatural Oversight Council to listen to us and allow a branch of the Academy here."

"That's great, Robin. Thank you so much for putting all of that together for us. I really appreciate it." Elizabeth sighed. Getting a branch of the Academy here was another thing on her quickly filling plate. She was grateful for any help she could get.

"Robin, would you want to take on designing a presentation to the Council? I feel it's absolutely vital, but I don't know how I'll find the time right away, and it needs to happen as soon as possible. It's already almost July. Even with magic, getting an Academy branch set up here before school starts in the fall will be challenging. And you have a better idea of what the current school is like, how bad it is. You can be more convincing on how much we really, really need the Academy here."

"I guess I could. I don't know why I didn't do it before. I mean, I know I've been frustrated with the way things are. So has every other parent I've talked to. I could do it."

"Thank you. Siofra will get me a copy of the plan that Crown Princess Drake and Brendan Casey presented to the Council for the Valerian's Cove Academy. Maybe it will help you with a plan for here. I'll let you know as soon as I have it."

"That's good. Maybe we can have a brainstorming session, see what everyone thinks we need most. Make it a town-wide event. I can rent the meeting house. We'll need fliers. It's Sunday today. Would Tuesday night be too soon? Or Wednesday. Let's say Wednesday. That gives us enough time to make sure everyone hears about it and has time to make plans so they can come."

Elizabeth grinned to herself as Robin did her own brainstorming at the other end of the phone.

"Rob, I need to go make stuff. I'll bring you the plan as soon as I get it, ok? Let's plan a girl's night out this week. You pick the day."

"Let's do it Friday. We can process the meeting together and anything else going on in our lives. Ok, that sounds great. I'll let Sarah and Sandra know. Have fun in the stillroom! I'll let you know how the planning goes." Robin disconnected the call.

Elizabeth shook her head as she unlocked the door to the still-room. Robin had always been driven like that. Give her an idea she could get behind, and she would run with it full steam ahead. Elizabeth wished she had some of that energy sometimes. She selected the herbs and crystals needed for the first batch of potions and got to work.

SIOFRA WAS SITTING IN THE KITCHEN AGAIN WHEN ELIZABETH AND Maia shuffled inside after a long afternoon brewing potions. Mary sat them at the island in the kitchen and handed each of them a mug of peppermint tea and a plate of shortbread cookies. With cinnamon on top.

Siofra grinned at them both.

"Hard day at work, ladies?"

"Maia, this is Siofra MacNamara-Brooke. She's partners with Brendan Casey of Casey's Nurseries in a venture to bring Fae plants to the Earth Realm. She's helping with getting a branch of the Academy here so you guys can finally get the magical education you need. Siofra, this is Maia, one of my apprentices. She's very good at potions. At some point, I would like to bring my apprentices to see the greenhouses at Casey's Nurseries. I want to see the Fae plants, myself."

"That's a fabulous idea. You could visit our Academy as well, and get a feel for it. Get some ideas for what you might want here. Hi, Maia. It's nice to meet you." Siofra smiled at the young Witch.

Maia smiled back.

"Where's Dervla today? Is Nathaniel watching her?" Elizabeth asked.

Siofra shook her head.

"Malia Casey-Gianetti's got her. She has a pair of twins the same age as Dervla. So does her twin, Marissa Casey-Thorndike. And we have a Phoenyx baby the same age, too. Keya Rose. We have a play-group set up once a week. We rotate which parent is in charge. It gives the rest of us a day off. So today is Malia's day to host. Malia is the mate of the Alpha of the Wolf Shifters in Valerian's Cove. They have a large house with an enormous garden. She also has two older sets of twins to help out. One set's hers, the other she and Tony are fostering. They're fine without me. We often take this time to get stuff done if it's not our day to host."

"That sounds like a brilliant arrangement," Mary said.

"It really is. Liz, you should come visit soon. I'd love to show you around Valerian's Cove."

Elizabeth tugged on her braid. It was something she did when she was thinking.

"I put my friend Robin in charge of making the presentation about the Academy to the S.O.C. She should come with us to see the Valerian's Cove Academy. Let me see what I can arrange. I want to bring all my apprentices, but I can't leave Morgan alone in the store. And I desperately need to create more potions. Our grand opening wiped us out."

"That's good, right?" Siofra said.

"It's great for the bottom line, but it means I will need to double production to keep inventory in stock."

"Would you consider selling things from other Potions Masters? I can contribute Fae potions, and Suzette Rousseau-Gianetti, Malia's cousin, is a Potions Master too. She graduated last year and has been working with the Potions Master at the Academy and at the Valerian's Cove Clinic as a Healer. Maybe you make some special potions specific to you, and we each contribute, too? I imagine your apprentices will contribute, too, once they are up to scratch? And you could make special orders yourself. That would free you up quite a bit. I have stock already available of certain Fae-specific things. You have a fairly strong Fae population here, don't you? Do you know how to make our potions?"

Elizabeth blinked. She hadn't even thought about that. Of course, there would be some Fae potions she couldn't make. She wouldn't even know what they were because that wasn't a part of her training. She wouldn't even know to ask about them unless something specific came up. Having Fae potions on hand would be a tremendous benefit to the community.

"That's a fabulous idea, Siofra. I would love to sell your potions. What kind of deal would you want?"

"Seventy-thirty? Would that cover overhead for you?"

"That would be fine. I look forward to doing business with you." Elizabeth smiled at the Aes Sídhe and held out her hand.

"When can I expect the first shipment?"

"What are the main Fae races here in Fairweather Falls?"

"Aes Sídhe, Brùnaigh, Gnomes, a few Trolls, Dryads and Pixies," Mary said.

Siofra nodded.

"I have most of the potions relating to those groups in stock already at the Casey's. I do most of my brewing there, now. However, I do still have my shop back home in Faerie as well. Though I mostly let my manager run that now. I send her potions when needed. She's an excellent Potions Master herself, so I trust her to make many of the things for that store. I can get you a shipment tomorrow."

"Why don't I bring Claire, the apprentice who is supposed to be brewing with me tomorrow, and visit Valerian's Cove? I can bring Robin too. Maybe I can meet Suzette? It would be great if I had more time to focus on the apprentices and my own children and life. It would certainly take a load off."

"No more cracking the whip in desperation. Life is meant to be enjoyed," Mary said with a smile.

Siofra grinned.

"Sounds good. Bring this young lady and any other apprentices you have as soon as you can. They will love the greenhouses at the Nursery."

"I'll bring Michael on Tuesday and Maia here on Wednesday if that's ok. If I have stock from Suzette, that will help us catch back up, so missing three days of brewing won't be so bad."

Siofra stood.

"Then I will let Suzette know. I'll see you tomorrow, Liz!"

Siofra vanished. Maia blinked.

"I really get to visit Valerian's Cove?"

Elizabeth made arrangements with Robin and got permission from the apprentices' parents' for the trips. Monday morning Elizabeth and Claire worked in the stillroom until lunchtime, then, after a quick meal, headed to the portal in town. Robin met them there. Stepping through the portal, the three women arrived in Valerian's Cove at ten in the morning. The Valerian's Cove portal was just outside the town proper. The friendly Dragon who ran it wished them well and a pleasant visit and gave them directions to the Casey's.

The three looked around as they stepped out of the portal area. Just to their left, at the start of the town center, was an ice cream shop. There were pink awnings and umbrellas providing shade, and the tables were set out, ready for customers. The sign above the gate proclaimed it *The Sweet Delight Ice Cream Shoppe.*

All three women looked at the shop for a long minute, then at each other.

"Oh, yes," they all said in unison.

"After we meet with Siofra and Suzette," Elizabeth said. "Remember, it's only ten in the morning here. We'll get an extra lunch if we're lucky. Then definitely, ice cream."

They turned right and walked up the road. Before too long, the women came to a sign that read 'Casey's Nursery and Garden Center.' They turned into the drive.

Apple trees lined the drive to the garden center. As they neared the end, they could see a building off to the right, surrounded by plants and gardens. A large white Victorian-style house with a wrap-around porch sat back and to the left, at the end of the drive. Behind the closer building that held the garden center, they could see the tops of the greenhouses rising.

"Let's go into the nursery. We'll ask them where we can find Siofra there," Elizabeth said.

A Witch with long, curly brown hair pulled up into a messy bun on her head was at the cash register. She smiled at them as they entered the shop.

"Hello! I'm Celine Benoit-Casey. Welcome to our home and shop. Are you Elizabeth, Robin, and Claire from Fairweather Falls? Siofra is back in the greenhouse with my husband, Brendan. I'll take you to them."

Celine called out to another Witch, who came and took over the counter.

Celine led the way through the building and out the back.

"Now, I know that you, Elizabeth and Claire, will probably want to get lost in here for hours, but it's my understanding that you are planning on visiting the Academy today as well. You can always come back again for more visits. We're happy to have you. I'll give you two hours. After lunch, Brendan will take you to the Academy. He has an afternoon class today, anyway. He's teaching a few classes for summer school for those who might need to catch up a little. He's the head Professor of Magical History there. He'll introduce you to the Potions Master there and to Maria Hemenway, the Headmistress."

Celine opened the door to a very large greenhouse with high, vaulted ceilings. Magic was wonderful at creating things that wouldn't otherwise be easy or possible. Birds flew overhead, some with brilliant plumage unlike anything seen in the wild on Earth. Other strange noises suggested there were more creatures calling the greenhouse home as well.

The little group found Brendan, Siofra, and Suzette in the middle of the greenhouse. They were looking over several trays of seedlings and a few potted plants. Brendan was making entries on a tablet on the table in front of him.

Celine clapped her hands as they approached. All three gardeners jumped.

Brendan smiled and came around the table to embrace Celine. He kissed the top of her head, then, keeping an arm around her, held out his hand to Elizabeth.

"I'm Brendan Casey. It's nice to meet you, Ms. Sloan. I've done business with your mother for years. I've been trying to get her out here as well. Maybe she could come with you next time?"

"She'd love to. She wants to see the Fae plants. And now that I've seen this greenhouse, you'll have to lock her out. You won't be able to keep her away. She'll want some of these plants for her own gardens. We have a large Fae population in Fairweather Falls, as I'm sure Siofra's told you. It would be great to be able to supply the plants as well as potions."

Siofra and Brendan looked at each other. Brendan raised an eyebrow.

"We don't have a branch of Casey Nurseries in Maine," Brendan said. "I think my parents intended to have one on the East Coast, but Saoirse wanted to go back to Ireland with them, and they didn't want to let anyone else run it. I would trust Nora Sloan-O'Brien. Maybe not a full Casey Nursery, but an addition to her gardens, with credit to us somehow? Maybe she becomes the East Coast supplier for our plants?"

"Like a franchise?"

"No, it would still be her own business. She has a good name for herself already, and she already carries some of our regular plants. But as a specialty part of the business. We could just sell them to her, I suppose. But she'd have to learn how to care for them, and she'd have to be willing to build a greenhouse like this for them."

"Maybe have her hire a Fae Earth Mage with plants as their focus to help?"

"And they would work for her, not us. But she would be the sole supplier of our plants on the East Coast. I suppose we could work it out. Do you think she would like that?" Brendan turned to Elizabeth.

"I think you need to talk to my mother herself," Elizabeth answered. "I'll make sure that she gets in touch and visits you soon."

Brendan and Siofra showed the group around the greenhouse, telling them a little about the plants and wildlife they had there as they went. A large bird, about the size of a Macaw, with brilliant red and gold plumage and a long tail, landed on Siofra's shoulder as they walked along.

"This is my familiar, Amaia. She's a firebird. They're not the same as Pheonyxes. More like a distant cousin. She's beautiful, isn't she? Firebirds don't shift to human."

Claire stroked the beautiful bird's head, running her hand down the bird's back as she did so. Amaia closed her eyes and trilled.

"That's her happy sound. She likes you," the Aes Sídhe told the young Witch. Claire blushed.

Brendan chose them each a little plant and had them all pick pots they liked. They replanted them as gifts to take home.

"Now, it's close to lunchtime, and Celine will get cranky and send someone after us if we're not out of here on time," Brendan said.

They all washed their hands at the sink on the wall of the greenhouse.

Brendan led the way outside and across the grass to the back of the big old Victorian house.

"My family has lived here for five generations since the first Valerian arrived in the Cove," Brendan said. "My parents retired home to Ireland almost thirty years ago now. They run a branch of the nursery over there, along with selling organic fruits and vegetables and handmade soaps, cheese, and yogurts. My sister Saoirse works with them, with her husband Kevin and son Declan, though Declan's passion is music. He may be moving on soon."

Celine had laid out food on the picnic tables on the patio at the back of the house. Several teenagers were helping her set out plates and utensils.

"Everyone, this is our daughter, Shari-Beth Meyer-Casey, and her friends Emma, Joshua, and Micah."

Everyone introduced themselves.

"My son's name is Joshua, too," Elizabeth said. "He's fifteen. How old are you?"

"We're all eighteen."

"My Josh is an Earth Mage. He's just learning how to use his powers. We lived in a human town while he was younger. It wasn't safe for him to use them there. I'm hoping we can get a branch of the Academy in our town this year. Our current school is a little light on magical education, even though it's in a Haven. Do you all go to the Academy here?"

"Yes, we do," Shari-Beth said. "Our family was responsible for a lot of the changes in the Academy here. We're related to Dragons, Phoenyxes, and Fae, and we needed training in the Gifts that came with that. Luckily, we had some very good friends, and the Headmistress and the S.O.C. were open to the changes. It turns out the Headmistress is part Fae, too, and never got the training she needed in her Fae Gifts. She's getting it now. It's really cool to see her as excited as any of us when she learns something new," Shari-Beth grinned.

Elizabeth asked the young people about their experiences with the Academy and what they thought about it. She was interested to learn about the combat training at the Academy.

"What's that about?" She asked.

Brendan cleared his throat.

"Our family is very powerful, magically. We've had some trouble. The Goddess decided it was a good idea to gather a strong fighting force around us. We now have Dragon, Guardian, and Phoenyx enclaves here in Valerian's Cove. The Guardians are treating the Fight Training program at the school as a testing ground for possible Guardians. They help us train, too."

Elizabeth blinked.

"But surely, that kind of fighting force isn't needed?"

"There has been some evidence that it is, or it will be soon. I don't know how much you know of the paranormal history here on Earth, but last year our granddaughter, Allison, was chosen as the new wielder of the Sword of Fire. She was just eleven. She'll be thirteen in the fall. A lot of the training was designed around her."

All three visiting Witches blinked.

"But isn't that just a story?" Claire asked. "Are you saying the Sword of Fire is real?"

"Yep," Shari-Beth said.

"Wow."

"Doesn't the wielder of the Sword have both Phoenyx and Dragon blood?" Robin asked.

"Yes. We have Phoenyx blood on my side of the family and Dragon on Celine's," Brendan replied.

"Cool," Claire said.

"And Fae, too," Celine said. "Through my side by marriage, and also through my daughter Marissa's mate, Theo. He's part Aes Sídhe. He's a distant cousin to Siofra and her brother, Ciaran."

The rest of the meal passed with the Caseys and Shari-Beth's friends catching the visiting Witches up on events in Valerian's Cove. Elizabeth took a moment to approach Suzette.

"Suzette, Siofra tells me that you're a Potions Master. I would be honored to carry some of your potions in my apothecary in Fairweather Falls if you think it would work out for you."

"Siofra mentioned the possibility. I would love to talk to you about it. I have some samples here that you can look at if you like."

The two Potions Masters thanked Celine for lunch and left the table early, so Suzette could show Elizabeth what she'd brought. Elizabeth was delighted with the quality of the potions she saw.

"I would be happy to carry these. Do you have your own branding and labels worked out?"

Suzette shook her head.

"I've been busy with the Clinic and the Academy and haven't taken the time to work on that yet."

"Robin is a graphic designer. She can help you out if you like. I would like to get these in my store as soon as possible."

They worked out a deal as they headed back to the group on the patio.

"Rob, Suzette needs help with branding and logos," Elizabeth told her friend.

Robin rubbed her hands together, grinning.

"Step into my parlor," she joked. Suzette went to sit next to her. Robin took out her tablet and began sketching ideas.

Celine cleared her throat.

"Ladies, Brendan needs to get to class. He'll take you all over to the Academy with him."

Robin promised to send Suzette her designs the next day for approval.

They said goodbye to the teens, Celine, and Suzette and followed Brendan to his car. Elizabeth asked Brendan questions about the nurseries while Claire listened and Robin brainstormed ideas for Suzette. Soon they were pulling up the drive to the Valerian's Cove Academy.

The Academy looked like an old English Manor House. It was covered in ivy. Brendan parked in the staff parking area and led the way into the school. He stopped in the office and knocked on the Headmistress's door.

"Come in!"

"Maria, this is Elizabeth, Robin, and Claire, from Fairweather Falls in Maine. They're the ones wanting to have a branch of the Academy in their town."

"The entire town wants a branch of the Academy. We're tired of the substandard education our children are receiving at our current school," Robin said acerbically.

Maria frowned.

"What's the problem with your current school?"

Robin explained.

"And nothing has been done, despite complaints?"

All three visiting Witches shook their heads.

"This is inexcusable. I will have a word with the Council myself. It is dangerous to send our children off into the world without the training they need. What are these people thinking?"

"We're not really sure. We just know they're not thinking about the well-being of the children," Elizabeth said.

Maria handed Robin a copy of the plan for the Valerian's Cove Academy.

"Look that over. Maybe it will help you. Let's show you around. Many of our students and teachers are on summer break, but some live on the Academy grounds. I believe there is a fight practice going on at the moment. There are also a few summer classes. The Academy here will be expanding into the University level in the next several years. We are selecting a sight nearby for that campus. We will share students with the Healer's Academy in San Francisco."

Maria told the visitors all about the Academy, explaining the long-term vision as they went. It was pretty all-encompassing. Elizabeth and Robin were impressed.

"What about you, Claire? Does this seem like something you would like?" Elizabeth asked as they watched a class through a window in the door. It was an Earth Magic class for younger children. It was fun to watch the children practice their Gifts. There were only three children in the class, as it was summer, but the looks on the children's faces as they figured out new ways of using their Gifts were pure joy.

Claire nodded.

"This is so much better than anything I could ever have imagined,"

Claire said. "I mean, I've read about schools like this, but I never thought I'd see one. This would be amazing."

Maria led them out to the physical practice area behind the school. Fight training was in session. A tall man with short brown hair was leading the practice.

"Malachai! Duck! Now roll! That's it. Good." He shouted. A young teen followed instructions, coming up inside his opponent's guard and winning his sparring match.

Maria led her little group up beside the man in charge.

"Ladies, this is Declan Muiran, our Fight Master. Declan is a Dragon from the Drake Clan. He's the nephew of Princess Aldona, the Crown Princess. His assistant is his cousin, Sean Drake, Aldona's son. Her daughter, the next Crown Princess, is usually around here somewhere as well. Her mate is one of our professors. He teaches Psychic Gifts."

Maria introduced the visitors to Declan. He shook everyone's hands.

"If we were to include a Fight Training program at our branch of the Academy, would you be able to recommend a teacher?" Robin asked.

Declan nodded.

"I would be happy to. Before I was here, I was my cousin Devra's bodyguard as she worked for the Guardians. We taught them how to use their Dragon Gifts. I know of several young Dragons and several Guardians who would make excellent instructors."

"Thank you. I'll want to talk to you about that soon," Robin said.

"Any time." Declan smiled and went back to his students.

Robin rubbed her hands again.

"I have so many ideas," she said, a sparkle in her eyes. "The S.O.C. better be prepared to fund this because I am not going to take no for an answer. We *will* have our own branch of the Academy this fall, even if we have to start a bit late and finish into the summer. This is happening. Watch out, Council. Here I come."

27

The three visiting Witches stopped for ice cream before taking the portal home. The portals were a Dragon innovation. The original idea had been for Dragons and other magicals with strong teleportation abilities to carry people where they needed to go for a fee. The Dragons thought that it would be much more efficient to have a portal system set up—managed by Dragons, of course. So they had broken out some ancient magical technology they had been sitting on and set up the portal network. They still charged a fee for its use, of course. But they rolled the cost into the magical taxes each paranormal paid so that the system was open to all. Yes, magicals paid two sets of taxes—those to the governments of the countries in which they lived and those to the Supernatural Oversight Council that helped fund the Council's work in keeping the magical world running and mostly hidden from humans. Even now that the magical world was out in the open, there were still parts of it that were better kept hidden. The Council was in charge of handling that. As well as handling magical criminals, making sure all supernatural beings were treated with respect and had healthy living situations, things like that. Over the last couple of years, the Council had been cleaning up the magical world, making a colossal effort to bring its people into the current century so that all its inhabitants got the respect they deserved, regardless of race, gender, or anything else. Each person was valuable in and of themselves. It was a lot of work, but the Council was up to it. They had already done quite a bit. Many magicals from harrowing backgrounds were already living much more beautiful lives.

Before returning to Fairweather Falls later that evening, the three visitors had taken some time to explore Valerian's Cove as they ate their ice cream. It was a beautiful town, full of friendly people of all kinds. The harbor was picturesque, with the boats moored there painted bright colors, and the Merfolk, the Fae of the Sea, playing in the water. Claire stared at them with eyes wide open for a solid minute. Elizabeth finally waved her hand in front of the girl's face to get her attention.

"Earth to Claire. Come on now; you've seen Selkies before. Surely this isn't so different."

"I had a dream when I was little that I swam with the Sea Folk. I didn't think I would ever see them in real life." Claire continued to stare at the cheerful group in the middle of the bay.

"You dreamed about us? Where are you from, Ms. Witch?" A young Sea Fae male said as he leaned up against the sea wall next to them. He was in human form and had been passing by, coming from the water, in time to hear Claire speak.

"Maine. Fairweather Falls." Robin said.

The young man blinked.

He turned and whistled at the group in the water. They all turned toward him, pausing in their game.

"Hey, Jed! Isn't your family from around the North Atlantic somewhere?"

Another young man swam up to just below where they stood at the wall. His iridescent green tail flashed in the water.

"Yeah, Atlantic side of Nova Scotia, though we come in to trade, sometimes. Why?"

"This young Witch had a dream about swimming in the sea with one of us when she was small."

The young man looked at Claire for a moment. His eyes opened wide in surprise. The young man swam to a ladder on the nearby pier and hauled himself out, shifting to human form as he climbed. He was fully clothed. He came up the dock and over to where they were standing. He looked at Claire, who couldn't seem to tear her eyes away from him. The young man reached out slowly, brushing a strand of hair out of the young Witch's face.

Elizabeth sighed. It looked like her apprentice had found her fated mate. She was only seventeen. Oh, dear.

"I thought it was a dream," Claire whispered.

Jed slowly pulled her toward him, holding her in a hug against his chest. Claire stayed with a sigh. Jed looked over Claire's head at Elizabeth.

"She's my apprentice. You're going to have to come to Maine and explain things to her family," Elizabeth told the young man. He nodded.

"My family are still out there, too. I came here for the Academy. I have one more year."

"So does Claire. We're working on getting a branch of the Academy opened in Fairweather Falls this summer. Would you come back when we succeed?"

"I am pledged to protect the next Seer, and she's here. I'm in training with the Guardians at the Academy as a bodyguard."

Elizabeth sighed again.

"We'll work something out. Claire, do you think your parents would let you come to school out here?"

Claire raised her head.

"I don't know. I'll have to ask them."

"There are good people here for you to learn from. You would do well here. And you heard Headmistress Hemenway. They are adding a University here soon. You could stay here for your further training if you wanted to." Elizabeth turned to Jed.

"Where is the Seer from? Where will she live when she's done with school?"

"I'm not sure what she'll do. She came here because the Goddess told her to, through the current Seer. She's from the Atlantic herself, originally. I'm not at liberty to say exactly where."

Elizabeth and Robin looked at each other. Robin took a compact mirror out of her bag and handed it to Elizabeth.

"She's your apprentice. You tell them."

Elizabeth called Claire's parents through the mirror. Claire's mother, Jennifer, answered.

"Elizabeth? Is everything ok? Are you guys having a good time in Valerian's Cove?"

"We had a fabulous time. We'll be home soon. We have run into a little wrinkle, though. Do you remember Claire having a dream about swimming with Sea Fae when she was younger?"

Jennifer froze, then sighed.

"It wasn't a dream. I'm half Sea Fae on my mother's side. Until she was six, I used to take Claire to see her cousins in the summer. I can shift, though I'm not as strong a swimmer as a full Sea Fae. Claire hasn't shifted, but she can breathe underwater. I, um, may have had her memories altered a bit. And possibly had that part of her gift bound. When Claire was six, there were rumors in the water that someone was after our children. A new, stronger Seer was supposed to have been born, and there were people looking for her. Several children vanished from the Sea. I realized that Claire wasn't the new Seer, but even so, I was afraid for my child. So I had that side of her bound, and we left the Sea. We haven't been back to visit since. What's happened? Are there Sea Fae in Valerian's Cove?"

"I believe a few of the children from your family's area are here. And one of them appears to be Claire's fated mate. We found him playing in the water of the harbor here. He's attending the Academy here with the new Seer, being trained as her bodyguard. His name is Jed."

Jennifer blinked, then smiled.

"Is he there now?"

Elizabeth turned so that Jennifer could see Claire and Jed.

"Jed, do you remember me? You're Noreen's boy, aren't you? I'm your Auntie Jennie. Your mother and I were best friends when we were young. We lived on the shores near you so that my mother could return to the sea when she needed to. You and Claire used to play when I would bring her back for the summers."

"I remember you! You would bake us cupcakes. Mom says it's your fault I like chocolate so much. She misses you. She understands why you stayed away, though. Once we reinforced the wards in our area, you had to choose between the Earth and the Sea. And you married the Earth, so I guess you had to stay there. Or, that's what Mom says, anyway."

"I would love to see her again. Do you think I could?"

"I think you'll have to, now," Elizabeth said.

"Why couldn't you have visited, even with the wards up?" Robin asked. "Surely they knew you and would have let you in?"

Jennifer shook her head.

"For a long time, the Sea Fae stayed to themselves. Once those wards were strengthened, no one was allowed in or out for about nine or ten years. I guess that's changed if Jed's in California."

"It changed when the Seer saw that Sinéad needed to come here to Valerian's Cove, about two years ago," Jed said.

"Sinéad is the new Seer?"

"Yes, Daughter of Sionna, the current Seer."

Jennifer was quiet for a moment.

"Claire, come home tonight, please. We'll tell your father. Jed, are your parents still here, or are they with you?"

"They are still closer to you."

"Then I will go find them tomorrow. Can I start my search from the same place?"

Jed nodded.

"Then, once I find them, we'll decide what to do. If you can contact them, tell your mother I'm coming to find her tomorrow, ok? We'll work this out."

Jed had walked them to the portal, kissed Claire on the forehead, and let them go. He had waved as the portal whisked them out of sight.

Claire wiped a tear out of her eye as they walked back towards her home on the edge of town.

"I never thought it was real. I used to wish it was. And I have a fated mate! But I'm only seventeen. How is this going to work?"

Jennifer must have been watching for them as she met them at the door. She hurried down the steps and pulled Claire into her arms.

"Oh, Sweetheart. I'm sorry I got scared and hid all of this from you. Here, take this. I knew that someday we'd have to tell you and give you back your memories, so the spell was tied to this shell. Break the shell, and you'll get your memories and your Sea Fae Gifts back."

Claire took the shell and looked at it for a moment. She dropped it to the ground and stomped on it. The shell held.

"The magic may have made it a bit stronger than normal," Jennifer said. "Hit it with a stone and say, 'break!'

Claire grabbed a large rock and smashed it down on top of the shell. The shell shattered.

Claire gasped.

"I remember! I remember everything! I remember Jed! He used to be so bossy. He tried to stop me from doing things with the others sometimes. He said I wasn't strong enough."

"He was right. He wanted to keep you safe. Noreen and I knew then that there was something special between the two of you. I was going to tell you when you finished high school. I guess the Goddess has other ideas." She smiled at her daughter.

"I know that you were trying to protect me, Mom. Is Dad home? Did you tell him yet?"

Jennifer nodded.

"He's home, but I thought we would tell him together. He knows what I am and that you have some of the Sea Magic. He'll be happy for you but probably will try to keep you from completing the bonding until you're thirty."

Elizabeth and Robin said goodnight and left them to it.

"Well, that was a surprising way to end the day," Robin said and yawned.

"Truly," Elizabeth agreed. "I never saw that coming. I might be down an apprentice."

"Meh. You'll find another one."

Tuesday morning Suzette and Siofra sent stock through the portal. Morgan got it all arranged in the apothecary so that Elizabeth could take Michael to Valerian's Cove. Magnus and Josh went with her. The boys loved Valerian's Cove. They had lunch with the Caseys again at Celine's insistence. Marissa and Theo joined them with their younger twins, who were about the same age as Siofra's Dervla. Theo promised an introduction for Joshua to his Grandfather, Guardian John Thorndike, also a Stone-based Earth Mage. Magnus approved.

They visited the greenhouses, and the Academy, since Robin wanted their opinions, too. She had stayed home to work on the proposal. The two boys would report back when they got home.

On Wednesday, Elizabeth brought Maia to Valerian's Cove. Maia's eyes widened as she looked around. She was in heaven at the greenhouses and thought Malia's art studio at the Casey's was the cutest thing ever. Elizabeth decided to talk to Maia's parents about setting up something similar for Maia at their house. The girl needed her own space. Maia thought the Academy was fabulous.

"I don't think the fight training is my thing, but everything is so exciting! This place must be so cool when everyone's here. I've never seen Dragons and Phoenyxes before. Do you think they shift a lot? I would love to see that! I wonder if they would let me draw them."

The boys and Maia had dutifully reported their impressions to Robin, who included them in her report and proposal to the Council. On Thursday, Robin took the portal to Council Headquarters. Brendan had told her to approach Council member Peter Brown, a Shifter. He had been instrumental in getting the expansion to the Valerian's Cove Academy arranged. Brendan had also warned Peter that Robin would be visiting and to make time for her. Peter was part of the arm of the Council that was actively dragging magical Clans, Packs, and Families into the present and had a thing for justice and protecting those who were being mistreated in any way. Once Brendan told him there were children involved, Peter was pretty much prepared to let Robin have her way.

Peter listened to Robin's report and proposal. She told him what the kids thought of their current school, what the parents and the townsfolk thought, and showed him the petition. She told him about the Mayor and the principal of the local high school, how they were more focused on academics than magical training, and how it affected the children in the community.

"How can they not see the importance of training magical youth? Aren't they magical themselves?" Peter Brown asked.

"They are, and no one really understands. We've been trying for years to change things, but nothing happens. Many people have given up. Some of us have been trying to train our children ourselves. The children are passing the mortal requirements. It's just their magical education that's failing them."

"If the children are not getting the magical training they need to be safe and effective members of society, something must be done. And what is happening to the money we give the school for magical supplies and training? We give them a standard amount every year to make sure that the children have what they need."

Robin shrugged. "I don't know about that. I didn't know they were getting extra funding for magical training. Beyond what any other public school gets. You would have to take that up with Principle Jones."

"Oh, I will. And so will the accountants here at the Council. That money comes from us, not the federal government. It's part of the deal between the non-magical government and ours."

Peter rubbed his hands.

"Ok. You'll get your Academy. Do you have land picked out?" They spent the next hour going over specifics. Robin left, feeling over the moon. Peter had promised a Fae Architect and extra help with building the Academy as well. Robin mentioned that Declan Muiran had offered to recommend fight instructors, and Peter said he would see about finding staff for the school.

"We'll ask Headmistress Hemenway for suggestions. Also, the Academy system has its own governing board. I'll call them this afternoon and get the ball rolling. They will send you candidates as well. Do you have a hiring committee set up?"

"I'll work on that as soon as I get home," Robin had promised.

Robin had called Elizabeth as soon as she stepped back into Fairweather Falls. Then she called all the other parents that had been teaching their children to use their Gifts at home. They all met that evening at the meeting hall.

"We won! We get our own Academy. We need a hiring committee. Mr. Brown says he will have the Academy governing board send us candidates for teachers as soon as possible."

"What's going to happen to the teachers at our current school?" A man asked from the back. His sister taught eighth-grade science.

"If they are good teachers, maybe we can poach them for the Academy," Robin suggested. "The problem ones will either stay at the current school or have to find new jobs. I'm not worried about them."

"Will the current school stay open, then? Won't everyone want to move their children to the Academy?" Tara Frances, who owned the hair salon in town, asked.

"I guess it depends on how many people want to keep their kids at the old school," Robin answered. "If that school closes, we'll make sure the teachers are all taken care of. Like I said, we can offer the good ones positions at the Academy, or maybe the Council can get them good retirement packages or something. We'll work it out." Robin paused. "So, the architect and the builders will be here on Monday, so we need to make sure we have land chosen by then. Does anyone have any good ideas?"

Elizabeth had already spoken to her family about that.

"My family owns the land along the coast for the next five miles. We will lease it to the Academy, on a hundred-year's lease. It would be best if you made sure that the Academy includes facilities for the Sea Fae, in case any of them want to send their children here. So our land on the coast is perfect. There are also caves and forests, so it's perfect for all races. With plenty of space for gardens and training fields."

They spent the next two hours hashing out what they wanted; then Robin spent Friday compiling it into a plan. By the time the architect showed up on Monday, they were ready to go.

28

With plans for the Fairweather Falls Academy underway and the shop and apprentice training running well, Elizabeth found her attention returning to the deaths of Aunt Gloria's friends and former teammates.

On Monday afternoon, after Magnus had picked up Michael and Josh for their afternoon training session in Stones and Metals, Elizabeth loaded new stock into her car and headed for town. After delivering everything to Samara's Garden and helping Morgan arrange it on the shelves, she ran over to The Flower's Daughter to see Clara and Lorien.

The chimes over the door sounded as Elizabeth walked in. Clara was helping a customer at the register. The tall Aes Sídhe smiled at Elizabeth, who waved and wandered off to look around as she waited.

Clara finished ringing out her customer, who left with an enormous smile on her face and several bags in her hands.

"Elizabeth! What can I do for you on this beautiful day?"

"I was wondering if Lorien had had any luck finding Daffydd MacNeil?"

Clara shook her head.

"Lor is getting quite frustrated. He's certain that Daffydd doesn't have the magical strength to shield himself this way and that someone must be helping him. Lor went back home to aid in the search himself. I believe that our Queen has asked the Guardians for help as well. She is quite angry that no one has found anything yet."

Elizabeth shook her head.

"It seems so strange that they could completely disappear like that. I mean, with all the magical means of tracing someone, surely we should have found something by now."

"Roger hasn't found anything in the Earth Realm yet, either?"

"No. No one has seen Daffydd in the last five years. All of his business interests are being managed by people in his company. They get their orders from the current president of the company, but Roger can't find out how that man is getting *his* orders, which means it's probably happening through magical means rather than electronic."

"And we're absolutely sure this company president isn't Daffydd under a glamor?" Clara asked.

"Roger says his background history checks out. Lukas and Elise have someone tailing the man. So far, he hasn't done anything suspicious."

"How long has this man been the company president?"

"For about ten years now, Roger says."

"Hmm. It's still possible that Daffydd could have removed the man and taken over his identity. If they haven't found him in Faerie by now, I think it's more likely that he is hiding here in this realm. My Queen would have found him by now, else."

Elizabeth thought about that as she drove home. She knocked on Roger's door. Roger answered, his hair standing up on end and his glasses crooked on his face. It looked like she had woken him up.

"I'm sorry if I woke you, Roger," Elizabeth began. "I was just visiting Clara, and she says she thinks that Daffydd and Sarah may be here, in the Earth Realm. She says that her Queen would have found them otherwise. Clara suggested that Daffydd might have taken over the identity of the president of his company here? Would that be possible?"

Roger blinked.

"I looked into that, briefly. The man is married, and there have been no changes in his habits that I can find. It would mean that either the man's wife is in on it, or she has been replaced too."

"Could Sarah be the wife?"

"I doubt it. The wife has her own life and is out and about a lot. I don't think Daffydd would allow Sarah that much freedom."

"Can you dig more deeply into their lives? There has to be something we're missing, somewhere. No one completely vanishes."

"No one in this realm can hide from me completely," Roger agreed. "There's always some digital trace. I'll look into it. I'll let Lukas and Elise know what we're doing, too. The more eyes on this, the better, though I'm sure I'll find something first."

Elizabeth thanked the Techno-Mage and made her way back downstairs. Waiting was frustrating and getting harder by the minute.

On Wednesday morning, Elizabeth and Maia were hard at work in the stillroom. Maia was turning out to be a fun person to work with. She had a strong talent for potions and an intuitive way of knowing which herbs and other ingredients would enhance them. The young girl would bring her drawings to show Elizabeth as well, which Elizabeth loved. Maia was a very talented artist. Maia and Robin had come up with beautiful branding materials for the shop. The logo was a blue line drawing of a potion bottle with a ribbon tied around the neck and a spray of stars and flowers swirling around it. The shop's name hovered overhead in a pretty, rustic font, while underneath the bottle were the words' bookstore, apothecary, cafe' separated by stars.

Elizabeth had included potion ingredients among her offerings in the apothecary section of the store. She had even designed several potion kits for those who wanted to brew their own. The kits were those simple potions that were easy to make and best brewed fresh. She had a simple healing potion, a calming potion, a happiness potion, and an invigorating potion. She was considering adding others, depending on the success of the ones already on offer. Claire was going forward with her plans for a line of cosmetic potions, though she was finding them a bit more challenging to make than she had expected.

Elizabeth put this down to the ineptitude of the current potions teacher at the high school, not to Claire's talents and abilities, which were growing quickly with practice. Of course, now that Claire was distracted by having found her fated mate and having him living across the country, who knew what might happen. Claire's parents were talking with Jed's. So far, they had not reached a decision. Both families had visited Valerian's Cove together over the weekend so that the teens could spend time together. Knowing that Jed couldn't leave Sinéad, Elizabeth figured the odds of losing her oldest apprentice were pretty high. Then again, with the Academy opening, there would be more people moving into the area. If she wanted another apprentice, she could probably find one pretty quickly. Or just hire someone to take over Claire's hours at the store.

Maia had just bottled a nerve tonic and was putting the labels on the bottles when Roger opened the door to the stillroom. Maia jumped, and the label she was trying to align properly went crooked. She sighed and began peeling it off again.

"Elizabeth, I think I found them. It's not the president. It's his assistant. He's a human male, was hired about six years ago. The previous one supposedly left to start a family, though she divorced soon afterward and moved away rather suddenly. He has a live-in girlfriend who doesn't go out much. She's supposed to be a graphic designer who works from home. She has a portfolio site online but rarely seems to do any actual work. They live in the next town over from the company offices in Richmond, Virginia. They don't socialize much, though they are seen around town occasionally, just enough to keep the gossips from talking about how weird they are. The assistant is slender, with black hair. He dresses in slacks and turtleneck sweaters and looks like he'd fit in in New York. He's a bit elitist, but not enough to have people hating him on sight. The girlfriend is quiet and a bit shy. She smiles but doesn't talk much when they're out."

"Does this assistant actually exist? Or are they made up, do you think?"

"No, they are based on real people. The young man, James, applied for the job and was hired six years ago. His girlfriend, Miranda, moved to town with him. She can work from anywhere, as her business is primarily digital. No one has noticed much of a change in them since they've been there—their lives seem pretty consistent. Neither of them talks to their families much. They met in school in Savannah. He went to Armstrong Atlantic, and she went to Savannah College of Art and Design. On a scholarship. She was quite talented. Her teachers expected her to do more than just be a graphic designer working for other people's dreams. James was pre-law but never went to law school. He took the job in Richmond straight out of college. At the time, James told his teachers he was taking some time to rethink his career. According to his professors, he was a smart student but lacked the drive to make a good trial lawyer. Lukas and Elise are on their way down to question the assistant and his girlfriend now. Lorien is going with them to break any glamours they might have on them."

"What are the odds those two young people are still alive somewhere if Daffydd really did take over their identities?" Elizabeth asked softly.

Roger shook his head.

"Not good, I'm afraid. I'm not sure how the S.O.C. is going to explain this one to their families. Though, I guess it's easier now that magic is out in the open."

Lukas and Elise reported in later that evening.

"We got them," Elise said, a tired smile on her face. "Sarah is fine. She wants to see everyone. We'll bring her up tomorrow. She's resting now. It seems that Sarah's Gifts include a kind of mind magic where she can make anyone see anything she wants them to see. And they'll completely believe it, even when presented with evidence to the contrary. Daffydd was using her to make sure his business deals went his way. He had amassed quite a large pile of wealth using her Gift. Sarah hates that Gift and rarely used it herself. She's not all that fond of her Bean Sídhe side, either, and had worked really hard to control it her whole life. It was easier than it could have been because she wasn't bound to a particular family. The family her mother was bound to passed away just before her mother died, passing her Gift on to Sarah.

And Sarah never took another family. She made the Supernatural Oversight Council her life but made sure never to be bound to anyone there."

"But she could still sense death?"

"Yes, that part she can't control. She just doesn't have to wail and announce the death."

"Wow. Sarah must be very strong-willed."

"She is. It's what's kept her alive so long. She feels horrible for everything she's done under her father's control. She is devastated that Daffydd used the lives and deaths of her former team members to control her. She feels it was her fault. It will be a long road before she can forgive herself, I think."

"She was caught between a rock and a hard place. And anything Daffydd did is on him. Not her."

"I know, but she still feels responsible. We're going to do what we can to repay the families in any way that can be helpful to them. We're doing the same for the families of the people that were affected by the manipulations Daffydd had her do. Many small businesses went under, and a lot of land was sold that would not have normally been. Families lost homes and lands that had been in their families for generations. A few are still intact and will be returned to the previous owners with a healthy monetary settlement as well. If Daffydd's company still holds them, those that were broken up and developed will be offered back to the families they were stolen from, or the families will be fully compensated for them. Daffydd's entire company is under investigation. Daffydd is going to be facing a lot of charges, both here and in Faerie."

"What will happen to Sarah?"

"She was a victim in this as much as anyone else. She was under duress and afraid for her life and the lives of others. That is being taken into consideration. I don't think she'll be charged with anything. She wants to help in making reparations. I'm not sure what that will look like. The S.O.C. will work with the King and Queen of the Unseelie to figure it all out. The Queen is insisting that Sarah be taken care of and given the best of care. I imagine she'll be working with Mind Mages for quite a while to get over the PTSD from this. They're going to have to take it slowly. Fifteen years is a long time. That's a lot of healing. The fear and anguish are firmly entrenched in her psyche at this point."

"I'll tell everyone you're coming up. Thank you, guys, for letting us know. I'm so glad you found her."

Elizabeth turned to Aunt Gloria, who was watching the video conversation over Elizabeth's shoulder. Ghostly tears were flowing down Aunt Gloria's face.

"I feel so awful for Sarah," Aunt Gloria said. "I hope we can help her heal. She deserves so much better than this."

"We'll help her as much as we can, Aunt Glo. Why don't you and Rosie help Eleanor make a room for Sarah? I'll let everyone else know."

❧

WHAT ELISE HADN'T TOLD ELIZABETH WAS THAT IT HADN'T BEEN easy to take Daffydd down. Elise, Lukas, and several other S.O.C. agents and enforcers had moved on the house in the evening after the 'assistant' had gotten home from work. They had watched from the shadows as he entered the house, closing the door behind him.

"Move out," Lukas had whispered, knowing that his team could hear him, thanks to the comms they had tucked in their ears. They were a mixture of magic and technology and couldn't be hacked. At least, they hadn't been, yet.

Agents had surrounded the house. A Witch and an Aes Sídhe worked together to take down the wards Daffydd had set up to protect the house and warn him of any intruders. Unfortunately, it seemed that at least one of the wards had been tied directly to Daffydd, and he knew they were coming. He had set off a spell buried in the soil around the house, causing the ground to explode around the agents already in place. The second wave of agents stormed the doors, front and back. They blew the doors open with magic, then moved forward, shields raised. Those entering the kitchen had found a meal cooking on the stove. A pot was just beginning to boil over. An agent stopped to turn off the stove, then followed the others into the hallway and the main area of the house.

Daffydd had retreated upstairs with Sarah, who had been in the kitchen. He pushed her into a bedroom, turning to fire a bolt of energy at the agents starting up the stairs. The Aes Sídhe ducked into the bedroom after his daughter and closed the door. He set a ward quickly, then started to open a portal. Portal magic was something he was marginally good at. The portal was nearly large enough to jump through when the door exploded behind him.

Daffydd fired off another bolt of energy. It struck a shield and glanced off, breaking a window on the far side of the room. Lukas and the Aes Sídhe on his team entered the room. Lukas made for Sarah as the Aes Sídhe took care of Daffydd.

"Daffydd MacNeil, you are under arrest for kidnapping, murder, manipulation, and illegal business dealings. I believe you will also be charged with torture in the case of your daughter, Sarah MacNeil. Surrender now."

The S.O.C. Aes Sídhe had snapped the portal closed before it could finish forming completely. Daffydd lost his temper and launched a furious attack on the taller Aes Sídhe. The agent easily deflected the attack and sent a stream of golden energy to wrap around Daffydd, binding him tightly. Another blast of energy knocked the rogue Sídhe out cold.

"The MacNeils were once a proud family. Never very strong magically, but wise and able to see opportunities that others would have missed. They were respected advisors to the Court of Faerie," the tall Aes Sídhe agent shook his head. "It's a pity that they have come down to this."

"I hear his son's a better person, and I will personally vouch for Sarah here. She's nothing like her old man," Lukas said as Elise came into the room and headed straight for Sarah. She hugged the other woman tightly.

"I'm so sorry it took us so long to figure out what was going on, my friend," Elise whispered to Sarah. Tears were rolling down Sarah's face.

Elise looked at Sarah.

"Can you talk?"

Sarah shook her head. She held up her wrists. Thin silver bands set with a black stone encircled both arms. The bands looked like pretty bracelets, but Elise could smell the magic on them. It gave off a bitter, biting sent.

"Lorien, can you get these things off of Sarah, please?" Elise asked the Aes Sídhe, who had followed her into the room.

Lorien looked at the bands around Sarah's wrists, huffing in disgust.

"These things were outlawed centuries ago. How did he manage to find a working pair? How dare he use them on anyone, let alone his own child?"

Lorien placed his hands on the bands and focused. He grunted, then focused more intensely. He paused for a moment, then called, "Wendy! Come here for a moment, please!"

The S.O.C. Witch hurried up the stairs and into the room. She looked at the bands on Sarah's wrists and made a face of disgust.

"Slave bands. How dare he."

Wendy sank to her knees next to Lorien, and together they focused on the silver and stones. After a moment, the bands broke, falling away into dust.

"There, you're free now," Wendy said, sitting back. "Can you talk now?"

"Yes, thank you," Sarah said. She wiped the tears off her face and took a deep breath.

"I wasn't allowed to speak or use my magic unless he told me to. He made sure to forbid me from asking for help if we were out in public. I had to do whatever he said." Sarah took a breath. "I fought the bands as much as I could. This was the fourth set. I broke the others. Each pair was stronger than the last. It took me a long time to figure out how to break the first two sets. When I figured it out, he started killing people from my old team as added insurance against my good behavior. He never admitted he had killed them or ordered their deaths. He would come and tell me about them. After I broke the third pair of slave bands, after John died, he started telling me their deaths were my fault. He bragged about interfering with Rosie's mind so that no one would connect the deaths or notice the pattern. He told me I would never break free, and the next time I tried, if I disobeyed him in any way, did anything he didn't like, he would kill someone else. I've been so afraid. In the last few years, he's gotten so much worse.

Even the slightest thing, even if it were imagined, could set him off. I never meant for anyone to die. I tried so hard to fight him, at first. I hate my Gift. I hate using it. It should never be used to control other people. It's meant to help with healing. To ease pain. I hate what he had me do with it."

Sarah sagged against Elise's shoulder.

Elise, Lukas, Charles, Lorien, and Wendy looked at each other. Sarah's road to healing would be an extended one. She had been in her father's control for far too long.

29

Elise and Lukas brought Sarah to Elizabeth's house early the following day. Charles opened a portal straight into Elizabeth's sitting room for them to step through. He let the portal close with a wave once they were safely in Fairweather Falls.

Aunt Gloria was hovering while Madelynn and Sharalee rushed forward to pull Sarah into a hug. They got her seated on the couch.

"What I want to know," Madelynn said coldly, "Is how that worm managed to block you from me. I truly thought you were dead. I couldn't feel you."

Sarah smiled up at Madelynn.

"I know I was never a strong part of the bond, Maddie. I was always running around, taking care of other things. Rosie was the one you were truly bonded to."

"You were included in the bond, though, Sarah. That should have been enough. There is no way that he should have been able to cloak you from me."

"He had slave bands on her. Could that have done it?" Elise asked.

Maddie looked shocked, then furious.

"He dared? On his own daughter? If he knew of the bond and had it specifically worked into the magic on the bands, then it may be that they suppressed the bond to me. I claim blood debt. Sarah is my family. I hope you have no lingering affection for your sperm donor, Sarah, because *he is dead.*"

Madelynn's face had become dried and lined. Her eyes were pools of deepest black. Her hair whipped around her face.

Sharalee paled.

"Someone had better call the Queen. She needs to know Madelynn has called blood debt before she sentences Daffydd MacNeil."

The Pixie looked up at the enforcers.

"Has Daffydd been transferred over to the Court, yet?"

Lukas shook his head.

"Since his businesses were in the Earth Realm, the S.O.C. and the Court are still sorting out who has first right of jurisdiction and what kind of punishments each will exact. I'll call it in now."

Lukas stepped outside for a moment.

As he was turning to come back inside, another portal opened into the living room. The King and Queen of the Unseelie, Darragh and Lorelei, stepped through, followed by several guards, a member of the S.O.C. and a Guardian. The sitting room was getting quite crowded. Elizabeth was grateful that the children were already off with their mentors for the day. As it was, Claire would be here soon for her day in the stillroom.

Everyone bowed to the royal couple.

Queen Lorelei looked at the Brùnaigh who had gone boggart.

"Madelynn, you have claimed blood debt against Daffydd MacNeil for his actions against his daughter, Sarah MacNeil, whom you claim as a part of your family, is that right?"

"It is. He will answer to me for his attack on one I call my own."

Queen Lorelei looked around the room.

"It seems that there are three parties with jurisdiction here. I will wave the right of the Court to decide punishment in favor of Madelynn of the Brùnaigh's claim. It is her right, as he has harmed her family."

The S.O.C. agent nodded.

"The S.O.C. has already seized all of Daffydd MacNeil's known Earth Realm assets. We will make very sure that we have found *all* of them. We will make reparations on his behalf to those who have been affected by his actions in this realm. We will defer further punishment to Madelynn of the Brùnaigh. I trust she will think of something suitable for his crimes."

Madelynn smiled. It was amazing how such a usually kind face could look so evil.

"Come, Madelynn. I will take you to him and deliver him into your hands," the Queen told the Brownie. The Royals, the Brownie, and those that had come with them stepped through the portal and were gone.

"What will she do to him?" Elizabeth asked.

"She's called in a blood debt. His life is forfeit. But death would be too easy for him. Slave bands are horrible, horrible things. You have no will of your own while wearing them, yet you are still conscious of what is happening to you, of what you are being forced to do. They trap your own will behind a barrier. You can only watch and do nothing. Sarah must be incredibly strong in her magic that she was able to resist as much as she did," Elise said. She hugged the other woman again.

"I think Madelynn will find a punishment that puts him at the command of someone who will not use him easily. She will make the punishment fit the crime. There are also the deaths of her other family members, the other members of the team, that he has to answer for. He really owes her blood debt for each member of the team that he had killed. Whatever she comes up with, it won't be pretty. You may not want to know."

Madelynn returned in time for lunch. Elizabeth and Claire found her sitting on the patio with Sarah when they took a mid-day break from potion-making.

"Claire, would you go ask Mary for some food, please?"

Elizabeth waited until the teen was safely inside the house before turning to the Brownie.

"What did you do?"

"I gave him to the Sluagh. He will live one hundred years for each death with them, used at their will, driven to the point of death, then healed and used again, in whichever way they feel necessary that day. Then, for using slave bands on his own child, something even the Sluagh find abhorrent, he will find himself the main course in a meal for some of those among the Sluagh that enjoy Sídhe flesh twice a month. Only, he will not be killed. He will be kept alive and healed after every meal so that he can serve again at the next one. His body will be completely regenerated after every meal. This will continue until he has paid for each death in service, after which whatever is left of him will finally be allowed to die. Or be completely eaten. It's up to the Sluagh, based on his behavior while in their care."

Elizabeth blinked.

Sarah looked fierce next to Madelynn.

"Never cross one of the Brùnaigh, or mess with our families," Mary said, as she came outside with a tray of food, Claire following close behind.

"How much of that did you hear?" Elizabeth asked her apprentice once they were back in the stillroom after lunch.

"All of it. Mary thought it would be good for me to learn what happens when you cross a Brownie and how important it is to be a part of a Brownie's family. I think I told you we have a Brownie living with our family? I knew she was protective of us, but this is next-level. I had no idea they took their bonds so seriously. I mean, I did, but.... I'm going to be extra nice to Susan from now on."

Elizabeth let it go at that. Mary had made her point, and Daffydd was taken care of. Elizabeth understood why the Queen had deferred to Madelynn. No one could think up a worse fate than the one she had arranged for the renegade Sídhe.

The rest of the afternoon went by quickly if a little more quietly than usual. As they were cleaning up at the end of the day, Elizabeth asked Claire about her plans now that she had met Jed.

"Jed is bound to protect Sinéad, so he has to stay in Valerian's Cove. Since I'm only seventeen, my parents want me to stay here to finish high school. We can visit each other on the weekends. Then, I'll go to Valerian's Cove for university, or wherever Sinéad is then. It's helpful that we're all in the same grade."

"And have you met Sinéad and the rest of the Sea Fae with her?"

"Yeah, they're all really nice. They understand the importance of the mate bond. Sinéad says I'll be a welcome friend when I join them for college. They don't have a Healer bonded to them yet, so she suggested I see if my Gifts extend that way. I hadn't really thought about it. I mean, I love potions, but I've always thought more about having my own skincare line than focusing on healing."

"You've already begun using salves for healing. It's not that large of a step. You can do both, you know."

"I know. I'm thinking about it. And if they stay in Valerian's Cove for university, the San Francisco Healer's College isn't that far away."

Elizabeth considered for a moment.

"Claire, you know that I think you've gotten a sub-par education in potions from your regular school. I know your parents will enroll you in the new Academy here this fall. I've already talked with them about it. You are going to have to work really hard if you want to be able to get into the Healer's College. You'll have a lot of catching up to do. If you are sure you want to explore this, we should see about getting you a second apprenticeship at the Clinic here one or two afternoons a week. Tuesdays and Fridays, maybe. At least for a trial period, to see if it is something that would truly interest you. I can talk to Healer O'Shoughnessy if you like."

Claire thought for a moment as she put a label on the jar of salve she had just filled.

"I think that's a good idea. I'm sorry I won't be able to cover as many of Maia's hours as I had thought. But I think you're right. I need to check it out, if the Healers will let me. Thank you, Elizabeth."

Elizabeth arranged for Claire to spend Tuesday and Friday afternoons with the Healers and discussed the change with Claire's parents. They saw the wisdom in it and agreed. They were still coming to terms with the idea that their daughter had a fated mate, and he was of the Sea.

"I just don't know how it's going to work," Jennifer, Claire's mother, said to Elizabeth. "I mean, Claire can breathe underwater, but she can't shift. She can't swim like the Sea Fae do. She could live on the cliffs above them, but what happens when they have children? The children will be able to live in the sea fully. With a full-blooded father and a partial-blood mother, they will be at least as strong as I am as a half-blood, probably more so. I don't see how this can end well for anyone."

"The Goddess is never wrong, Jennifer. You know that. It will all work out. And this all means that you can be back in touch with your Sea Fae family and friends, too. That's good, right?"

Jennifer had agreed. Then she sighed.

"It's going to be rough on my husband, though. I mean, there are enchantments to allow him to breathe underwater for a time. My son can breathe underwater like Claire can. I guess it will all work out. And I guess we'll be moving again, when Sinéad returns home. At the very least, back to the coast of Nova Scotia, near Jed's family. Most likely, we'll all move to wherever Sinéad is based. My son is not happy about any of this."

"It will all work out. You'll see."

"I know. Thank you, Elizabeth."

30

Elizabeth decided that she did need to hire two full-time staff to help Morgan, now that her two older apprentices were also studying with their other mentors and had less time to spend in the shop. And Maia was in the stillroom with her most of the time now. She talked to Morgan and Samara about it on Friday afternoon. She had brought a delivery into the store and was helping put everything away as she waited for Jonah. Maddie and Josh were having dinner and a sleepover at her sister Lucy's that night.

"Things are continuing to move so quickly," Elizabeth said as she placed a bottle of hair tonic on the shelf.

"With Michael spending time with Josh and Magnus and Claire with the Healers, you definitely do need more help, Morgan. Do you know anyone you think would fit in here? Do you, Samara?"

Morgan shook her head.

"I don't know of anyone off the top of my head. Most of my friends back home are already settled into places they like. I think we'll need to get the word out that we're looking to hire. It worked with the apprentices. And me," she grinned.

"I think Morgan is right," Samara said. "I have been mostly sleeping since Jackson closed the store. I haven't really been keeping an eye on the people in the town, just on the store itself, until you opened it up again."

"Ok, then we'll do that. I'll have my mother put the word out and ask Robin to come up with an ad we can post to the nearby Havens. Hopefully, we'll find the right people quickly." She looked at the shelves where Siofra and Suzette's potions were displayed. Siofra's were almost gone already, and Suzette's were half-gone.

"How are the potions from Siofra and Suzette doing? It looks like we need to order more already?"

"They're doing great. Siofra's especially," Morgan replied. "I already placed additional orders with each of them. The Fae in the area are thrilled to have potions and remedies here specific to them. And made by Siofra MacNamara. Apparently, she's quite the Fae Potions Master. She's well known. I've had several people tell me we're lucky to have her things here and ask me when we are getting more."

"I'm glad it's working out," Elizabeth smiled. "Have you told those people they will soon be able to get Fae plants through my mother?"

"I mentioned it to a few people. They were excited. I think it's going to be a good market for her."

"She'll be happy to hear that."

ROBIN HAD AN AD READY TEN MINUTES AFTER ELIZABETH HUNG UP the phone. She even sent it to the other Havens via email. Each Haven had a town message board, as well as their own local newspaper.

"You owe me for the ads in the papers. Sixty dollars, please... or credit at the shop. I'll probably spend it there anyway," Robin grinned at Elizabeth Saturday morning. She had stopped by the stillroom to report.

Michael and Maia were deep in their potions. They were making calming bath bombs this morning. Michael was planning on taking a few home to his mother. Maia wanted some for herself. They were making lavender, orange blossom, and rose. The stillroom smelled like a flower garden in the warm summer sun.

"I'll pay you, Rob. You deserve the cash. What you do with it's up to you," Elizabeth smiled back. "I really appreciate all the work you're doing for me. You're fantastic at this graphic design stuff."

"Maia is too. She was a great help on the logo," Robin smiled at the girl.

Maia blushed.

"I'll happily take a couple of those bath bombs, though, if you have any spare," Robin said, looking covetously at the balls of salts, scents, and baking soda in their pretty bags. The apprentices had tied the bags with ribbons whose colors matched the aromas of the flower-flecked spheres.

Elizabeth handed her two of each.

"Enjoy."

"Oh, I will. I certainly will."

ELIZABETH AND THE KIDS WENT OVER TO NORA AND ELLIOT'S FOR dinner that night.

"Mom, Morgan says that she's been telling people about you getting the exclusive contract to sell Siofra and Brendan's Fae hybrids on the East Coast. She's had a lot of people interested already. I think you're going to see an enormous boost in business."

"I already am. I have a waitlist that's growing by the day. Brendan and Siofra are going to come and help me set up a greenhouse here for the plants since they need a unique growing environment. It will be a masterpiece. I may sell tours. I went to Valerian's Cove yesterday to talk to them about it. The greenhouses at the Casey Nurseries are enormous and so full of beautiful plants! I have plant envy. I can hardly wait to add to my stock here. This is going to be an extremely beneficial relationship for all of us, I can tell."

"I'm glad it's working out for you, Mom. Siofra's potions are selling well in the shop, too. It was a powerful stroke of good luck that we all connected."

"Brendan told me that the Goddess takes a personal interest in the Casey Clan and has done for years. She finds them all fated mates and has gathered a large group of fighters and extremely important people around them. He thinks something big is coming, but not for a few years yet. He figures that we play into it somehow, but we'll have to wait and see how, exactly. At any rate, I am happy to be building a stronger connection with them! They are a wonderful family."

Nora turned to the children.

"Tell me what you have been learning this week? Is everything still working out with Mags and Magnus?"

"Mags is great!" Maddie said enthusiastically. "I want to show you what I've learned, but Mags says we have to do it after dinner because it has to be outside."

"Why is that, Sweetheart?"

"Because she's been teaching me weather and fire magic."

Nora looked at Elizabeth in some alarm.

"Mags says Maddie was already starting to influence the weather, and she needs to know how to be aware and use her talents consciously and with caution," Elizabeth said with a shrug.

"Mags also says that Maddie will be even stronger than we thought and wants to know if we have any Dragon blood in the family. She hasn't seen an Elemental Mage with Maddie's degree of talent in a long time, if ever."

Nora looked at Elliot. He shrugged.

"Not to our knowledge, darling. It's always possible, I suppose. Maybe we should have Maddie tested for Dragon Gifts? If her magic really is that strong?"

"Mags suggested the same thing. I'll have to ask Ciaran or Siofra if one of the Dragons in Valerian's Cove would be willing to test her. Maybe we should all be tested. All of our family are fairly strong in our Gifts."

"That's probably a good idea."

"I'll ask Siofra tomorrow, then."

SIOFRA AGREED TO ASK THE DRAGONS. THE AES SÍDHE WOMAN arrived at lunchtime on Sunday, a young male Dragon in tow. Siofra had Dervla on her hip. Nathaniel appeared behind them, a large covered basket in his hand.

"We brought food. Dragons eat a lot, and even though this one had breakfast not long ago, I know he'll be hungry again soon. And it *is* just about lunchtime here," Siofra said with a grin.

She turned to the Dragon beside her.

"Elizabeth, this is Sean Drake of the Fire Mountain Dragon Clan. He's the assistant fight trainer at the Valerian's Cove Academy. He will test Maddie and anyone else that wants to be tested."

Sean smiled and held out his hand. Elizabeth shook it, smiling back.

"Thank you so much for agreeing to do this. We've no record of any Dragons in our bloodline, but Maddie's teacher, Lady Margarethe Laughlin, suggested it. Apparently, Maddie is the strongest Elemental Mage she's ever seen, and Maddie's powers are still coming in."

"It's not a problem. Just be aware that just because she's extremely powerful, magically, doesn't necessarily mean Maddie has Dragon blood."

"Oh, I know. Still, it seems like the wise thing to do."

They stepped out onto the back patio. Mags and Maddie were already there.

"Mags, this is Sean Drake of the Fire Mountain Dragon Clan. Sean, Lady Margarethe Laughlin of the Unseelie Aes Sídhe."

The two nodded to each other.

"Are you going to see if I'm part Dragon?" Maddie asked the tall young man.

Sean nodded.

"Ok. What do I have to do?"

"Why don't you sit over here on the ground, please, Maddie. Now, close your eyes. I want you to take a deep breath in, hold it for a moment, now, let it out. Take another deep breath in, now let it out. In your mind, with your eyes still closed, I would like you to imagine yourself on a large rock ledge in front of a cave. You can see the stars all around you. No one else is there, but you feel perfectly safe. You're enjoying looking up at the stars." Sean paused for a moment. Maddie had a smile on her face.

Sean nodded and continued.

"Now, reach deep inside yourself where you feel your magic. You feel your elemental magic first. It's always with you, and you are familiar with it. You know how it feels. Now, look even deeper inside you. Is there another magic there? It may be warm and red or gold, or it may be blue or green and cooler-feeling. In this magic, you sense someone looking back at you. They are a part of you. They will always protect you. This being can help you grow your magic and learn to soar. If this new magic could stand up and take form, it would have vast wings with which to soar upon the winds. Now, thank your new friend, and slowly step back. Take a deep breath, and begin to wiggle your fingers and toes. When you are ready, you may open your eyes."

Sean looked at Elizabeth and shook his head.

"Maddie, what did you think?" He asked the girl.

"I don't know. I loved looking up at the stars. I could almost feel them sending me light. They were talking to me, but I couldn't quite hear what they were saying. I didn't really feel the Dragon energy at all. I could see in my mind what you were saying, but it just felt like when I imagine something. It didn't feel real."

Sean nodded.

"That's fine, Maddie. Elizabeth, Lady Margarethe, I don't believe that Maddie has any Dragon blood. I think she may have some Aes Sídhe, though. Have you tested her for that yet?"

"I did when I first got here. I didn't get the feeling that there was anything there. We can try again, I suppose," Mags moved to stand with her hands on Maddie's shoulders.

"Ok, Maddie. We're going to do something similar. Take another deep breath and close your eyes. Go back to the cliff, surrounded by stars. Breath in the starlight, then breath out, imagining you are sending your own light to the stars. Feel the ground beneath you, supporting you. Feel the breeze on your skin, the slight moisture in the air. Feel the warmth in the light of the stars. Do the stars speak to you? What do they say?" Mags paused for a moment before going on.

"Now, Maddie, thank the stars and the elements. They are your friends, your family, and are with you always. You know the feeling of them, of the magic they hold. You know the feeling of the magic within you. Does it feel any different from before? Take another deep breath. Let it out. Breathe in again and slowly move your fingers and toes. You can open your eyes now."

Mags looked at the other adults.

"I still don't get the feeling that Maddie has any Aes Sídhe blood."

Maddie opened her eyes. They were glowing. Sean, who was facing her, blinked.

"Maddie, what did you see when you were on the cliff?"

"I saw a woman who glowed. She told me that I was special, that my whole family was special. That we had a spark of something that hadn't been woken up until now. She said it was extra strong in me. But Josh and my Mom have it too. Everyone in my mom's family on my Grandpa Elliot's side does. She said that one of our ancestors came from the stars. And now it's time for us to wake up."

Sean looked over Maddie's head to Elizabeth, then Siofra and Mags. They all stared back in complete and utter shock.

31

"What does this mean, that we came from the stars?" Elizabeth asked.

No one answered.

"There are stories that there are realms where the stars are living beings," Siofra said slowly. "There are even stories that they somehow crossed the realms and played a part in human evolution on Earth. I never took those stories seriously before this."

"It sounds as if Maddie spoke with the Goddess," Nathaniel said. "Maybe Fionnuala and Milena could help? They are used to channeling divine communication as a part of their Illusionist Gift."

"That's an idea," Sean said. "We can ask them. Maybe the Seers can help too?"

"We can ask Fionnuala and Lily when we go home," Siofra offered.

Nathaniel and Sean nodded.

"Who are Fionnuala and Lily?" Elizabeth asked.

"Fionnuala is Aes Sídhe, a powerful Illusionist. She teaches at the Valerian's Cove Academy. Milena Casey-Thorndike is Marissa's daughter. Marissa's mate is part Sídhe, and Milena has the Illusionist Gift too. Lily is a Dragon. She is ancient and the strongest Seer we have," Sean said. "She's currently living in Valerian's Cove, too, since her grandson is teaching at the Academy and his younger sister is a student there. Bethie is an extremely strong Seer, too. Lily actually says that Bethie is, or will be, stronger than Lily herself. Though Bethie is only twelve and still growing in her Gifts."

"If the entire family has this spark, how would we awaken it?" Elizabeth said.

"I would guess with a meditation somewhat like I just did with Maddie," Sean said. "You would have to go within and find it within yourself. But focused on Star energy, rather than Dragon or Fae."

Elizabeth looked troubled.

"We know nothing about this energy or these Star Beings. All we know right now is that their energy boosts our Gifts, and in Maddie, it's made her exceptionally strong. We don't know of anyone who can teach us or help us use these Gifts. But if Maddie is already so strong, if this spark awakens fully in her, it could cause problems. We need to be taught to use it safely. What do we do?"

"First, let's talk to Lady Fionnuala and Lily and see what they say. Then, we go from there."

❧

SEAN USED THE MIRROR IN THE SITTING ROOM TO CALL FIONNUALA. Luckily, she was at home and answered.

"Lady Fionnuala, we could use your help," the Dragon told the elegant Aes Sídhe woman. He explained the situation to her. She paled a bit, then nodded.

"Milena and I will help. I appreciate your thinking of us. I will let you know what we find."

Sean ended the call, then stroked the mirror's frame again, thinking of Lily.

"I know what you want, boy. Bethie woke me up this morning talking about it. We have already looked. Tell the Witch not to worry. A teacher is coming. Oh, and their new Academy will have to include studies for the Star Born. More families are awakening and will make their way to Fairweather Falls. As our Academy has specialties for the Dragons, Fae, and Phoenyxes, the new Academy will need a specialty for those with the blood of the stars as well. The new Academy should also offer the other courses but will have more students of the Fae and Star Born bloodlines. And maybe one or two others." Lily smiled and ended the call.

Sean sighed. Lily loved to be mysterious and difficult whenever she could. The ancient Dragon said it added spice to life. She was also a mischievous prankster, a trait she had passed down with glee to her granddaughter, Bethie.

Sean made his way back out to the group on the patio.

"Fionnuala and Milena are seeking answers. Lily said to tell you that a teacher is coming and that the new Academy here should expect other families of Star Born and should include a curriculum for them."

"There are more of us?" Elizabeth exclaimed. "Why have we not heard of this before?"

Sean shrugged.

"I don't know. But at least you're not alone."

FIONNUALA REPLIED AFTER LUNCH, CONFIRMING WHAT LILY HAD said.

"The Goddess was quite certain that a teacher is coming. She said not to worry and to keep in touch with those in Fairweather Falls. She said we should all work together. I think she is continuing to build the network and fighting force she started in Valerian's Cove."

Sean sighed. That fighting force included children. Magical children from several distinct races. Several of those children were turbo-charged with extra magical energy. After an initial set of events had drawn the group together, things had quieted down a bit, and the last year-and-a-half or so had been largely peaceful, allowing more time for training and for the kids to be, well, kids. The adults involved had hoped that they would have more time before things began to get out of control. Evidence had started popping up that there were tears in the Veil between the realms and that Demons and other darker forces were making their way through. So far, the S.O.C. had kept things contained. Still, the nature of the alliances formed and the significance of the races who had come together suggested that before too long, more considerable trouble was coming.

Sean relayed the message to the other adults present, who were watching as Maddie and Oreo played in the field. Maddie was using the air to fly with Oreo, who was teaching her aerial gymnastics from the looks of it.

"Wait, fighting force? Children with extra Gifts? How have I not heard of any of this?" Elizabeth said.

"You were away from the Havens for a long time, Liz," Mags said gently. "It hasn't come up since you've been back. And let's face it, you've been extremely busy since your return. There's probably a ton of things you haven't been caught up on yet. And as Sean said, things have been rather quiet lately. The S.O.C. has handled everything so far, with help when needed. The age of those with supercharged powers seems to indicate that the main trouble is still some years in the future."

"I certainly hope so. Maddie is only eight! She will not be fighting Demons!"

"We all hope not. Allie and the other Casey twins and their friends were ten when they started to come into their Gifts and get into trouble. Allie was eleven when she bonded with the Sword of Fire, and the Phoenyxes returned. She fought a much older Dragon-Phoenix hybrid, then. She had a lot of help from her twin and from a large group of adults, though. The point is, these children have a vast support system. None of them will fight alone, and we will make sure they stay out of the fight for as long as possible. Though, in Allie's case, that's a little more challenging," Sean grinned. "That girl has a fiery temper and a huge sense of justice."

Elizabeth was profoundly shaken.

"I'll have to talk to Robin about the curriculum at the school. We'll need to make sure we have a strong fight program. And courses in Star magic, whatever that looks like. I don't even begin to know what to do with that."

"I'm sure the teacher who comes will be able to help you with that," Sean replied.

"But when are they coming? How will they find us? I mean... I don't even know what to do with any of this."

"From what Lily and Fionnuala said, I would suggest that the teacher is coming sooner rather than later. Until then, carry on as you have been. Let Lady Margarethe teach Maddie as much as she can, and you continue with whatever you do. Make the rest of your summer as normal as possible. When the teacher shows up is soon enough to worry about everything else."

❧

SEAN, SIOFRA, DERVLA, AND NATHANIEL RETURNED TO VALERIAN'S Cove. Mags took Maddie off for more adventures, and Elizabeth called her mother.

"Mom, you are not going to believe this," she said when Nora answered the phone.

Nora was flabbergasted.

"What? Star Born? That's just a myth! You can't be serious. Are you sure?"

"Apparently, yes. Will you tell Dad? When this teacher shows up, he'll have to join the classes. So will Lucy and her kids. Mom, this is crazy. I have no idea what to do with any of this. I'm freaking out here."

"I think that's quite understandable, darling. Come over for dinner. I'll make sure Lucy and her family are here, too. We all need to talk about this, as a family."

❧

ELIZABETH CALLED ROBIN NEXT.

"You said what now?" Robin gasped as Elizabeth wound down from her story.

"Wow, Lizzie Grace. That's unbelievable. I can't even imagine trying to explain why we need courses in Star Magic or what that even is! Will they need special buildings or teaching areas? How do I change the plans? The building has already started! When is this teacher getting here? It's a good thing I had already included the fight training facilities in the plans. I hope the fight teacher is chosen soon. Star Born. Whoever would have thought that was a real thing?"

"I know. And now I need to hire two more full-time staff for the store. I feel like my life is spiraling out of control. It's different from when I was living in the human world and felt like I was losing control after Jared died. At least there, I knew I could come home. But here, there's nowhere left to run to hide my head in the sand. And with how strong Maddie is, that's not safe, anyway."

"One thing at a time, Lizzie Grace. The Star teacher hasn't shown up yet. Let's deal with what you can do something about right now. The fliers and adverts for new shop assistants have already gone out. You should get replies soon. Morgan may have gotten some already since I put the number for the shop on the ads. Mags has Maddie well in hand for now. Magnus has Joshua. You haven't noticed anything weird with your Gifts yet, have you?"

"No, not yet. They're as strong as they've always been, no changes that I can feel."

"Ok, then. Keep making potions and teaching your apprentices. Focus on the shop and all the good you are doing already. Focus on your relationship with Jonah. That's going well, right?"

Elizabeth blushed.

"Yeah, that's going well. I'm having a good time getting to know him again."

"Good. Let's make Wednesday nights a permanent Girl's Night Out night. Or Saturday, whichever works best for everyone. I think you need your crew. And we could all use a little more fun. I'll call Sarah and Sandra. First Weekly Girl's Night Out is this Wednesday. We'll go to the diner."

32

Sarah Faraday went home with Madelynn and Sharalee Monday morning. They took Carl with them as well.

"They can stay with me for as long as they need to," Madelynn told Aunt Gloria. "You can come visit whenever you want. You're not bound to Fairweather Falls, are you?"

"No, I don't appear to be," Aunt Gloria answered.

"Good. And you don't feel the need to move on?"

Aunt Gloria shook her head.

"I am going to stay as long as I can. Elizabeth needs me. Life is not going to be easy for her these next few years. There will be a lot of things happening for her and the children. Lizzie will need all the help she can get. She still needs me to continue her potions training as well."

"Then we will expect to see you often."

"Mads, do you think Sarah and Carl will be ok?"

Madelynn smiled.

"Yes, they will. Queen Lorelei has already asked that Sarah join her in Faerie as soon as she is able. Now that Daffydd is out of the way, Sarah is free to go home. She stayed in the human realm for so long, partly to stay away from him. She will visit here often, as most of her friends are here, but I think it will do her good to go home for a while."

"As for Carl, that will take a little bit longer, I think. His partner's betrayal and what happened with his sister's family severely traumatized him. I think he blames himself for not figuring it out sooner. He's fallen so far down into that bottle that it may take a while for him to pull himself out of it completely. I'll make sure he continues to work with a Mind Healer for as long as is necessary. And that he goes to a twelve-step program, too. There are a lot of programs that focus on magicals now. We'll get him the help he needs."

"Thank you, Madelynn. You always were the glue that held us together. Will you come back to say goodbye to Mathilda before she passes on?"

"Yes. We will all come back for that when it's time."

MORGAN RECEIVED A SLEW OF APPLICATIONS FOR EMPLOYMENT AT Samara's Garden. Many were from high schoolers who were looking for after-school work for the fall, while others were from those who had actually read the job description stating that full-time was desired. She narrowed the pile down to five people, four women and one young man.

"Let's have them all come in on Thursday, Morgan," Elizabeth said.

Thursday morning at nine, Elizabeth was in the store with Morgan. Claire was taking a long weekend to visit Jed in Valerian's Cove. Her parents had gone with her, as had Jed's. The two families were spending a lot of time together, something Claire's mother, Jennifer, was pleased about. She was glad to have her childhood best friend back in her life.

Promptly at nine, the bell over the door chimed as a tall, slender young man walked in. He had long brown hair pulled back in a ponytail down his back. With his broad shoulders and otherwise lean but muscular frame, he looked like he would be better suited to working outside on a farm than inside a store, even one that dealt in herbs and potions.

Behind the young man, four women entered the shop.

The first was an older woman, with round cheeks and a cheerful smile. Then a serious young woman with shoulder-length black hair pulled back from her face. The next was a slender woman with long, straight blond hair that looked somewhat like your stereotypical movie elf. She could have stepped straight out of a Tolkien novel. The last had curly reddish-brown hair and blue eyes. She grinned as she looked around the store.

"Thank you all for coming," Elizabeth said. "I realize that having you all come in at once is somewhat unusual, but since I believe that a good business is only as strong as the people working it, it's vitally important to see how we would all get along. There's no point going further if our personalities clash." She smiled at the newcomers.

"Why don't you all introduce yourselves and tell Morgan and me a little about you? Like, where you're from, and why you think you would like to work at Samara's Garden?"

"My name is Aidan. I'm from Rhode Island, originally, but I went to college in California and have spent the last ten years out there. I studied different farming methods, particularly organics and biodynamics. I have an interest in herbs for healing. I'm an Earth Witch, medium power. Eventually, I would like to have my own farm and herbal line, so I'm looking for experience in the business end of running a shop."

The older woman went next.

"I'm Helen. I taught English for years before the magical world came out of the broom closet almost twenty years ago. Let me tell you; it was much more fun teaching afterward when I could use my magic to make the lessons come alive for the students. I retired several years ago, and I'm bored. I miss interacting with people and helping them learn. I figure a book store is perfect for me. I am willing to help out in the other areas of the shop as well."

"I'm Joan. I need a job. They fired me from my last job because a customer complained after I told him off for hitting on me after I shot him down several times," the dark-haired girl said.

"My name is Marilee," the woman who looked Fae said. "I am recently come from Faerie and am looking for a way to occupy my time and get to know my new community. I feel that working in a shop such as this would be a good way to do both."

"I'm Arianna," the last young woman said. "I'm taking a gap year from school. I finished high school with excellent grades, but I don't really know what I want to do with my life. I'm great with people, and I enjoy helping them figure things out about their lives. I don't want to be a Mind Healer or a mundane therapist. Maybe a life coach? I don't know yet. But I'm great at customer service. I worked at the ice cream shop in my hometown all through high school. So I have shop experience."

Elizabeth and Morgan looked at each other and then back at the candidates.

"Let's show you around," Elizabeth said. "I have three apprentices right now, who take turns in the shop. Their hours will, of course, be much less once school starts up again. Michael is here now. Claire is away for the weekend, and Maia is in my stillroom brewing potions. Michael is in the back at the moment, getting the cafe ready for the day. Let's start here in the bookstore part of the shop."

Elizabeth and Morgan showed the candidates around the shop and introduced them to Michael.

"Now, there is one more thing I should tell you about the shop," Elizabeth said towards the end of the morning. "The shop is named for the Spirit that inhabits her. Samara has been with the shop since it was first begun, centuries ago. Samara has no limits in time or space, and she has to approve all new hires. We can't have anyone here that she doesn't get along with."

Samara appeared in front of the group. She smiled and waved.

Aidan smiled back. He blushed a little. Samara was exotically beautiful.

Helen grinned at Samara.

Joan nodded, unsmiling.

Marilee inclined her head with a faint smile.

Arianna grinned. "Hey! It's nice to meet you. My grandmother's house has a House Spirit. Her name is Nancy. She was my grandmother's great-aunt. I'd love to hear your story sometime."

Samara grinned back at the young woman in delight.

❧

Elizabeth, Samara, and Morgan sat in the cafe once the candidates had left.

"I really like Arianna and Helen," Morgan said.

"I agree. Though I do like Aidan, too," Samara nodded.

"I like all three. I don't think that Joan or Marilee would be a good fit here. I might tell Clara about Marilee, though. I think the girl would be much happier in a store like The Flower's Daughter. Joan, though, as much as I would like to give her a chance, there is just something off about her. I wouldn't feel right about hiring her."

"I wish we could hire all three," Morgan said. "Couldn't we have Aidan and Helen full time, and Arianna part-time and to cover whenever we needed extra help? Oh, and did we forget to ask where they all live? Would they be commuting from their homes through the portals, or do they live nearby?"

"Oh, that's a good question. I forgot to ask," Elizabeth said. "I think you're right. Let's see if that arrangement would work for the three of them. Aidan has already said that he plans to have his own farm and business someday. So we know he'll be moving on, eventually. And Arianna admits not knowing what she wants to do with her life. I think having an extra set of hands is a good thing. Are we all agreed?"

Everyone nodded.

Elizabeth called Aidan, Helen, and Arianna after lunch. All three were excited and agreed to start work the following Monday.

"I'm at the end of my lease where I am now," Aidan said when Elizabeth asked him where he lived and how he planned to get to work.

"I'll come back tomorrow and start looking for a place in Fairweather Falls. Until I find one, I'll commute through the portals."

"Aidan, I was thinking," Elizabeth said. "My mother runs her own nursery and garden center. She has recently arranged with Brendan Casey of Casey Nurseries to be the exclusive East Coast distributor of a new line of Fae-Earth hybrids that he has developed with Siofra MacNamara-Brooke. If you are really thinking about setting up your own herb farm someday, you may like to spend some time working with my mother, too. Or at least visiting her gardens."

"That would be great, Elizabeth! Thank you. That's an awesome suggestion. I appreciate it. I'll visit her garden center when I come tomorrow to look for a place to live."

Helen, it turned out, lived several towns away from Fairweather Falls in a mundane town.

"My husband was garden-variety human," Helen said. "He passed away just before I retired. I've mostly stayed here because this is where I've lived most of my life. I was going to drive in every morning. I don't mind the drive—I do my best thinking when I'm driving, sometimes. Plus, I can put on the music and sing at the top of my lungs without hurting anyone's ears."

"I live in Silver Falls," Arianna said. "Madelynn told me about your shop. Her niece owns the ice cream shop I worked in through high school. I'll take the portal in every morning. It's an easy trip."

So that was sorted, then. Elizabeth went out to the stillroom to check on Maia. This was the first time she had left the young apprentice alone for so long.

Maia looked up as Elizabeth entered the stillroom. She had been making herbal soaps all morning, and the room smelled wonderful. Curing soap molds lined the shelves around the room.

"How did it go this morning, Maia? I apologize for leaving you alone for so long."

"It was great! I had a lot of fun making these soaps. I might make a line of these myself if that's ok with you. These would make great gifts. They're easy and smell great. And you can do so many things with them. You can set them in pretty molds; you can carve them. I like making soaps."

"You can do similar things with candles," Elizabeth said. "I've seen some lovely carved candles at maker's fairs and renaissance fairs. They can be layers of different colors, have things pressed into them... the possibilities are endless."

Maia's eyes were shining as Elizabeth finished speaking.

SATURDAY MORNING ELIZABETH AND MAIA WERE IN THE STILLROOM looking at catalogs for candle molds when Elizabeth sat up suddenly, looking around.

Maia looked at her in confusion.

"Are you ok, Liz?"

"Don't you feel that? There's a strange kind of buzzing. I feel like my whole body is vibrating."

Elizabeth stood and left the stillroom. She looked around the garden, then turned to look down the field. Standing in the field were three tall figures. They glowed so brightly that for a moment, it hurt to look at them. Suddenly, the glow faded, leaving Elizabeth wondering if she'd imagined it.

The three figures started up the field toward Elizabeth. Soon two tall women and an even taller man were standing before her. They smiled at Elizabeth.

"Good morning, Elizabeth. I believe you are expecting us. I am Malcolm— or, that is the name I once went by in this realm. These two lovely ladies are Melissa and Rowena, my daughters. We are here to teach those in this realm who are Star Born. Oh, and I suppose I should tell you, Elizabeth. I'm your grandfather, several generations removed."

THANK YOU!

Thank you for reading *Herbs and Homecomings*! This was Book One in the Return to Magic— Fairweather Falls series. If you liked the book, please leave a review. As an indie author, good reviews help ratings, which in turn helps sales. So they are really important! Also, I enjoy hearing from readers who have read my creations. Honest opinions help me to know what I can do better to improve my storytelling. Please let me know what you liked most! If there is a character that you would like to see developed further or even given their own story, please let me know. You can contact me through my website at www.hettycate.com. Thank You!

STAY IN TOUCH!

Want to stay in touch? Join my newsletter for updates on new books and other fun stuff from me! There will be no spam-just news about upcoming releases, sales and promotions, freebies and some fun facts about the worlds and characters in my books.

ACKNOWLEDGMENTS

To all of my friends and family who have supported me thus far in my author journey, thank you. I love you.

Also, I would like to thank my mother, Teren de Cossy, for reading and editing for me! I really appreciate it!

Thank you!

ABOUT THE AUTHOR

H.C. de Cossy (Hetty Cate) writes paranormal fiction. She lives on the Pacific Coast with her son and two cats. Hetty Cate has family all over the place. She loves to travel, paint, dance, and sing. She occasionally makes her own clothing, chocolate and costumes. She has always felt close to fairies, nature and the paranormal world.

www.hettycate.com

ALSO BY H.C. DE COSSY

PARANORMAL FICTION

The Valerian's Cove Series

Waken the Witch

Broken Bonds

The Sword of Fire

Alliances

The Sola Blake Trilogy

Hidden Witch

Spirit Walker

Fate Weaver (Forthcoming)

The Return to Magic Series (Fairweather Falls)

Herbs and Homecomings

www.ingramcontent.com/pod-product-compliance
Lightning Source LLC
LaVergne TN
LVHW050616100826
845148LV00011B/1615

* 9 7 8 1 7 3 7 9 6 3 2 1 9 *